MAGPIE

a Novel

M.A. Reyes

ROTOR Publishing, a Division of ROTOR Consulting, LLC.

MAGPIE

Extensive efforts have been made to present a correct and complete work, but even editorial nitpickers make mistakes. If you happen upon one, please email the details to: MAReyes.AUTHOR@gmail.com

Cover Illustration © 2014 by Clyde Steadman

Graphic Art by Faith Rumfelt

Editing by Priscilla Bohl and Alexa Poteet

Poetry by Robert S. Warshow

I welcome contact from readers, so please feel free to drop me a line:

MAReyes.AUTHOR@gmail.com

Or

www.facebook.com/M.A.REYES.Author

Follow me on Twitter:

@MAReyesAUTHOR

The Magpie

I walked one day
In the Garden of Wasted Things,
And there I found
The bitter ghosts of all that had been spent unwisely,
Or lost through brutal circumstance.
I found the childhood
That some labourer's child had never known;
I found the youth that some young man had squandered;
There I found some poet's genius
That had gone unrecognised.
I saw the ghosts of idle words,
And small talk,
That men had used to waste away the hours.
I saw the hopes that had been smothered,
And all the dreams
That never had come true,
And Laughter that had died for lack of bread.
I met with all the lives that had been misdirected,
And spoke with dreary shades
Of loves that might have been,
And songs that never had been sung.
I met with all these ghosts,
And many more;
And each of them
Sat silently in the shadows,
Brooding over quirks of mad Creation,
And puppets' dreams.

Robert S. Warshow

BOOK 1

Spring

CHAPTER 1

April's Dribble

I despise April Fools' Day. Even as a child, I hated the idea of playing tricks on people. My friends and family had grown accustomed to my "sensitive nature," a label my mother slapped across my forehead when I was in first grade. Eventually, I learned to stay away from mean people, saving my mother the embarrassment of admitting her eldest was a crybaby. By the time I reached adulthood, I'd come to know the source of humankind's dark side: Fear, a fundamental emotion that drives ghastly behaviors and prompts oblivious conspirators to revel in the suffering of others. In the end, all of my brouhaha kept me at arm's length from the people I loved most, including my sister.

Hunting for the phone buzzing on my nightstand, I finally answered, "Hello?"

"Is your refrigerator running?" A familiar voice asked on the other end.

I squinted at the clock and barely made out the time. "Katie, it's five in the morning, what gives?"

Even when I was angry, I'd never used my baby sister's given name, Katherine; she'd always been Katie to me, and everyone around her. I often wished for a formal name. People inevitably expected more than "Maggie."

"Oh come on, Maggie, it's a classic! What would April Fools be if not for my annual wake-up call?"

Ordinarily, I cherished Katie's playfulness, but not today. Her crack-of-dawn prank calls were an April 1st farce I'd endured since we left home; before then, she'd invent other, equally annoying ways to rouse me for her amusement.

"Katie, I've got a helluva day ahead of me. Please just leave it alone."

I didn't want the call to drag on. Chances were things would escalate, as had been the pattern lately. I had far too much on my mind to spend time tiptoeing around Katie's feelings.

"What a drag, Mags. Just trying to make you laugh, which you haven't done lately, by the way."

Katie was like a puppy—not a purebred, but a sweet mutt, capturing the attention of anyone within petting range. Simply put, Katie managed to keep an innocent outlook on life and people adored her for it.

"I know, I know. It's just the worst day possible, okay? How about dinner later this week?"

I had to put a stop to the conversation, and a dinner offer usually worked, especially when I picked up the check, which I did often.

With detachment, Katie said, "Sure, sounds fun. Well, hope whatever it is you're worried about today goes okay for you. Talk later."

I disconnected the call before I could hear the click of her indifference to my situation.

ॐ

My *situation*. What was it, exactly? Arranging the noise in my head, I dissected my life and jotted two words on a notepad,

Personal then *Professional*

Straining to expand the two categories, I realized I needed coffee to delve further into my fragmented life. I grabbed the notepad, stepped into my slippers and cozied into my favorite red robe—the one Jack gave me the Christmas before he died. The sky was turning my favorite shade of peach, and I stared out the bedroom window yearning for the longer, warmer days of summer.

"Oh for Pete's sake, Cody," I said, tripping over the chocolate Lab we adopted almost 10 years before.

I made my way to the kitchen to make a pot of *Café Pajaro*, an organic fair-trade blend that had become a favorite the day I to learned to make coffee for just one. The strong coffee gave me the oomph I needed to get through those tortuous days; the particular brand provided interesting coffee talk, distracting concerned friends and family from my anguish,

Wow, this is great coffee, Mags. What is it?

It's from Trader Joes, a Fair Trade blend that helps sustain Central America's economy and environment. It guarantees farmers a minimum price, and links farmers directly with importers, creating long-term sustainability...

Very cool! Do you have any cream?

Strangely, I couldn't imagine drinking any other kind; the brightly colored image on the cardboard canister soothed me like a child's favorite blanket.

Catching my balance, I scratched my old dog's head, "Cody, you're going to kill me, you know that?"

Oblivious to the message but responding to my gentle tone, he wagged his way into the kitchen.

"Coffee first, then food, buddy."

I wasn't lonely; at least I didn't think I was. I missed the commotion of family—plain and simple. Memories had become haphazardly arranged like scraps of fabric I'd collected over the years, stowed in opaque plastic boxes crammed into the closet of my rarely used sewing room. I wanted to hear my son's clumsy steps first thing in the morning; sense my husband's gentle breath on my neck as we woke in unison; and laugh at our carefree conversations over breakfast. More than anything, I wanted to feel the love between us, even if it meant just one more time. As I had for seven years, I tucked those memories away, straining to close the closet doors to my mind.

"So, Cody, here's the deal, buddy. I forgot to get your food yesterday. My bad. So, I can make you eggs and throw in some yogurt, sound alright by you?"

He approved, his tail told me so.

Scrambling a couple of eggs brought me back to ruminations about my dual existence. I wondered if most people spent as much time dwelling on their lives as I did. Coffee in hand, I sat at the breakfast bar and began to elaborate,

Personal
>   *House*
>   *Grandkids*
>   *Vacation!*
>   *New car?*
>   *New man? Yeah, right...*

I pondered my personal life for a moment, then went on to the other column,

Professional
>   *Asshole boss*
>   *New project – ugh!*
>   *Staff reorg*
>   *Raise??*
>   *New job – start looking?*

Before I could give my life anymore thought, the phone buzzed with a text,

Today, 5:47 AM
KATIE: You mad?
MAGS: No, just busy
KATIE: Just trying to cheer u up!
MAGS: I know its okay
KATIE: What r u doing?
MAGS: Katie pls
KATIE: Okay, just don't be mad
MAGS: I'm not, really
KATIE: K
MAGS: K
KATIE: Latr

"Cody, why don't you chew up my phone like other dogs do, huh buddy?"

I put my cell phone down and scratched Cody's neck, thinking how I dreaded the day he'd be gone because, in large part, he was a constant reminder of good times. Other things—sights, sounds, smells—brought about sad memories, which made me understand, to a degree, why Carrie, Michael's wife and the mother of my grandchildren, moved back to California. Her parents were there and the painful memories of Michael weren't.

They died on the same day; Jack from cancer and Michael from a bullet. Jack was in my arms and Michael was 8000 miles away in Afghanistan. Along side four of his brothers...but not me. I wanted to hold my son as I had with his father, but the only thing left to hold onto were memories, and an 8 X 10 photograph from his Navy SEAL graduation.

I got up for a second cup of coffee, pouring the heavenly brown liquid into my favorite green mug Jack picked up in Wyoming—a beefy hunk of unbreakable ceramic that holds two cups, not one. Before sitting back down, I stopped at the backdoor window and stared at the barren yard, longing for the first signs of spring. Gardening had become an indispensible escape from all the discord and demons; soul-crushing squatters intent on inflicting pain, while refusing to vacate my body. Shaking off painful memories, I heard the buzz of a text— the third one and it wasn't even 7:00.

"Oh, for fuck's sake, Katie!" I said aloud, and looked at the screen,

Today, 6:23 AM
TOM: Hey gorgeous
MAGS: Oh hi
TOM: Whoa! What's with the mood
MAGS: Bad start - How r u?
TOM: Horny
MAGS: Not me
TOM: Can I call?
MAGS: Maybe latr

Tom, Match Date #1, was the first guy I'd met on-line since my friends convinced me to start dating. He was an attractive, well-educated and opinionated banker. Still, his on-line profile stood out from the rest, and I was instantly attracted. I found it clever, light hearted and sexy,

Maybe it's just me, but describing myself in 2000 characters is not my idea of fun. I'd rather be doing something useful, like lying on the couch watching Golf Channel. Apparently, though, this is a critical procedure in meeting new ladies, so here goes, I'll be gentle; I think I'm generally considered by everyone who knows me to be a decent, intelligent, all-around good guy. I have heard I'm handsome, funny, focused, laid-back, distinguished, good lover (I could swear I've heard that one, may be wishful thinking), generous, and fun. I'm better looking than my photos indicate. (No, really, I am. Really. I swear. Maybe.) I do tend to be intense in some activities. My humor can be wicked at times. Physically, I'm lean with an athletic build, so petite/slender women work better for me, and they ride better on the back of the Suzuki. (KIDDING, lighten up!) Just a regular guy. No issues, warrants, skeletons, or weird stuff...

We had a few dates, and I was pleased he picked up the tab on each. I offered, of course; I never understood the "guy always pays" rule. Still, something bothered me about Tom. He was, as he described, a thin, toned guy...handsome as hell. I was, as truthfully described in my own profile, "curvy" with "a few extra pounds." I also disclosed that, while, "I am active and enjoy outdoor activities," I'm not "athletic and toned." Tom's desire for petite, toned women made me wonder if his interest in me was a flesh fetish some men discover in middle age. I never found out, because during our third date, Tom casually asked if I'd like to go back to his place to get to know each other better.

Don't get me wrong. I'm no prude, and like sex as much (or more) than the next 50-something gal. But sex so soon? Our first date was simple: coffee at a local coffee joint near his office. (I was playing it safe.) The second one involved lunch halfway between our respective offices. (Not near either of our homes, not yet). Date #3, dinner at a trendy sushi bar. (Closer to his home than mine.) I didn't go by any hard rules, but a general sense about a guy gave me comfort, knowing his last name even better. Unless, of course, it was a one-night stand, in which case I didn't want to know anything about him.

I politely declined Tom's offer to come over and immediately began avoiding his calls. There was something about his hyper-confident nature, I concluded, that prevented him from accepting my rejection. So he began texting me, friendly notes at first. Then, as he sensed my continued disinterest, he began to toy with me, using flattery and sexuality to...what? Get me in the sack?

Tom's text this morning was no different. I could have—*should have*—deleted his number, but I was intrigued by his inability to let go; it made me feel less crazy about my own.

Guilt consumed me. How could I go from memories of Jack and Michael to thoughts of Tom, an over-sexed banker who fell for a woman who wasn't even his type? Hell, it took me three years to begin to go out with girlfriends, four to attend parties that involved drinking, dancing and...men.

Five years after resentfully earning the title of "widow," I went on a date. Not a real date, like the kind you get all dolled up for. A neighbor—a man who had to be close to 70—watched me as I worked my ass off in the garden one Sunday afternoon. Around 4:00, he came over and hollered over the fence, asking if I'd like to join him for a beer and a hamburger on his patio. I agreed and walked over an hour later, wiping my soil covered hands on my cargo shorts—I didn't even think to shower first.

I poured another cup of coffee and checked my work inbox: 56 new emails. Time to get my ass in gear.

⚬⚬⚬

"So, how's the dating scene, Mags," I heard a familiar voice ask as I plopped my computer case on my desk.

Tony, my admin and professional lifesaver, is a tall, olive-skinned man, with piercing blue eyes who could easily be a Calvin Klein underwear model. Tony anticipated my dating details like a child standing in line for ice cream. He knew when and who I dated because he kept my calendar. I gave him the details of my dates because he was my friend and confidant. Tony *got* me, and I trusted him—wholeheartedly.

"None since Tom. It's completely dried up. Wait, not me! I mean the scene!"

We laughed together like teenage girls, which aroused the interest of the rest of my team.

"Come on folks, move on, nothing here to see!"

Mimicking an officer directing traffic, I herded people back to work. Though part of a large tech company, my team was close and behaved more like a family than colleagues.

I was curious about my mail, not in Outlook, but my Match.com inbox. The Internet had revolutionized the workplace and created a continuous dialog about personal use vs. business use. The old guard hated it, thought it slowed productivity. Not me. Like a coffee break or a quick walk around the block, surfing the web was a release for many employees, including me, and I permitted it.

A year after sharing burgers and beers with my neighbor, I'd been convinced by a few determined friends and my sister to create an online profile. Grudgingly, I sat down at my breakfast bar, opened my laptop and scratched out a few sentences. After selecting several recent pictures, I uploaded my profile, including an 87-word blurb drafted with the intent to attract a good egg...or two,

> *I am a professional who works in the technology industry. Aside from work, I'm devoted to my family and friends—including my four legged one. I love the outdoors and live and play outside as much as possible. I'm particularly known to pack a bag and hit the road for a few days...or more. When I'm home, I can be found working in my gardens and taking an occasional break in my hammock. I'm looking to meet new friends and, if it works out, a serious relationship. Oh, and please NO "Flirts," "Likes" or "Favs" – I only respond to original notes.*

I scanned it for errors and, accepting I had no creative-writing ability, I hit "submit," instantly becoming part of the online-dating community.

Within weeks of joining Match.com, I realized I didn't have the patience to search for "matches." Instead, I'd answer penned (so to speak) messages, look at the guys who had viewed me, and ignore the saps who could only muster hitting a "flirt" or "favorite" button. Though I stated clearly in my profile I didn't answer flirts, I received more of those than regular messages. Funny, because so many men said they were "old fashioned" and had "traditional values," yet couldn't jot a simple note of introduction. *Ugh.*

Having successfully logged on to my account, I noticed I had one message. Whoa, he had pictures...and a complete profile—an anomaly in the online-dating world.

I called Tony into my office, "Tony, can you come in here for a quick sec?"

I'd developed a terrible habit of having someone else open my Match mail because, quite honestly, it made me nervous. I preferred Tony, but more times than not it was Katie. We'd meet after work, Katie scouring the site for potentials, while I gulped a glass of wine to summon the courage to check them out.

Eyes shut, I asked, "Can you take a look at this one?"

He knew to open the profile and vet the candidate before saying anything.

Breaking that rule, however, Tony said, "Hey, I like this guy, Mags."

I couldn't open my eyes, "What does it *say?*"

"Hold on, wait *just* a minute," Tony's voice lowered an octave. "Mags, he lives in Georgia. Why the hell is he writing you?"

Tony was clearly annoyed—at himself and the suitor—and scrolled to close the tab, when I stopped him and said, "Hang on, let me see."

Why did a guy from Georgia reach out to me, a Colorado native? I skimmed his intro,

> *Looking for a great friendship first, which hopefully leads to a long-term relationship with someone special, someone to share my interests*

as I will share hers. Looking for a relationship where we both make each other better versions of ourselves.

Intrigued, I leaned back in my chair and glanced at the few pictures of "setpnt58." He had nice eyes, great legs (guys always seemed to include close-ups in shorts if they had nice legs) and a genuine smile. I liked setpnt58.

Tony saw what was happening and, in a warning tone, he said, "Mags, come on. It's never going to happen. You're going to get hurt."

Ignoring his concern, I blurted out, "I'll just read his note and respond politely with a 'No, thank you.'"

After brushing my friend off, I opened setpnt58's message,

> *Dear MGroadie,*
>
> *We live approximately 1600 miles apart. It's ridiculous to think anything would come of us. But I had to write and tell you how beautiful your eyes are. I wish you all the best in your search for Mr. Right. BTW, what does MGroadie mean?*

I thanked Tony for his guidance, but explained I'd take it from there. He huffed out of my office, clearly irritated. Ignoring his silent outburst, I settled into my chair and began drafting a response in my head. What could I say to a man who lived 1600 miles away?

> *Dear setpnt58,*
>
> *You are kind, thank you. Yes, it seems 1600 miles is too much to overcome. I, too, wish you well on your search. Re: my profile name—the "MG" are my initials, and "roadie" is a reference to my addiction to road trips. Never saw the other meaning until someone asked if I was really grody...May I ask about your profile name?*
>
> *MG*

Leaving the site open, I switched to Outlook. Damn, 112 new emails and I hadn't opened one.

I didn't leave the office until 7:00. I spent a good deal of time deflecting pranks and avoiding conversations about who did what to whom and how terribly funny it was. My stealthy avoidance drained every last ounce of cerebral muscle, forcing me to shut my door at 3:00 to get a few things done. I made a mental note to work from home on the first of April next year.

It was raining and dark when I got into my car, Jack's ratty 2001 hunter green Toyota 4Runner; a relic I refused to sell or worse, drop off at a bleak junkyard. After starting it, I patted its dash, a practice I'd picked up from Jack. I wanted the jalopy to last forever, filling the void.

Once, driving to Boulder to visit a friend, it died. I managed to steer it onto the shoulder as it chugged to a slow, pitiful stop. I felt almost breathless as it came to a standstill, as if something inside me had ground to a halt, too. Not wanting to experience that again, I had my temperamental sidekick overhauled at a neighborhood shop. Watching the guys work on it brought about an almost maternal sense. *It needed a name*, I thought. Thereafter, my mechanical companion was known as "Beater" because, well, he was one.

Turning out of the parking lot, my stomach growled and I realized how famished I was. Thanks to my co-worker Sarah, who Saran-wrapped the refrigerator closed, I hadn't eaten lunch that day. I heard only playful guffaws over the April Fools' stunt while I moped about, missing my heat-and-serve low cal slop. I opted to stop by a local joint that served pretty good noodle dishes. My phone buzzed with a text while waiting for my food,

Today, 7:32 PM
TOM: Horny yet?
MAGS: I can't do this anymore
TOM: What?
MAGS: This horny stuff
TOM: Come on, having some fun is all
MAGS: It's not fun, more like childish - Let's just say we had a good run and call it quits

okay?
TOM: Serious?
MAGS: Ya

Tom didn't respond. Thank God. Easiest break-up ever.

The disinterested and freakishly pierced youth at the counter called my name and handed me my food. "Thanks," I responded automatically, to no one in particular and walked out the door.

The food smelled wonderful, and I couldn't wait to get home. One more stop for a half bottle of Prosecco, and I'd be set. I'd learned, during a particularly bad spell, I could blow through a full bottle in no time. Since then, restraint and I had become friends...sort of.

Placing the to-go container next to the stove, I took Cody for a quick walk around the block. The smell of the mouth-watering pasta lined our nostrils as soon as we stepped through the doorway, reminding me I'd forgotten Cody's food. I felt terrible, so I pulled out a single portion Angus-beef patty and defrosted it while I ate. Poor guy just stared at me in disbelief. I couldn't help it; I was starving. In between bites, I fried the patty, leaving it mostly pink. I let it cool for a few minutes and placed it before the soppy jowls framing Cody's sweet face.

"Hope this makes up for it, buddy."

Cody, like most Labs, had no capacity for grudges.

My phone buzzed, and I glanced to see who was texting,

Today, 8:51 PM
KATIE: Got the promotion!
MAGS: Great
KATIE: Still grumpy?
MAGS: No, just ate so I'm good
KATIE: Mags, it's going to be so amazing!
MAGS: Dinner thurs is a must, am thrilled for u!
KATIE: What r u up to?
MAGS: Gunna chk email then bed – u?
KATIE: Out with friends to celebrate!

MAGS: Okay, be safe
KATIE: Thx MOM!
MAGS: ☺ Nite

That wasn't so bad. Katie and I had finally figured out how to resolve our silly spats. Jack's calm nature had an influence, I'm sure. He possessed unique insight, especially about people. Gently inserting a comment or two (often one of his terrible jokes), he'd extinguish the heat between my baby sis and me, leaving us laughing at ourselves. I acknowledged him occasionally for his spot-on insights, but not enough. I didn't do or say lots of things nearly enough. About two years ago, I quit asking God to give me five more minutes with him; now I just talk directly to Jack and leave God completely out of it.

After being woken up so early, I was tired. Normally, I'd read for a bit, curled on my comfy sofa with Cody at my feet, a nice cup of chamomile tea and light jazz leavening the mood. That night, however, I skipped my routine. A quick face wash and tooth brushing and I'd be ready to fall into bed, which I did with relish.

Nearly asleep, I sat straight up, remembering the guy from Georgia. I never checked back to see if he responded to my message. I grabbed my iPad off the nightstand and turned it on. I'd downloaded the Match.com app on my phone but not this device, so I did it the old-fashioned way and entered the URL.

"What the hell is my password?" I said out loud and rubbed my eyes, as if it might help me recall the information I so desperately needed.

"Why can't this autofill like my fucking phone?"

A funny thing happens when you live alone for a long time: Profanity flows like rain in spring.

Finally, I entered the correct sequence of characters and noticed a red circle above "Messages," which showed the number "1." Tony and Katie were not available to open the message for me, and I fumbled for a few seconds wondering why it was so damn difficult to do it myself.

"Okay, Maggie, just do it," I whispered as though there were people in the house sleeping.

The message was from setpnt58. I didn't know when he

sent it; Match doesn't timestamp messages. I wondered if he waited to write it until he got home from work.

No time like the present, as the notable "they" say,

> *Dear MGroadie,*
>
> *It is clear to me from your gorgeous pictures you are NOT grody. Only a fool would ask such a question. (So now you know one thing about me: I'm no fool.) My profile name is a reference to tennis, a sport I've played since college. I love it and attempt a game or two every week, weather permitting. Do you know what a "set point" is, MGroadie? (Will I ever know your real name?) You know my age from my profile, so you know I was born in 1958. Pretty simple. What if 1600 miles were 16? Would you care to meet?*
>
> *Have a splendid evening,*
>
> *Daniel*

Daniel. Nice name. "Evening" meant he wrote it earlier, especially since he was two hours ahead of me. Hmm...a tennis player. I dated one in high school. Nice legs, too. I tried tennis myself once—a complete disaster. I possess the coordination of a slug, making sports uninteresting. Jack played hockey, something I could watch because it was fast, which complimented my self-diagnosed Attention Deficit Disorder. And, of course, because he loved it.

I felt like I needed Tony to help me respond, but it wouldn't be very professional to contact my employee at 10:00 at night with a dating question. Propping myself against a stack of pillows, I reread Daniel's message. I smiled with delight at his playfulness. Daniel was sweet, a word most men hate, but a "must have" quality for me.

Feeling frisky, I wrote, hoping he'd get the reference,

> *Daniel my brother, you are older than me...*
>
> *I couldn't help it, it's late! But you really are older*

than me—I was born in '59. Never took you for a fool, BTW. Not a real sports person, though I can appreciate the athleticism (is that a word?) of tennis. Actually, I was glad to see something about you that is so different from me—makes the point there never will be an "us" easier to swallow. Would I care to meet if 1600 were actually 16? Good question—may I sleep on it?

Sweet dreams,

Maggie (not short for anything, it's really my given name)

I hit the "send" button and realized I was flirting with a man who lived hundreds of miles away, yet I'd set him up for a response. Giggling quietly, I felt my face flush with a heat I hadn't felt in years. I closed the Match tab on my iPad and set it down. Calmly, I turned out the light and dozed off to sleep, an impish smile brushed across my face.

୨ৎ

For the next few weeks, Daniel and I traded messages. I continued to flirt, and he volleyed back. I didn't tell anyone about him. I lied to Tony when he asked about setpnt58, explaining I hadn't heard from him since the first message we read together weeks back. When Katie asked how my online dating was going, I'd shrug and tell her I rarely checked the site, too damn busy. In reality, I checked the site daily, looking for Daniel's sweet, clever messages.

"Good morning, buddy! Want your bunny basket?" I asked Cody, making my way into the bathroom.

It was Easter Sunday and the weather was going to be fantastic. I planned an early morning walk with Cody followed by brunch with Katie. It was our tradition. Our folks lived on the Western Slope in the same house we grew up in. We attempted to go back home every few months, but not this Easter. Snowfall in the mountains had reached record numbers, and we didn't want to get caught in a spring storm that could render I-70 a parking lot.

I threw on some yoga pants (none of the four pair I owned had sullied a studio), fleece jacket and my "outside" sneakers. Cody knew the routine and was dancing in circles.

"Hang on, Cody! Just wait, let me get your leash."

I'd made an effort to keep his 85-pound frame in good shape, hoping like hell he'd live a long, healthy life. I snapped the leash to his loose collar, and we headed out. Cody lived for his walks, and I delighted in giving my pooch what he longed for.

I was happier than I'd been in years, thanks in part to Daniel's fun and flirtatious messages. We hadn't traded personal contact information yet; I'd learned to be cautious after a few crazy online-dating experiences, which had ended before I met the weirdoes in person. Daniel's messages had become a little more suggestive but not in an obnoxious way, like those I'd received from so many other guys. He had a way with words that made me think he was a writer, either professionally or as a hobby. He excited me, what can I say. Unfortunately, our budding romance made it difficult to concentrate at work and I'd missed a few deadlines, a rarity during my professional career. Damn, it was easy to daydream about Daniel...

Before I knew it, we were back home. Cody made a beeline to the sofa, while I jumped in the shower.

Katie and I agreed we'd make reservations at a new place every year for Easter. Mom and Dad loved Village Inn and ate there on Easter Sundays when we weren't visiting. They would call afterward, excited about running into friends who shared similar beliefs and opinions, most of which were straight out of the fifties. Pinkies interlocked, my baby sister and I vowed never to grow old minded, though we knew age was beginning to take a toll on our bodies.

Thank God for Spanx, I thought, simultaneously making a mental note to check the state of my miracle undergarments.

I made my way to the restaurant and, spotting Katie, called out, "What a cool place!"

I gave her a bear hug and held on for a few extra seconds.

Sensing the shift in my affection, Katie said, "What's up with the mongo hugs Mags? You get laid?"

She always went *there*. Though she rarely shared details, I knew Katie had a healthy sex life. So did I. Before Jack died, I recalled. Sexually, I'd shut down since then. My grief had robbed me of my youthful passion and I'd boxed it up. Until now.

"Nope. No man in my life. I just love spring. It's gardening season, and when, pray tell, will you be joining me for a day of tilling?"

"Why do you need to say stupid stuff like *pray tell*, it sounds uppity," she scolded.

Katie had earned a degree in marketing, which consequently didn't require much reading or writing. She often chided me for my word choices or references to current events. Simply put, Katie's world involved more socializing and less critical thinking. Strangely, our differences were the stickum that kept us close; had we been more alike, one of us would have strangled the other long ago.

Inside the restaurant aptly called, "Above Bored," I counted nine tables: a mixture of four tops, two tops, and several tall tables where a few couples stood, a new dining trend in which I was wholly uninterested. We followed the hostess to a small table near the front window facing a beautiful greenbelt across the street.

Minutes into our brunch, Katie asked, "So, what's the deal, Mags? I can see something's going on with you. Plus, you've lost your winter weight and I *know* you haven't been going to the gym."

My sister was on a roll, and I lowered my eyes, scanning the menu to avoid her stare.

"Did you meet someone? Online? Who is he?"

I raised my eyes, locked onto hers, and told the truth, just not all of it, "Katie, I haven't met a man. I'm just happy, and I think I'm finally moving on after Jack and Michael."

"You're lying, Mags."

God, I hate my sister sometimes.

CHAPTER 2

Budding Things

My phone buzzed, stirring me from a deep sleep. I could identify a couple "4's" on my digital clock, but had no idea what time it really was. I knew Katie wasn't up yet—too damn dark outside—and no one from work would dare. Finally putting two and two together, I smiled, knowing the author of the text before I looked at the screen,

> **Today, 4:45 AM**
> DANIEL: Thank you
> MAGS: For what
> DANIEL: A great night's sleep
> MAGS: Me too
> DANIEL: Sorry its early
> MAGS: Well, what puts us to sleep could work the other way
> DANIEL: Hmm
> MAGS: Ya
> DANIEL: ☹ can't – meeting in 15
> MAGS: Effin time zones
> DANIEL: Tonight?
> MAGS: Tonight

Less than a month into it, Daniel and I had agreed to share our phone numbers and email addresses. We'd been swapping Match.com messages several times a day and decided logging on to an awkward dating site stymied our getting to know each other. Once direct communication lines were made, my intuition about Daniel being a writer was confirmed. He worked for an online sports rag, writing about tennis, soccer and lacrosse. He was also a talented creative writer. We used email for lengthy discussions about work or current events and, though we knew a bit about each other's personal lives, we avoided delving too far; didn't want to be bogged down with details that had the potential to interrupt our carefree virtual world.

Daniel hadn't missed a beat; within minutes after swapping phone numbers, he'd called,

Hello, Maggie Garrett.

I knew I'd love your voice.

Hi Daniel, what took you so long?

You intimidate me, what can I say.

Aw, you'll get used to me.

It felt like we'd known each other forever; in just a few weeks, he'd managed to peel back layers most of my closest friends couldn't. Strangely, sharing the loss of my husband and only son came easily. I explained I lived alone and hadn't seriously dated for some time. I worked very hard, I told him, which was true, leaving little time for romance. My family, I said, were extremely important to me. My folks were still alive and living in the house I grew up in, while my sister, my best friend and part time nudnik, lived right around the corner. Most importantly, Daniel understood I was a Colorado girl and had no plans to move. Ever.

Likewise, I came to know Daniel had been divorced for five years and was married twice; his adored teenage daughter, Sami, a product of the first. His second marriage was a mistake, a rebound that didn't last a year. Unlike me, his parents were gone. Like me, Daniel had one sibling, an older brother named David who lived and worked overseas. Most importantly, I knew Daniel was a Southern man who had no plans to move. Ever.

So, I know what you look like, how you write, and now I know what you sound like—the only thing left, really, is to know what you feel like.

Twelve words from 1600 miles away, and I'd become instantly aroused. He'd known I'd react that way, and secretly

I'd hoped his voice would have the same effect as his texting, which it had...and then some. His voice, radio announcer smooth, had sent me over the top, reeling with thoughts of fucking his brains out. Out of control and my mind spinning, I couldn't form an adult sentence,

Yeah, uh, I have to go...have a meeting in a few. Talk later?

You got it, Mags! Have a splendid day.

I adored how Daniel used the word "splendid." My online thesaurus showed alternatives like, grand, superb, impressive, marvelous, wonderful, and magnificent. Half of the selection would have sounded ridiculous, the other half, unimpressive. "Splendid," on the other hand, was...Astaire like. How did Daniel know I was a word junkie? Versatile speech tickled me— everyday prose was a bore.

Like people, I thought.

As much as I enjoyed talking with Daniel, I cherished our secret virtual world of texting. It had started innocently,

DANIEL: Hello Mags

MAGS: Hi!

DANIEL: Nice not to have to log on

MAGS: Indeed

DANIEL: What r u doing?

MAGS: Fixing dinner, u?

DANIEL: Reading

MAGS: What

DANIEL: Boring work stuff

MAGS: Like what

DANIEL: Rafa, a tennis pro

MAGS: Oh, not "Raffi?"

DANIEL: The children's songwriter?

MAGS: Ya! u know him?

DANIEL: What parent doesn't

MAGS: Hmmm

DANIEL: Hmmm what?

MAGS: Just Hmmm

DANIEL: Guess what

MAGS: What

DANIEL: U r making me a better texter

MAGS: Don't u text your daughter

DANIEL: Yeah, like "how r u" then, "fine, u?" then "good"

MAGS: That's it?

DANIEL: She's embarrassed her dad texts her

MAGS: I wish I saved Michael's texts

DANIEL: I can only imagine, Mags

MAGS: Ya, kinda sad

DANIEL: Let's call it a nite, talk tomorrow?

MAGS: Sure and thanks

DANIEL: For what?

MAGS: For not feeling sorry for me

Without speaking a word, we'd cut through all the bullshit with which a budding relationship is typically fertilized. Texting had become our regular form of communication and it felt like we'd known each other for years. Was it easier with Daniel because of the geographic cushion? Could people be more real in an unreal world?

I didn't know and didn't care. It was fun and seemed harmless, so I was just went with it.

No one knew about the steamy virtual affair I was having with a guy some would call a complete stranger. After all, what did I know about Daniel? I hadn't run a background check on the man. Why would I? I didn't find him threatening, and, even if he were an ax murderer, he'd have to travel a long way to knock me off.

I'd dozed thinking of our first call and text. Coming to, I tried to shake off a terrifying scene my imagination had concocted: Me, alone on a class-five river, frantically navigating jagged boulders with no end in sight. I squeezed my eyes shut, hoping it was my ridiculous imagination and not a premonition.

A quick glance at the clock showed more than 15 minutes had elapsed, consumed by imagined portraits of Daniel. Welling from my gut, they became the main ingredient in an emotional soup expertly spiced with guilt, regret, doubt and fear. Guilt seasoned everything I did, said, touched and felt; regret coated my throat, making the future hard to swallow; and doubt soaked through every layer of my skin, impossible to rinse, no matter how hard I scrubbed. Over time, however, the strength of those spices waned. They were nothing more than epicurean bungles best concealed with sugar.

Fear, on the other hand, burned the inside of my mouth. Its vapors stung my eyes and scorched my nasal passages. If not perfectly balanced, fear would ruin every attempt at sensory satiation.

Mags, focus...

Hoisting myself out of bed, I made my way to the kitchen.

ॐ

I love the month of May. Snow long gone (with the exception of a freak storm), my gardens begin to form, mostly green foliage with tulips and iris scattering brilliant colors in between. Chilly nights force me to keep the furnace going, but during the day, I open the windows for long-awaited fresh air. This time of year challenges my professionalism. I struggle to leave home in the morning, usually taking a few extra minutes to enjoy a third cup of coffee, listening to the birds and watching Cody frolic from my perch on the back deck.

Thankfully, things had begun to slow down at work. My last big project had ended a few weeks earlier on May 1

May Day—*Out with the old, in with the new...how fitting*, I thought, the corners of my mouth fighting an impish grin.

The first quarter of every year generated more projects than my team should have been able to handle, yet we'd always managed to execute on time and within budget. Still, by the middle of the second quarter, we all were ready for a break. For Christmas the year before, Tony crafted bumper stickers for everyone, poking fun at project managers: "PM's: Perpetual Maniacs."

I didn't even know what a project manager was when I was in college. I thought about going to law school after I graduated, but I met Jack, who was two years ahead of me studying engineering. When it became clear we were meant for each other, I decided one graduate student in a young marriage was enough. Jack resisted, saying I'd make a great lawyer; I said I'd probably make a better wife.

Soon after our wedding, Jack enrolled in the geological engineering graduate program at Mines, which happened to be located in Golden, less than half an hour from our home in Denver. I'd applied for a job at a mid-sized tech firm, well known for customized telecommunications software. I wasn't tech savvy and feared I wouldn't make the cut. Nevertheless, the position was administrative in nature and I successfully convinced the hiring manager I could make my way around an office. Over time, I proved to be an exceptional project manager. I earned my Project Management Professional certification, courtesy of the company, and later became a Six Sigma Black Belt. As the director for a unit within the innovation division, I led a team of brilliant PMs, all of whom were Type A personalities.

Possessing the same personality type, I nevertheless appreciated down time and often stole a few extra minutes on sunny mornings to soak in early spring's splendor. It was Friday, and I'd decided to take the day off and head to my favorite spot for shopping: Home Depot. But first, a latte, made perfectly at an eclectic coffee house operated by a charming Lebanese man whose eyes were brilliant green, flecked with gold. Sometimes I wondered if I stopped there for no other reason than to gaze into his exquisite pools.

"Hey Adnan, ready for a day of sunshine and brilliant blue Colorado skies?" I asked.

I didn't know what was more hypnotizing, Adnan's eyes or the flash of his perfect white teeth as he welcomed me with his genuine smile.

Earnestly, he said, "Maggie, even if it was snowing, you'd brighten my day!"

"How's Jamie? I hope to see more of her this summer now that she's out of school. Has she found a job yet?"

Jamila was Adnan's wife, a real beauty with smooth, honey-colored skin and golden eyes. Aside from her striking looks, she was quite intelligent, having recently defended her dissertation—something to do with bioengineering. I loved talking to her about Lebanon, strife in the Middle East, and life as a Muslim woman in such a male-dominated field.

"Yes, she did! A start up contacted her and offered her a very attractive deal. They are in Boulder, so the commute may be rough, but the work is exciting. It's a biomimetics firm specializing in artificial intelligence. Anything more, you'll have to ask Jamie."

Adnan was proud of his wife and beamed whenever I asked about her. I couldn't wait for them to have babies.

"Thanks, Adnan, heading out to Home Depot to begin my spring ritual."

Already with another customer, Adnan nodded and flashed his mesmerizing smile.

I jumped into Beater, placed my latte in the cup holder, and adjusted my rearview mirror to make sure I hadn't been talking to Adnan with a crusty nose. Dad always said God played a practical joke when he made me. I loved the outdoors, gardening especially, but my immune system reacted violently to pollen. He urged me to "muscle through it," which I did, never looking back. Mom, less of a Catholic and more of a realist, said it was no practical joke, but flawed genes. When I got older, I often reminded my mother I took after her side of the family more so than Dad's.

My phone buzzed just as I started the engine,

Today, 8:12 AM
DANIEL: Betcha I know what u r doing
MAGS: Ya?
DANIEL: Slowly tracing your swollen pussy, thinking of me
MAGS: Nope, not even close
DANIEL: ☹
MAGS: Betcha I know what u r doing
DANIEL: Ya?
MAGS: Stroking your incredibly engorged cock
DANIEL: Yup
MAGS: W/o me??
DANIEL: Yup
MAGS: U'll have to finish w/o me, I'm driving

DANIEL: Latr then
MAGS: Latr

What had started as late-night exploits now trickled into mornings, lunch hours...even late afternoons. We were so comfortable with our arrangement; choosing not to play wasn't a sign of rejection, but simple postponement of something delicious to which we both looked forward. Daniel worked from home and could step away at almost any time, which electrified me. I never knew when I'd get a text and what kind of text it would be. The thrill of our "arrangement" seeped into every moment of the day.

There were times when I wanted to share my on-line fling with Katie. I struggled keeping it to myself because we shared almost everything—always had. I'd begun to feel guilty when we hung out, so I minimized those occasions. Her new position was demanding, making it somewhat easier to keep our distance, thankfully. Worked for me, otherwise I'd worry she'd detect my secret, something easily teased out of me with a glass of wine or two.

A few hours later I was loading Beater with flats of alyssum, baby blue eyes and African daisies for sunny spots, and a few flats of impatiens and begonias for the shady areas. I grabbed a few bags of potting soil for my containers, and mulch and soil amendment for my perennial gardens. Sweat was beginning to drip down my neck; it was only 10:30 and I guessed the temperature to be around 75 degrees. Pretty sure the thermometer would reach close to 90 by midday, I ramped my pace.

Properly hydrated, I unloaded my garden essentials and worked non-stop until 5:00, or thereabouts. I'd left my phone inside, freeing myself from the ties of technology, and dedicated my full attention to my botanical world—except for the part of my brain processing a steady stream of '60s and '70s folk music blaring from my iPod.

Finished for the day, I schlepped up my deck steps and remembered about dinner with Katie. I drank a glass of cucumber water before picking up the phone to call and cancel, when I decided not to; I didn't want to deal with her disappointment. I texted instead,

> **Today, 4:53 PM**
> MAGS: Hey
> KATIE: Hey
> MAGS: Been in the yard all day – can't even move now, rain chk?
> KATIE: God I forgot! Sure, that's fine cuz we have tix to Adelle!
> MAGS: Oh I forgot – why did we even plan tonite? LOL!
> KATIE: I know, right
> MAGS: Will call next wk?
> KATIE: Sure
> MAGS: xxxooo
> KATIE: x 2

Before I could text Daniel, my phone buzzed with a call. It was Bill, Match Date #2.

Fuck.

"Hello?" I answered with an uninterested tone, hoping he'd catch on.

Normally, I didn't play games, but this guy couldn't read a cue if his love life depended on it. Not long into our date, I'd posed the notion we didn't have much in common, hoping he'd agree. He didn't; blowing past my comment like a lead NASCAR driver, Bill went on to brag about having an autographed copy of Ann Coulter's *How to Talk to a Liberal*, followed by a detailed description of his mission experiences in Indonesia, including a proud moment where he and his church fellows had managed to "save" the indigenous people who'd graciously hosted their trip. I'd shared a few highlights of my political, social and religious beliefs, certain they would scare off this clueless chump. At the end of dinner, awaiting the check, I'd added a closing remark, hoping to underscore our mismatch:

Bill, thank you for dinner. But I'm not sure we're a "match," as they say.

I thought we had a great time tonight, Maggie. What did I say or do to put you off like this?

Almost everything, really.

Ha! Such a joker. Can I see you again?

No, Bill, I don't think so. Hope you can understand.

Disbelief had pooled in Bill's eyes. Had he really not understood?

Shaking my head back to reality—and Bill's call—I listened for a response, "Hi Maggie, it's Bill. How are you?"

Pissed you don't fucking get it, Bill. How the hell are you? I so wanted to say.

"Oh hi, Bill. I'm whipped, been in the garden all day. How are you?"

Please read between the lines.

"Well, it sounds like you could use a nice dinner and glass of wine. I know it's last minute, but I've been thinking about you lately."

Uh huh...

"I know we got off to a rocky start, we probably shouldn't have talked about the things they tell you not to talk about on the first date, right?" He said, chucking over his   obviously amused with himself. I couldn't get a word in, before he said, "Look, no strings, no hidden agenda. I seriously like your company and find you so damn interesting. Nothing like the twits you get on Match."

'Twits' you get on Match?

"What do you say, Maggie? My treat, of course."

Even Cody begged with more style. Still, I could sit through a conversation with him if it meant a great dinner at one of Denver's premier steak houses.

"Well, Bill, you make an interesting offer. No strings, just dinner? No convincing me to convert?"

Don't poke the bear, Mags.

"You make me laugh, Maggie! No, just conversion, I promise...this time anyway."

My God, he was completely in love with himself! No wonder he had no need for a twit.

I rolled my eyes like Katie used to do when our mother directed her to clean her room. I rarely employed such an adolescent tactic, and was surprised at my reaction. With a tone of indifference, I said, "On one condition, then. We go to Del Frisco's. How we get in on a Friday night is your problem, deal?"

A few seconds lapsed before Bill pronounced, "Deal!"

Bill had suggested we meet around 7:30. Del Frisco's was a good 30 minutes from my house, which meant I had to feed Cody, shower and find something decent to wear in 90 minutes. Utterly do-able.

My skin tingled with a slight burn as I showered and shampooed my hair. Thankfully, I had my mother's coloring, which tanned easily. Her folks were French, while full-blown Irish was Dad's claim to fame—as much fame as one can claim in western Colorado. Poor Katie got the Irish tones: pink and pinker. When I get a little sun, my skin turns golden, a color people try and replicate in tanning booths. *Bons genes*...touché, mom.

I didn't need much time to get ready. I'd quit straightening my hair years ago, and I wore very little make up—none on the weekends. My parents thought I was pretty, in a natural sort of way. Jack's nickname for me was "beautiful;" not just for my outward appearance, so he said. If asked, I'd probably say I was "nice looking," probably adding "for a 55-year-old." On the other hand, Daniel insisted I was gorgeous.

"Gotta love the limits of technology," I snickered to myself.

I found a black sleeveless maxi dress in the back of my closet and pulled it out. I'd worn it only once, having scored it from a sale rack at H&M last fall. It hung nicely on my body, unlike most straight skirts and dresses. I was curvy, always had been; my ass attracting more glances from ethnic men than white. I'd come to appreciate my looks, pitying women who had body-image issues. Fretting over a couple extra pounds was too damn exhausting, and I simply had better things to do with my time.

It was a cool May night, so I grabbed a teal knit shrug and paired it with a scarf of similar shades. I chose a necklace and matching earrings Michael had picked up for me in Milan when he was stationed in Italy. He said they matched my eyes, the color of shallow Caribbean waters. I hadn't thought of Michael lately, though my eyes instantly brimmed with tears. He'd be 29 years old now; his children are seven, twins. They look so much like their papa, a bittersweet pill because every time I see them, I see Michael. They'd come to Colorado every year since Michael died, except that first year. I could have gone to California; Carrie's invitation was open ended. But I never took her up on it...some things I just couldn't do.

It was almost 6:30 according to my phone, which buzzed with a text from Daniel,

Today, 6:27 PM
DANIEL: You sore?
MAGS: Terribly
DANIEL: Sorry
MAGS: It's okay – love gardening
DANIEL: It's fri nite, do you know what that means?
MAGS: Ordinarily
DANIEL: ??
MAGS: Going out – on a date
DANIEL: Oh
MAGS: Not a real date tho
DANIEL: Do tell
MAGS: A 'match' guy thats not a match at all
DANIEL: ED?
MAGS: No, never got that far
DANIEL: Good to know
MAGS: Can't be possessive, Danny boy
DANIEL: Not, just protective
MAGS: LOL!
DANIEL: Want a nite cap later?
MAGS: Indeed
DANIEL: Will await your command
MAGS: ☺

I left the house a little after 7:00, thanks to my text binge with Daniel. Still, rush hour had long passed; worst case, I'd be five or 10 minutes late. I glanced in the rearview mirror, noting my clear nose, and smiled at the color on my face.

"Lookin' good, Mags," I said steering Beater southward.

The parking lot was full so I drove up to the valet stand. Ignoring the stares of patrons whose kids owned better cars than my relic, I focused on the attendant who cared only about his tip...and whoever was texting him on his blinking cell phone. I got out, smiled and thanked the young man.

Del Frisco's was a strange place. Located in the Denver Tech Center, it attracted swanky folks. Of note were the barflies, women who tried very hard to look several generations younger by way of bleaching their hair, leatherizing their fair skin, and dieting to maintain their boyish figures. A few of these gals stared as I entered the foyer. Unlike the male attention I seemed to arouse, the females at the bar checked me out as if I were competition.

Don't worry, ladies. I am not interested in your prey.

"Maggie, you are radiant!" Bill appeared from nowhere and took my arm.

"It's called overexposure to the sun," I said wryly, but with a smile.

"Then I'll be careful. Please, let me take your sweater."

"No thanks, I'm fine with it on."

In truth, I was chilled—the air conditioning didn't relieve my slight burn; rather, my tender skin recoiled from the cool air.

A young hostess seated us, and Bill's eyes lingered as she walked away. So did mine—she was exquisite. I couldn't make out her ethnicity and deliberated with myself for a moment or two.

"What a looker!" Bill bulldozed my thoughts like a Mack truck.

"Yes, quite lovely," I said as I scanned the wine list.

The date wasn't bad. Actually, I had a good time. We avoided serious topics and talked about movies, travel, and of course, food and wine. The lighting was low, enhancing the dark cherry-wood paneling covering the walls. Brass fixtures, though not my style, added charm to an otherwise formal atmosphere. Servers in crisp white shirts and aprons approached each table with finesse. Ours was handsome, about 25, and unusually tall. He bent practically 90 degrees to take our order. My back would have protested after the first order of the evening.

Halfway into the wedge salad we'd decided to share, our nerves settled, and I began to enjoy Bill's company. He was 60, but looked younger, and had a full head of hair. It was mostly gray, which complimented his steel-colored eyes. He was tall, about six feet, and had a strong frame, probably played sports as a young man. I couldn't recall his Match.com profile; didn't think to research the guy before our date.

"What kinds of things do you enjoy, Bill?" I managed to say before stuffing a wad of bread in my mouth.

Our steaks hadn't yet arrived, and the few sips of wine were beginning to take effect.

"Well, let's see. I played football in high school and college. I watch a little of it on TV, but I don't like devoting my weekends to armchair antics."

That's worth a few points, I thought.

"I love to sail. My dad had a boat, and I took to the sea like a dolphin. Haven't done much of it lately. Work has me pretty tied up. I scuba dive, too. Do you like the water, Maggie?"

My head was in the clouds when he asked me about water.

"Oh yes, I do. Dad taught us to swim at an early age. My younger sister, Katie, learned to scuba dive first; she's been single all her life and has a lot more free time—and money— than me." Tired of the sound of my voice, I quickly finished the story, "When she explained what it was like, I registered for the next class at a local dive shop. I only dive in warm seas though, no cold water for me."

I sat back after sharing the account of my diving history, my mind skipping among bittersweet memories of my last dive trip. It was right before the twins were born. Michael was on a leave from a mission he couldn't talk about, and Carrie was restless; both deserved some time to make up for their military imposed separation. Jack had been working crazy hours, and it'd been an unusually cold winter, even for Colorado. All told, we needed to get away.

Throwing caution to the wind, the four of us took off for five days, Saint John our destination. We'd learned of a small cottage situated on a bluff overlooking Cruz Bay and we didn't hesitate to book it; we preferred quiet and simple and the charming yellow hideaway fit the bill. One evening in particular stood out: Michael and Carrie swinging lazily on the front porch, the breeze off the bay blowing her hair. He tenderly brushed a strand that had fallen across her face, kissing her forehead afterward. Not wanting to intrude, I stepped back, but not before I heard my son begin to sing, "Here Comes the Sun" into his wife's round belly.

"Maggie?"

Bill had been talking for some time and I hadn't heard a word.

"I'm sorry, Bill, what were you saying? I think all my hard work is catching up to me."

I tucked those memories aside, thinking I might want to revisit them again soon.

"It's perfectly understandable. A risk I assumed when I asked you to dinner after a long day in the garden. Just wanted to know if you'd like another glass of wine."

I don't think that's what he was saying, but saving face was the least I could offer the gentleman who so graciously allowed me to ignore him for a minute or two.

"Yes, I think I would."

We shared a few more stories and some laughs over a fabulous dinner.

Bill had ordered lamb, two perfectly cooked chops, laying crisscross next to a ramekin filled with mustard shallot sauce, heavy on the Tuscan Sangiovese. My appetite for steak was satisfied by an eight-ounce filet mignon. Cutting into it, I was pleased to see it was prepared exactly as ordered: rare to medium rare. We ignored the side of asparagus. Delicious as it looked, our carnivorous instincts wouldn't let us miss even one meaty morsel, leaving us stuffed to the gills. Once our table was cleared, we ordered lemon cake for dessert but only ate a few bites. I'd take the rest home and savor it the next morning with a steaming cup of coffee.

I began to fade, and was happy when the check came. Bill walked me to the valet stand and waited until Beater appeared. He didn't flinch at the sight of my vehicle, which impressed me just a smidge. Either he had one hell of a poker face, or he was a decent guy and didn't put a whole lot into what people drive. I stuck with the latter assumption.

"Thank you for such a wonderful, impromptu evening," I said truthfully.

"My pleasure, Maggie. I did too. I hope we can do it again." He smiled as he spoke.

Smiling, I said, "I'd like that, Bill, I really would."

I meant every word.

Pulling up, I realized I'd forgotten to leave any lights on. I gingerly felt my way to a light switch and found Cody on the sofa. Jack and I didn't mind dogs on the furniture, but we didn't encourage it. Cody had been doing it more, though, particularly when I went out at night.

"Hey, buddy boy, let's go to bed."

I led him to my room and watched him plop on his oversized, memory-foam dog bed. I noticed a little more gray hair under his chin, sending a pang of sadness through my heart. I changed into my comfy jammies and washed my face. Almost didn't brush my teeth then thought twice.

Placing a dollop of paste on my electric brush, I heard my phone go off. Toothbrush still vibrating across my teeth, I ran to my purse to check out who it was and shivered with delight,

Today, 9:57 PM
DANIEL: Hey
MAGS: Brushing teeth, hang on
DANIEL: K

I shut my toothbrush off before the proper two minutes were up and spit clumsily into the sink. Wiping my mouth on my sleeve, I raced to my bed and checked to see if I had any water left from the night before, but the glass was nearly empty. I sped into the kitchen and filled it up, almost spilling as I ran back to my room. Cody was fast asleep—a good thing, given how awkward it felt wondering how a dog perceives strange noises and vibrations coming from its master's bed. I grabbed the phone,

MAGS: U were supposed to wait for my command

DANIEL: Oops

MAGS: I forgive

DANIEL: Were you a naughty girl tonight?

MAGS: No, well yes

DANIEL: Yes?

MAGS: Thought about you on the way home, panties soaked by the time I changed

DANIEL: Still wet?

MAGS: Yes, you hard?

DANIEL: As a rock, I'm throbbing

MAGS: So, what r u gunna do to me, Danny boy?

CHAPTER 3

Fast Forwarded Flashbacks

Memorial Day isn't a real holiday, not for me. Endless American flags displayed in store windows, proudly hanging from pillars and poles, and waved by enthusiastic crowds inspire me little. Family and a few close friends know to leave me alone; they respect the way I approach grief: in silence and solitude. For the past seven years, I'd spend the last Monday in May thinking about Michael and Jack, leafing through mental scrapbooks containing shards of cherished memories. Sometimes I'd flip through old faded photo albums, carefully placing the palms of my hands on the faces of my late husband and son, hopeful for one last brush. The pain has subsided somewhat, but the need to remember hasn't. It was *my* day, and I was very protective of it.

Like hundreds of cities and towns across the country, Denver hosts an annual Memorial Day parade. I've never gone. Didn't think to go before Michael joined the navy, and I didn't dare after he died. For seven years, I've made a point to stay away from the parade route and all the peripheral activities that follow. My 20-minute commute to the Tech Center takes me in the opposite direction, anyway.

Keeping to my ritual, I headed southeast, away from all the commotion, stopping only for a jolt of caffeine.

Adnan greeted me, "Good morning, Maggie. Working on a holiday I see."

He didn't know about Michael, only Jack.

"Best time to get things done," I said flatly, a tone with which he was unfamiliar.

I thanked my friend for the warm concoction and made my

way to the office. It was going to be a long day, indeed.

Settling into my chair, I stared at two large stacks of mail. One was made up of manila inter-office envelopes; the other was mostly junk mail. *I'll start with that,* I thought, when my phone buzzed,

> **Today, 9:03 AM**
> DANIEL: How's your day
> MAGS: Okay, yours?
> DANIEL: Slow, corp peeps are all out
> MAGS: Best time to work tho
> DANIEL: Not going to dwell, but I know what today means to you

Sharing personal bits and pieces was easier in a long-distance relationship, especially a virtual one. I often wondered if the geographic boundaries insulated me from the pain of sharing sad details about my life with Daniel. How could it be so easy to text about Michael and Jack but so damn hard to talk about it?

> MAGS: Thx
> DANIEL: Talk?
> MAGS: Dunno
> DANIEL: U have my #
> MAGS: I know, thx
> DANIEL: Take care, Mags
> MAGS: Will do

Daniel was a kind and thoughtful man and, on this particular day, I appreciated the hell out of him. He began using my nickname soon after we swapped personal contact info, said it was easier to text "Mags." He didn't know only my dearest friends and family used it. In return, I began using his childhood nickname, "Danny." No one used it anymore, he'd said, making it special that I did.

Staring at my blank computer screen, I recalled the nicknames Jack and I gave Michael: "Little man" because he was a preemie; "bubba" because he doubled his weight in under three months; "tough guy" because he was such a dare devil; and

Jack's favorite, "asswipe," a term reserved for their garage projects that doubled as male bonding sessions. We never called him Mike, Mick or Mikey—to us, he was Michael.

Still in a trance, my mind shifted to early memories: The day I found out I was pregnant; Jack's elation when I shared the news; the day our baby was born; the string of birthday's we celebrated in the mountains because Jack and I despised those places where manufactured parties are given (on behalf of hyperactive kids and their oblivious parents); graduation from high school, then college...and the day Michael sat us down at the breakfast table and proudly informed us he wanted to be a Navy SEAL.

"Fuck you, fucking navy assholes," I said with contempt.

I was so goddamned pissed at our government for getting paid to fuck things up around the world, absolving themselves of any responsibility locally by handing me an expertly folded American flag. Michael gave his life and I didn't even get his dog tags—was told the mission was classified, his body never recovered.

"Oh, Michael, I'm so sorry. I'm so sorry you aren't here to see your babies. I miss you so much, so much," I shuddered, burying my face in my hands.

The pain of Jack was different. Ours was an abundant marriage; perfect, no, but fulfilling, absolutely. I contemplated leaving him about a year before he got sick. We'd come to an impasse, or so I thought. Jack, chuckling in a way that always lightened the mood, shrugged it off as a phase we were going through. His ability to center me was uncanny. We didn't have time to figure it out, however, because he was diagnosed with stage IV pancreatic cancer and died eight months later. As difficult as that year was, Jack and I discovered a kind of intimacy we'd never experienced before. I was prepared, or as much as one can be, when he died. We were at home, hospice care in full force, giving us cherished moments until his last breath escaped his dry, tired mouth. Kissing him goodbye, I sensed the early morning sun gleaming through the bedroom window.

Three hours later, the doorbell rang. I answered it thinking it was yet another delivery of comfort food for which I had no more room in my refrigerator; liquor would have been my preference at that point. Instead, I was staring at two naval officers in dress uniform, one holding a large envelope. Not knowing how much time had gone by, I awoke on my sofa with my head in Katie's lap, a full glass of red wine in her hand. It was only 10:00 in the morning.

"Enough, Maggie, enough," I said with a determination.

Not wanting to spend another minute in the office, I walked out and headed to Home Depot. My gardens had begun to fill out and my containers looked great. I'd amended the soil in all the beds, weeding and mulching thoroughly. I had no reason to shop at my favorite spot, but then I remembered I needed citronella oil for my lanterns.

I parked Beater in a space that seemed miles from the front doors. Memorial Day had kicked off the gardening season and the place was packed, frantic customers vying for the best geraniums available. Little did they know America's favorite container plants were like weeds; you could practically kill them and they'd come back even stronger. Oh well, wasn't my job to hold gardening clinics on my dime.

"Can I help you?"

I turned to see an overly enthusiastic employee I'd never seen before.

Must be new, I thought, *I know all the garden center staff.*

Paying little attention, I responded, "No, thank you. I know what I'm after."

"Do you, now?" The fellow said.

I turned to get a closer look at the guy and felt a vague sense of familiarity.

It hit me just as he spoke, "It's Brett, you probably don't remember me. Brett Benson."

Oh, but I do.

"Oh my God, Brett, hello! I didn't recognize you. Wow, how funny to run into you after all these years."

Not funny, awkward. Brett and I had one crazy summer the year before we graduated from high school. Since succumbing to the spell of Facebook about five years ago, I'd managed to connect with a good number of high-school buds but no former flings. Cringing at some of the things I did back then (and with whom), my mind couldn't escape the spectacle of our young love.

I'd lost track of Brett soon after high school. I stayed put, attending Colorado State University, while he went on to Arizona State, largely because of a football scholarship. ASU was his kind of school: round-the-clock party time and no foul weather to get in the way. I'd been awarded a partial academic scholarship to CSU, but needed to work nonstop until I was handed my diploma. Even if Brett had lost his scholarship (which, amazingly, he didn't), his folks would have paid the bill; a luxury available to just a few...me excluded. He was an only child, and his folks doted on him as if he were a royal prince. No matter our proximity, we would have drifted apart.

Stammering a bit, Brett asked, "So, what are you doing now?"

I hated those reunion-type questions. *Google me if you must know,* I felt like saying.

"Oh, just working, you know."

Please, please don't ask...

"You married? Have kids?"

Oh hell...

"No, you?"

I wasn't going to delve into details about my marital status or worse, explain I'd lost my only son in combat; not to a former high-school jock who I fooled around with during an otherwise unremarkable summer.

"Divorced. Three kids, all girls. They're grown now, living on the east coast near their mom and stepdad. Proud as hell of each one of 'em. They all went to college and have great jobs. None of 'em are married, though. That's okay, I can wait for grandkids."

Brett was rambling, and I could see he was uncomfortable.

"Well, it was really good to run into you, Brett. Gotta run. Take care."

As I turned to find the damn oil, He stepped in front of me and said, "Hey, Maggie, want to go out some time?"

I said half-heartedly, "I suppose we could go grab a beer or something. I'm so busy with work, though. I just don't know when..."

I chided myself for not having the courage to spit out the words forming in my head: *No fucking way.*

"Great! Okay, so here's my number, when you're ready."

Brett, the ever-cocky jock, spun around and walked off. I looked at the Home Depot "pick up" slip he'd handed me with his number scribbled at the top and laughed out loud at the ridiculous metaphor.

Brett Benson. What a blast from the past. He still looked good—really good, in fact. Just under six feet I guessed, muscular, tanned, intense green eyes and wavy light-brown hair. No gray, which was interesting.

Did Brett dye his hair?

We hadn't gotten around to questions about our careers, and I was curious why he was working at Home Depot. Don't get me wrong, my ideal retirement gig would be working in Home Depot's garden center 20 hours a week with winters off, migrating South with all the other snowbirds. Maybe a beer with Brett and a trip down memory lane wasn't such a bad idea.

I finally found the citronella, checked out and headed home. Thoughts of Brett and our adolescent romance filled my head, and I barely noticed the buzz of my phone.

I fumbled for a second before answering, "Hello?"

"Mags, it's Tina. You were *so* on my mind today, and I wanted to check in and see how you're doing," she said, concern coating every word.

"Tina, it's good to hear your voice. How are you?"

I honestly was interested in how my best friend was doing. Tina and Katie had kept me alive those first few months after losing Jack and Michael—she might as well have been my sister.

"Good, chica, good. I know it's last minute, but I want to talk you into lunch. Smothered burritos and ice-cold Coronas, on me."

Tina was in a constant state of motion and good cheer. We'd met at a personal development seminar a few years back, and her authenticity instantly drew me in. We'd been great friends ever since.

I didn't have to consider the invitation for more than a second, "I'm in, sister. When and where?"

Half an hour later, Tina and I were sitting at a table in a local dive that, not coincidentally, had the best burritos and coldest beer in town.

Halfway through an icy Corona, she asked, "How've you *really* been, chica?"

Tina, a Latina with strong features and long black hair, grew up in southern Colorado. Sixth generation, she'd been the first to leave the world of ranching in pursuit of a college degree— the first in her family to earn one. She fell into her vernacular easily, providing a cultural leave from her professional life as an assistant district attorney in Denver.

"Rough morning, Tina, not going to lie."

It had been one of the roughest, I realized.

Inhaling deeply, I said, "Got really pissed, pissed at the government, pissed at Jack, even pissed at Michael. As you can imagine, my guilt crept up and bit me on the ass. Of all the people to survive, *me*."

"I can't even pretend to know what it's like. But I do know you, and I know you'll come out of all this miserable horse shit a stronger and happier person. Hell, you're halfway there, I can see it!"

See what, I wondered.

"Yeah, I know, I just want today to be over."

I polished off my beer and ordered another. Our food hadn't arrived yet, so I nibbled on a few chips.

"So, what's new with my badass DA?"

Tina smiled, "First, I'm not *the* DA, I'm an assistant district attorney, 'assistant' being the operative word. Second, and this has nothing to do with work, we're finally going to get hitched! For real, Mags. In California, not here. Civil unions are for wimps."

Tina was beaming and her joy began to soften my hardened veneer.

"Tina! Oh my God! I am so happy for you guys. Did Trish pop the question or did you? Hell, I didn't even know you guys were seriously talking about it."

I was speaking so quickly, Tina started laughing.

"Trish did. We went camping a few weeks ago...I think I told you. We have a favorite spot in New Mexico where it's pretty warm this time of year."

Stopping briefly to catch her breath and take a swig, she continued, "She tied my ring to Bella's collar and patiently waited for me to find it."

I could see Tina's mind was back at the campsite, reliving the experience.

"We were getting ready for bed, and I gave Bella a bear hug before crawling into my sleeping bag. That's when I felt it." Grinning from ear to ear, she went on, "Trish had put it in a velvet bag, and I couldn't quite figure out what it was. Then I opened it and screamed, of course."

Screaming was Tina's way of expressing all emotions, good and bad. I cracked up every time I heard her signature shriek.

"Why aren't you wearing it?" I asked tentatively.

"Are you fucking serious? Come on, Mags, we may live in a progressive city but the DA's office is full of stiffs. No way, not now."

She lowered her eyes, not out of shame, but frustration over her career choice.

I raised my beer bottle and said, "Salud, chica! To the most amazing couple I know."

We gobbled our food and had another round before she asked, "So Mags, get any cock lately?"

Choking on my beer, I said, "Holy shit, Tina, there's a family right over there."

We looked at the table across from us, packed with a large Latino family with kids ranging from toddlers to a preteen boy who looked exactly like his mom and nothing like his dad. They were oblivious to our conversation and I sighed with relief.

"Seriously, a few beers and you're worse than any one of Michael's sailor friends!"

I didn't even think before the words spewed out of my mouth.

Tina looked at me with reservation, but I spoke before the conversation became strained, "I'm okay, Tina, really. I love talking about him. Makes my kid less of a ghost."

We smiled at each other and both took another sip of beer.

"So, I have a secret. Something Katie doesn't even know about," I said coyly.

"Oh yeah? I'm listening. Come on, what it is?"

Tina had little patience for conversational set ups, so I just blurted it out, "I'm having internet sex."

She choked on a corn chip and tried to recover her voice but not before I continued, "Wait, that sounded really dumb. I think I'm drunk! Okay, what I meant was this guy and I text and, well, it's pretty hot texting, if you know what I mean."

Clearing her throat, Tina barked, "What the fuck are you talking about, Mags? No, I don't know what you mean. This sounds really creepy, seriously."

She'd put on her professional hat and was looking at me like I was a victim of some horrific crime.

"Tina, chill, Christ. You haven't even heard the full story."

I was beginning to regret bringing it up, when she said, "Look, Mags, I know it's been rough for you, which makes you vulnerable. I see so much shit, terrible shit, Mags. I care about you, I just want you to be careful."

She meant every word, I could tell. But Tina didn't have the full story, and I tried to convince her this guy was actually a good one.

Making my case, I said, "First, he doesn't live here, not even close. He lives in Atlanta. Or at least somewhere within that area code."

"Jesus-fucking-Christ, Mags, seriously?"

I didn't like where this conversation was going and needed to put an end to it.

But, before I could, Tina said, "I just don't want to see you get hurt, chica, really. I see this kind of thing all the time and the women always get hurt, physically, emotionally and financially. You've got to put a stop to it, okay?"

Knowing there was no getting through to her, I said, "Yeah, you're right. We don't text much anymore, anyway. It was just a dumb fling. Please don't worry. Plus, I'm dating a guy from high school, if you can believe that."

Subject closed, lesson learned.

I told Tina about running into Brett but concocted a story that convinced her we'd been dating for a few weeks, which made it easy for me to dump "ATL," a name she quickly ascribed to Daniel. I couldn't help feeling deflated after our lunch.

In some ways, I was closer to Tina than Katie. We traded

details of our lives I couldn't imagine sharing with my sister. Like the time I had a three-way in college (two girls and a boy), or the time she fucked a guy in her car while she was on break from her waitress job during law school; she hadn't yet come out at work and was trying to fit in.

Were my trysts with Daniel dangerous? Had I gone too far? I'd learned to trust my gut over the years, and my gut was not warning me of danger. Ironically, it was urging me to take it up a notch. I was tired of questioning myself, and I just wanted to go home, shower and see if Daniel was available for some hardcore sexting.

Having had a few too many, I walked around the neighborhood after we left. I loved to walk and, luckily, was wearing comfortable shoes. Within minutes, I was rambling the Cherry Creek Path, an outdoor hot spot Jack and I used to walk and bike. Thinking back, I realized I hadn't been on it since he'd died. The wide, concrete swath was packed, and I enjoyed watching people fly by on bikes and inline skates. I lingered on a young couple strolling along, soaking in the brilliant Colorado sun; regret welling remembering how we used to promise each other we'd spend more quality time together.

By the time I got back to the restaurant parking lot, the sun had started to set. The sky over the mountains was brushed with hues of pink and orange, and the few clouds above were rimmed with gold.

"Spectacular sunset, Jack. I miss you," I whispered.

I jumped into Beater and headed home. The dash clock read 5:30 and I couldn't imagine where the afternoon had gone. I stopped by the market for a spinach salad and some fresh fruit. Cody greeted me with gusto, partially because he thought I was just that cool; more because he was hungry.

I poured a cup of long-awaited kibble into his dish and scratched his head, "Here you go, buddy, bon appétit!"

Stripping off my clothes on the way to the bathroom, I was ready for a good rinse. I started with my hair, massaging my scalp with moisturizing shampoo because my curly hair was dry, especially in Denver's semi-arid climate. Using my new exfoliator, I gently scrubbed my face; I had decent skin, and I wanted to keep it that way. I grabbed my buffing cloth, a free gift

I received for spending way too much money on skin care products at Macy's. Admittedly, I liked the way if felt and took an extra few minutes to massage my tired legs. My hand moved higher on my left thigh, unexpectedly arousing me.

The last time I masturbated in the shower had to have been before Michael was born. Since then, I hadn't had the time, or the inclination quite frankly. Jack and I often had sex in the shower, and elsewhere, I recalled fondly.

So why, out of the blue, was I horny as hell?

Still covered in lather, I slowly ran my hands over my breasts, squeezing them gently. My nipples were very sensitive—always had been—and perked to pinches and nibbles. Only being able to manage the former, I worked them unusually hard until they stuck out like plump raisins. I was getting wet and throbbing like crazy.

A breath escaped my mouth, and I said, "Danny Boy, I could fuck you right now."

I stopped abruptly and quickly rinsed off. I wanted Daniel's expert assistance, and I got out of the shower, barely drying off. No need for my PJ's, I ran to my room and jumped into my bed. The digital clock glowed 6:47 P.M., which meant 8:47 his time. Most nights, Daniel went to bed late, so surely he'd be awake,

Today, 6:47 PM

MAGS: U up?

I waited exactly four minutes for a reply. It felt like hours,

DANIEL: In what way do u mean?

MAGS: Mmm

DANIEL: U wet?

MAGS: How'd u know that?!

DANIEL: I can smell your sweet pussy from here

MAGS: Don't make me cum fast

DANIEL: My cock is hard, throbbing wanting you to sit on it

MAGS: No, need it from behind

DANIEL: Want to flip you over, bring your ass

high in the air
MAGS: Squeeze my tits
DANIEL: Oh yeah, got both of em in my hands, squeezing
MAGS: I need it fast and hard tonight
DANIEL: I can do that
MAGS: Wait – go slow first
DANIEL: Working up to it, slowly pumping your throbbing pussy
MAGS: Can't type anymore
DANIEL: Okay, let's finish it
MAGS: Me 2

I put the phone down and screamed, almost in agony. It was one of the most intense orgasms I'd had in recent memory—one of the fastest, too. I came so easily with Daniel; just thinking of him stirred every cell in my body. I caught my breath and reached for my phone,

MAGS: So fucking good
DANIEL: Yes it was and so are you
MAGS: It's only 9 and I could fall asleep
DANIEL: Then do and dream of me
MAGS: Mmmm
DANIEL: You make me crazy, Mags
MAGS: You make me crazier
DANIEL: I wanna kiss your pussy goodnite
MAGS: I wanna lick your cock goodnite
DANIEL: Uh oh
MAGS: ?
DANIEL: Ready for round 2?
MAGS: Oh yeah

A good stretch was in order to avoid post-coitus stiffness, a condition from which I began to suffer after turning 40. Letting out a deep sigh, I pulled the lightweight duvet just beneath my chin and closed my eyes. I was drained, in a very good way, and couldn't move a muscle. As parched as I was, I couldn't muster the strength to reach for my water. Lying on my back, listening to the hum of the ceiling fan, I smiled thinking about what just happened. Sexting had become my new favorite hobby and I was elated at the promise of one sizzling, sexy summer.

BOOK 2

Summer

CHAPTER 4

Summer's Solstice

May flew by like a scene from a fast-moving train, leaving me physically and emotionally depleted. One night in early June, I watched a decent adaptation of one of my favorite books—*Eat Pray Love*. Elizabeth Gilbert made suffering seem so...all the rage. That's Hollywood, I thought, and made a promise to myself to avoid any more drama. As the credits scrolled, I dedicated the next few weeks to finding renewal and serenity.

I'd slept in and, feeling pangs of guilt, I pulled myself out of bed and headed to the kitchen. Giving a sideways glance as I passed the hall mirror, I shrugged at my reflection: Lightweight flannel robe (mint green striped), jersey pajamas (lavender polka-dot print), and worn brown-fleece slippers that doubled as snuggle bunnies for Cody when I wasn't home.

"No drama in that scene," I muttered with Cody at my heels.

"Morning, buddy boy. How 'bout some yummy breakfast?"

I placed a dollop of Greek yogurt on top of Cody's kibble because sometimes, like anyone, he needs a treat.

Pouring a steaming cup, I settled at the breakfast bar. I started leafing through a stack of seemingly unimportant papers then paused at a familiar scrap.

Scanning it, I wondered where my head was when I wrote it. What the hell did I mean by "House?" I added a few question marks in red and moved on. What was I smoking when I wrote "New car?" I put a line through that one, scratched out "Vacation!" and underlined "Grandkids;" time spent with them *is* my vacation, and I couldn't wait to plan their trip to Colorado. Skipping over "New man?" had more to do with superstition than shrewdness. After all, I might jinx the possibility of a man coming into my life, "or snatch," I sarcastically said out loud.

Nodding to myself, I approved the changes,

Personal

House???
<u>Grandkids</u>
~~Vacation!~~
~~New car?~~
New man? Yeah, right...

I moved on to the other, less interesting column. Funny, the "asshole" boss had since moved on to greener pastures and a bigger jerk had taken his place; a strained-face woman whose mouth twitched every time she attempted a smile. I scratched out that line and wrote "TBD." I scrolled down and stopped at "New job—start looking?" My new boss was difficult, to put it mildly, but she wasn't a reason to leave. Honestly, I couldn't remember what led me to think about looking for a new job; I scratched a particularly thick line through the last item.

I took a look at my work before accepting the revisions,

Professional

~~Asshole boss - TBD~~
New project – ugh!
Staff reorg
Raise??
~~New job – start looking~~

It was time to move on to more exciting plans so, filling the monster green mug for round two, I grabbed my laptop. Logging on to my Frontier Airlines account, I realized I had enough miles for a free fare. Giddy, I began booking two round-trip tickets. Frontier is one of the most kid-friendly airlines I'd worked with, primarily because children over five can travel unaccompanied. I'd been flying the twins out since they'd reached that age. I clicked on "find flights" and plugged in a route from San Diego to Denver. I selected July 1 as the departure and July 15 as their return. Two full weeks with Timmy and Lisbeth was hardly enough, but it suited my work schedule and Carrie's anxiety level, which rose exponentially after the 14-day mark. I didn't blame her and was grateful she trusted me.

Smiling, I confirmed the purchase then hollered, "Okay, kiddos, Nana's house, here you come."

Thrilled Saturday had arrived, I indulged in a third cup of coffee. I'd had a particularly difficult week with my new boss settling in; most of my team wasn't entirely convinced they liked her and, though I had similar reservations, I couldn't let them show. Consequently, not a whole lot of work got done, which frustrated the hell out of me.

I rinsed my green mug and left it in the sink; I'd get to it and all my other chores later. I thought about fixing oatmeal but decided otherwise. There was a really good breakfast place in the shopping center a few blocks away, so I threw on my cargo shorts and a T-shirt, along with my beefy sandals I often hiked in. I topped off my casual look with Jack's old ball cap, something I'd kept around as a reminder, now a part of my weekend wardrobe. I coated my face with sunscreen, opting to leave my legs alone. I needed a little color and it was still fairly early in the day, a sunburn was unlikely.

"See ya, buddy. Be home in a bit," I said to Cody as I walked out the side door.

I'd gotten in the habit of using the side door; it felt safer, don't know why. I tucked my phone in the pocket of my shorts just as it buzzed with a text. I hadn't talked to Daniel in a couple of days and hoped it was him,

Today, 9:13 AM
BRETT: Hey
MAGS: Hey

Mr. Cocky Jock. It had been a few weeks since I'd run into Brett at Home Depot. I'd texted him a few days after. Polishing off a second glass of wine, I said it was nice running into him. Didn't even occur to me I'd just given him my number.

Duh...

BRETT: Been awhile
MAGS: A while since what?
BRETT: Home depot!
MAGS: Oh, ya
BRETT: Is this a good time to call
MAGS: Going to breakfast
BRETT: Just want to see if u r up for a few
brewskies tonite

Brewskies? A last-minute date? Don't think so, Brett,

MAGS: Tonight? prob not
BRETT: I know it's a same-day thing
MAGS: Ya
BRETT: Have plans?
MAGS: Kinda
BRETT: Doesn't sound fun, meet me

I reflected on the few dates I'd had over the last few months. I'd approached them so reluctantly but then ended up having a good time. Maybe a few beers with Brett could turn into a fun night. Oh hell...

MAGS: Where and when?
BRETT: Varsity grille
MAGS: Near DU?
BRETT: Yes, know it?
MAGS: Drive by it every day, seems young
BRETT: We are!
MAGS: Ha
BRETT: 8?
MAGS: Okay
BRETT: Okay

Holy shit, I just got asked out by Cocky Jock via text not even 12 hours before game time! I reached the breakfast joint just as I put my phone back in my pocket. I was seated at the community table and served a glass of water by my favorite waiter who quickly brought me a cup of coffee.

"Thanks, Carlos," I said inattentively as I contemplated what to wear on my beer date.

Just then, my phone buzzed,

Today, 9:34 AM
DANIEL: Morning, sexy
MAGS: Hardly morning for you LOL
DANIEL: Hoping you'd still be in bed, naked
MAGS: Sitting in a public place, drinking coffee
DANIEL: Public huh
MAGS: Yeah
DANIEL: Pussy getting wet?

I'd concluded several weeks into our fling my vagina was linked by way of radio frequency to Daniel's phone number—whenever he called or texted, my panties instantly became dripping wet. Enjoying the steamy banter, I continued,

MAGS: Yeah
DANIEL: My cocks hard for you, baby
MAGS: Danny, I can't
DANIEL: Sure you can, be creative, I can wait

Strangely, Daniel's text made me think of Jack. Sex with him was glorious. Early on, our lovemaking was exhilarating; everyday worries rarely entered our passionate realm. On occasion, it was frenzied, chased by ever-increasing life stresses. Mostly, though, our sex life was relaxed and fun. After decades of marriage, our bedroom had become a sanctuary, balanced between emotional intimacy and physical pleasure.

Sex with Daniel was different. Putting aside our obvious differences, our sexual expression was raw and untethered. My body reacted almost angrily to Daniel's urgings. Over time, I became ravenous for him.

One night, not too long ago, he called. It was late for me, which meant *really* late for him. I answered groggily, "Hi, baby."

"Wanna play?"

Daniel's voice, like velvet, always managed to make me take a deep breath.

"Always."

Our words had become few, but extremely to the point. I stripped off my pajamas and, two hours later, I'd cum three times and Daniel twice. Our pillow talk between orgasms was light and sexy, nothing too deep. I appreciated the levity of our relationship.

I texted back, sneaking sideways glances hoping no one could see the color intensifying in my face,

>MAGS: Thinking bout your cock, getting so wet
>DANIEL: Ride me, baby, your tits in my face
>MAGS: My clit rubbing against your balls
>DANIEL: Your pussy juice drenching my cock
>MAGS: Fuck I'm gunna cum, hang on

I was startled by how fast I'd become aroused and close to orgasm. Again, I glanced from side to side, hoping the patrons at the community table were too engrossed in conversation or their newspapers to notice my shallow breathing. I'd never climaxed without some form of manipulation. Still, here I was, fantasizing about this mysterious man, ready to explode.

I put my phone down, closed my eyes, and took in several sharp breaths. I quick burst of sensation between my legs came and went in mere seconds. I opened my eyes and sucked in a deep breath this time. No one, it appeared, had a clue. Picking up my phone, I texted,

>MAGS: Ur so fucking bad, but so fucking good
>DANIEL: Was it good?
>MAGS: Intense, short, amazing
>DANIEL: Perfect
>MAGS: What bout u?
>DANIEL: I'm fine, got some work to do, just wanted to say good morning
>MAGS: OMG, forget good, you are pure bad!
>DANIEL: I get badder...
>MAGS: Gotta eat now
>DANIEL: Mmmm
>MAGS: Bye
>DANIEL: Ta-ta

I ordered two eggs, over medium, crisp bacon, sliced tomatoes, and whole grain toast. Normally, I enjoy a steaming bowl of steel-cut oats. That morning though, I splurged. As I waited for my food, I couldn't stop thinking about what just happened. Was it normal? Do other people do this? Was Tina right?

"Here you go, Maggie," Carlos said as he dropped off my breakfast feast, and then swiftly moved to take an order from the older couple sitting across from me. I prayed their senses were severely impaired.

Halfway into my breakfast, a thought occurred to me: What about my bikini line? I wasn't one for a Brazilian wax. I'd survived one once, though it nearly sent me to the ER. I was terrified three layers of tender flesh had been torn in one quick "shrrrpp!" of the cotton strip that had so fully adhered to my pubic hair. The idea a "landing strip" (or worse, a completely bald pubic triangle) was somehow sexy puzzled me beyond belief. My French heritage left me with tresses best suited for... beavers.

What if Cocky Jock wanted more than a few beers and my marvelous company? What if I did?

Fumbling with my phone, I Googled, "nearest salon," and was amazed by the number of salons nearby. Unlike Katie, I didn't have a regular spot. Every so often, she'd invite me to an afternoon of pampering, never forgetting to smuggle cheap wine in Dad's old Stanley thermos. There was no time for reminiscing; I clicked on the one with the most generic sounding name, which happened to be the closest.

I scarfed the rest of my food, paid the bill, and headed out the door.

I dialed *It's Your Time Day Spa and Salon*, and a chipper receptionist answered the phone, "Good morning, this is Andrew. How may I help you?"

I had to face the fact Andrew was ready and willing to make an appointment for the shearing of my bush.

Hesitation in my voice, I said, "Hi, Andrew, I've never been to your spa before, but I desperately need to make an appointment for today."

"What can we do for you exactly, honey?"

His dulcet tones, albeit higher in pitch, made me think of Tony, and I drew an unsupported conclusion about Andrew.

Feeling a bit more at ease, I answered, "A few things, actually. I need a mani-pedi and, if at all possible, I mean, if you have the time and a person available to conduct...Wait, not conduct. That's dumb! I mean I need, well, um...a wax. A bikini wax."

There, I spit it out.

"What's your name, honey?" He said with a hint of compassion.

"Maggie, do you need my last name?"

I had no idea why, but I was nervous as hell and beginning to sweat.

"Okay, Maggie, we have the best esthetician in the beautiful state of Colorado, Rebecca, who happens to have an opening at one-thirty this afternoon. It was a cancelation actually, so this is your lucky day!"

Andrew was so pleased with himself; it made me smile and I lighten up, just a smidgeon.

Chuckling, I said, "Book it, Andrew! Did you include the mani-pedi?"

"Oh, honey, I didn't forget. I want to find just the right time slot to make your day with us fantastic. Hmm, let's see. I can put you with Melissa after your wax. Perfect!"

Delighted with himself, my new spa buddy confirmed my appointment, "We have you down for two o'clock, honey, a manicure with a with a spa pedicure immediately following."

"You got a deal, Andrew. And thank you for being so accommodating to this ol' gal," I said, much more relaxed than when I first dialed.

"I can tell *old* is not your problem, Maggie—staying out of trouble is!"

I smiled as I disconnected.

৩৵৶

My mind drifted as I drove home, settling on my last date. It was with Bill, sometime in mid-May. I struggled to recall details, but I managed to remember that, like Cocky Jock, Bill had called the same day he wanted to take me out. I couldn't recall the last time I'd been asked out well in advance of the date.

How would I ever get used to the world of online dating?

It was almost 6:00 when I got home; goose bumps on my legs and arms reminded me it was early summer. After I fed Cody, I flipped through the mail and sat on the deck with a brimming glass of mint water. I didn't drink soda—hated it actually. I'd become fascinated with infused water and had begun experimenting with different flavors, my palate wanting nothing more except a caffeine fix in the morning and dizzying nectar at night. My mind wandered for a good stretch and, realizing the time, I jumped from my favorite cedar Adirondack chair and headed to the closet.

A dress was out. Cocky Jock didn't deserve it, and I didn't feel like wearing one. I scoured the row of slacks and found a simple pair of black capris. I'd dress them up with a bright sweater and flirty sandals. Having decided on an ensemble, I stripped off my clothes and hopped in the shower. No time for feeling myself up, I had to get moving.

My phone buzzed just as I slid the mascara wand in the tube,

> **Today, 6:12 PM**
> DANIEL: Good day?
> MAGS: Yes, actually
> DANIEL: Whadya do?
> MAGS: Aside from cumming in public? LOL!
> DANIEL: ☺
> MAGS: Went to the spa, mani-pedi and a wax
> DANIEL: Brazi?
> MAGS: No! Why do guys think thats sexy?
> DANIEL: Makes eating pussy delish
> MAGS: Guess u wont be eating me
> DANIEL: Oh yes I will
> MAGS: Can't fool around tonight
> DANIEL: ☹
> MAGS: Hot date
> DANIEL: ☹ ☹
> MAGS: Old hs flame

DANIEL: ☹ ☹ ☹
MAGS: Awe, u r my one and only virtual lovr!
DANIEL: Gunna fuck the guy?
MAGS: Maybe, if I feel like it
DANIEL: Text later, we can have a virt 3 wy
MAGS: Might just do that
DANIEL: Send me a pic of your tits bf you go
MAGS: No time
DANIEL: ☹
MAGS: Cry baby
DANIEL: Will await all the nasty details, lovr
MAGS: Mmm, will gladly give if there r any
DANIEL: Ta-ta

If Tina knew I'd sent compromising photos to Daniel, she'd have me institutionalized. I wouldn't even be able to get a word out about the precautions I'd taken before she'd have 911 on the line.

Daniel had started it, sending pictures a few weeks into our sexting spree. I'd been at work and was getting ready to leave for the day, tying up a few things before I left when the phone buzzed with a text from Daniel. I opened it and stared at an image of an incredibly erect cock. Quickly scanning my surroundings, I was relieved to see most of the office had cleared out. I glanced back at the photo and became intrigued by its shape, color and slight bend to the right. I'd never been concerned with penis size—ability and skill mattered more. However, the blatant shot of Daniel's impressive cock made me rethink my opinion.

I later reciprocated with a shot of my breasts, dripping wet from having just stepped out of the shower—no face, no recognizable background...nothing leading back to me. I made sure to disable GPS tracking on my phone before taking the picture and sending it. Daniel was thrilled, and we began enhancing our late night escapades with photos and a few videos, agreeing to delete images after every rendezvous. I never knew if he did, but I complied each time; less out of respect for our agreement and more for fear of Katie (or the twins, God forbid) getting a glimpse of my forbidden world.

With not much time left, I dabbed a little makeup; my skin had bronzed over the last few weeks and I didn't need much. I'd cropped my hair for summer, so all I needed was a little product to tame my curls and...Voila! Primping was complete.

I found one of my favorite lightweight sweaters near the back of my sweater drawer, an open-weave, boatneck number in the most brilliant shade of pink—not quite magenta but almost. I wore a lace camisole underneath, finishing the outfit with a pair of fine leather flip-flops with sparkly rhinestones. I was pleased the color of nail polish I'd selected earlier at the salon matched my sweater perfectly. A quick look at my reflection and a swipe of lip gloss completed my routine. From shower to car door, I never spent more than 45 minutes getting ready to go out; date night with Brett was no exception.

The Varsity Grille was an upscale dive near the University of Denver, the oldest private university in the Rocky Mountain region. DU attracts domestic and international students with wealth and privilege, the common thread uniting an otherwise diverse campus. Housed in a renovated 1920s bungalow much like mine, "The Grille" was noted for its vintage furnishings from the antique and second-hand stores lining Broadway for 20 solid blocks. Unlike most other college hangouts, The Grille had an eclectic clientele; a mixture of students, professors, neighbors and professionals gravitated to this cozy and upbeat place.

I parked several blocks away knowing nearby street parking was unlikely on a Saturday night. It was 8:05, almost fashionably late. Thankful for lingering daylight, I took a look in the rearview mirror and dabbed on a little more lip gloss, running my fingers through my curls one last time.

Brett was standing on the front porch, a coveted piece of real estate where several bistro tables were occupied. As I approached, I noticed he was standing in front of the only one still unclaimed, staking it with masculine pride.

Waving, Brett said, "Hey there. I found a table outside. Does that work for you?"

It was feeling more like high school every minute.

"Sure," I said with a cautious smile.

We embraced like first cousins at a wedding. I did manage to feel very muscular arms through his thin Led Zeppelin "United States of America 1977" T-shirt.

After a few awkward moments, Brett got up and said, "What would you like to drink, Mags?"

It was definitely a beer night, so I replied, "Stella, please."

Brett asked if I wanted a glass, which totally threw me; hadn't expected such attention from Cocky Jock. Politely, I accepted the offer of a glass, and he moved through the door with a confident stride.

People-watching was one of my favorite pastimes. Airports offer the best subjects, but bars come in a close second. With only a few tables outside to observe, I locked onto a young couple engrossed in a debate about Obamacare. Interestingly, they were playing "footsy" and were able to separate discussion from passion, or so it seemed. Sitting at another table were three professional women, older, about my age. Unlike the young couple, they weren't talking about anything of political or social importance. Men—black men to be specific—were the topic for the animated bunch. Before I could get any juicy tidbits, Brett walked over with my beer and his: a pint of Guinness.

"Guinness, huh?" I said, as if it were an illegal import.

"The best. Can't handle piss water like we drank in high school." He took a sip, which left a foamy mustache on his upper lip he wiped with the back of his hand.

In a challenging tone, I said, "Do you think Stella is piss water?'"

"For me, yeah. But if you like it, that's all that matters."

Surprised and a bit bothered he wasn't annoyed, I said, "Yes, as a matter of fact I do," and took a long swig.

"Want to talk beer or catch up a little?"

Brett didn't falter when he asked the question; instead of a beer debate, he seemed genuinely interested in getting to know one another...again.

Already feeling a buzz, I acquiesced, relaxing into what seemed to be the beginning of a fun date.

We ordered a couple of sandwiches and more beers. Conversation came easily, and I found myself really enjoying Brett's company. As the night wore on, I began to see Brett differently. Sure, his edges were frayed, but he was so comfortable in his own skin. He knew where he stood and what mattered to him. He didn't stay in shape to impress others, particularly women. Or so I gleaned from his lack of interest in any of the young, minimally dressed women who walked by our table.

I shivered as the evening cooled. Brett reached for a worn leather jacket hanging on the back of his chair.

Handing it to me, he said, "Here, put this on."

"You ride a motorcycle?" I said in an unfamiliar octave.

"Yeah, have since ASU. Nothing like riding through the desert with no one in sight. I know it sounds cliché, but I love the freedom and the sense nothing else exists but you and the road."

A single comment about motorcycles had revealed a new side to Brett, exciting me enough to send a tingle down my back.

I smiled and said, "It's not cliché. I know exactly what you mean. After my husband died, I spent a year taking road trips; sometimes I'd go for a few days. A few times, for several weeks. Folks at work were so good to me. When my leave dried up, they gave me unpaid leave."

I grabbed the chance to chase a few memories that managed to sneak out of lock up.

Calling my thoughts back to the present, I continued, "A bike probably feels very different physically, but I think we're talking the same thing—emotionally and spiritually."

I shifted in my chair, feeling a little vulnerable having just expressed something very personal. It seemed Brett's ease had somehow rubbed off on me.

With a sly grin turning at one corner of his mouth, Brett asked, "Want to go for a ride?"

"Probably not, unless you have an extra helmet."

I wasn't about to go anywhere on a bike without one. I was still "death shy;" probably will be until I die.

"You can use mine," he said, and before I could protest, he got up and went inside to pay the tab.

I don't know a lot about motorcycles, but I do know what I like. We walked halfway down the block and came upon one of the hottest looking bikes I'd ever seen. A cruiser type, I noticed it was a Triumph when I walked up to it.

"I thought Triumphs were cars."

I regretted my remark as soon as it escaped my mouth.

What a ditz, I thought.

"You're not the first. Here, put this on."

Brett handed me a Darth Vader-looking helmet with a tinted screen and full facial coverage. He noticed I was struggling to put it on and came over to help.

"Here you go...what a fox!"

This time, his juvenile comment made me laugh. I had to admit I was having a terrific time.

We rode around the neighborhood, slowly at first, so I could get used to it. Brett walked me through the rules of riding "bitch," and once he got a sense I had it, we took off west to Santa Fe Drive where he turned it up a few notches. The wind on my skin was thrilling, and I giggled inside the dark chamber of the helmet. We drove for about 30 minutes until he turned around and headed back to The Grille. I was sad to see our spontaneous trip come to an end, but I didn't let my disappointment show as I hefted myself off the seat.

"Wow, Brett, thank you." I was still reeling with the thrill of the ride.

"Want a ride home?" He said with the same sly grin he gave earlier.

Probably his signature smile...

"Hmm, not sure," I said, instantly bemoaning my answer.

"I don't bite, Mags. It's just a ride."

True, I mused.

As if reading my mind, he continued, "And I'll come get you in the morning to bring you back to your car. How's that for a gentlemanly gesture?"

Smiling, I put his helmet back on and gave him my address. We pulled into my driveway, maneuvering to an expert stop. Luckily, I'd remembered to leave the porch light on. Some deep, primal part of me took over, and stepping off Brett's bike, I asked if he'd like to come in. He didn't hesitate and walked along side me, stepping back only to let me through the door. Cody greeted us but jumped back on the sofa, somehow sensing the tension between the stranger and me.

Turning to ask Brett if he wanted anything to drink, he grabbed my arm and swung me around. He found my mouth, and kissed me hard. I caught my breath and kissed him back with furious heat. Brett began exploring me through my clothes, grabbing my ass and squeezing my breasts. He ran his hand between my legs, heat instantly racing through my body. Lingering on his muscular arms, I slowly moved my hands along Brett's back, which twitched with my touch, arousing me unexpectedly. I stepped back, tracing my hands along his hips to the zipper of his jeans, where I felt his hard cock straining against me. Breaking away, I led Brett to the bedroom. He ripped off his shirt and was unzipping his jeans when I took over. Sliding my hand down his snug boxers, I began to stroke him and coaxed him out of his pants.

Brett wasted no time and carefully pulled my sweater over my head. Capris came off next as he kissed and licked each leg as he went. Inhaling deeply, I reached for his body, though he kept his distance, teasing me with each move. Finally, he stood and backed me up to the bed, removing my camisole in one smooth motion. He found my right breast and took it in his mouth, pinching the other nipple while grinding against my thigh.

I couldn't breathe. My head was spinning, and it wasn't from the beer or motorcycle ride. My arms had gone limp, and I instinctively spread my legs. Licking his way down the center of my belly, Brett tilted my hips just as his tongue found my pussy. Muttering unintelligibly, I closed my eyes. I completely surrendered to the magic of Brett's mouth and savored every lick, his tongue investigating each swollen, throbbing fold. My hips began to move involuntarily, my breathing intensifying with each pivot. Purring turned to screaming and Brett took me with his entire mouth, sucking and pulling away, giving me a clitoral blow job. I began to cum in slow motion. I felt every sensation from head to toe—tingling, burning, throbbing. Brett yielded to the force of my orgasm allowing me to cum long and hard, screaming incoherently. Squeezing my breasts, I pinched my nipples hard to make the orgasm last longer.

Minutes passed before I could open my eyes. Gazing back at me was a man who had given me an erotic gift, something I thought I'd never experience again. Gently, he lifted himself on top of me and slid his engorged cock inside, pumping hard and fast until he came in short bursts of ecstasy. A few minutes later, Brett flipped me over and began fucking me from behind. Long, deep thrusts took my breath away, and I began to shake. He moaned deeply. His thrusts were more powerful than ever and within minutes we came again, both of us falling over onto the bed, drenched in sweat. We fucked like maniacs, hungry for something that felt out of reach.

Thirst finally overcame me. Getting up to go to the kitchen, I looked back at the man lying in my bed, an image I hadn't seen in seven years, and a wave of emotion ran through me.

Fun times ahead, Maggie.

Making my way to the fridge for a glass of lemon water, I glanced at my purse, which I'd tossed on the floor near the front door. Curiosity got the best of me, and I pulled my phone from the outside pocket of my bag. Four missed texts from Daniel. Ignoring them, I put my phone away. June's longest day had turned into one hell of a night and I wasn't about to let anything—or anyone—fuck it up.

৩০৫৩

Serenity didn't manifest during the month of June. Renewal, on the other hand, had. Throwing caution to the wind, Brett and I rekindled our relationship with playful afternoons, sleepy weekend mornings and erotic, sleepless nights. My lust for life (and sex) had ramped, nearing full throttle. I couldn't have been more satisfied.

The Varsity Grille became our hangout, and we managed to snag our "first date" table more times than not. More confident on a motorcycle, I bought a pair of beefy motorcycle boots and wore them proudly. I had enough T-shirts and jeans in my closet to look the part of Brett's ol' lady, a secret identity I kept from everyone, even Daniel. Our passion had no bounds. We fooled around like teenagers in movie theatres. We rarely texted; instead we talked on the phone or met in person. Ours was a tangible relationship; unlike the virtual, emotionally pixilated one I had with Daniel.

I felt so alive with Brett, like I'd been given a second chance at life. There was a part of me, very deep inside, that began to regret flying my grandkids out in the middle of the summer amidst my torrid romance. The thought of two weeks without Brett was excruciating, and I prayed the days of June would last forever. Still, big girls like me know fairy tales don't last...

CHAPTER 5

Dependence Day

People move to Colorado for the weather, among other things. Hot July days followed by cool, breezy nights keep them here. Occasional rain showers in the afternoon last long enough to cool things off, freeing the air from suffocating humidity. Just a few innocuous insects buzz about, eliminating the need for screened porches. People play, work and eat outdoors; some even sleep outside. A couple of times last year, I fell asleep on my double chaise under a huge ash tree that shades most of my backyard with its massive trunk and thick canopy of almond-shaped leaves. It's easy ending a long day in the garden wrapped in an old quilt, sipping tea under protective branches. I can't imagine a better place to live.

The twins were scheduled to arrive around noon on July 1. The day before, I'd gone through the house, making sure all was in order. The guest room needed to be set up to accommodate two seven-year-olds, which meant packing up ceramic knickknacks, glass picture frames and other breakable items, and replacing them with stuffed animals, books and puzzles. Several years ago, I'd purchased a nightlight with cut out images of dragonflies, illuminating the ceiling with soothing blue tones. I'd pulled it out of the closet, setting the gem of a find on the nightstand. Timmy and Lisbeth preferred to sleep together, making the full bed perfect for the inseparable duo. I'd picked up a set of colorful sheets that matched their color scheme back home, along with a matching comforter. From start to finish, I'd spent just a little over an hour preparing their home-away-from-home.

Celebrating the Fourth of July with the twins left me feeling tentative; it was an exhilarating holiday for children but a painful reminder for me. Still, I vowed to keep my grief at bay and scoured the paper for a parade that would delight the kiddos. Cities and towns across the Centennial State boasted of the best Fourth of July festivities, so I took my time perusing the special Holiday section of the newspaper, hoping to find a more traditional, less commercial event (or worse, political). Well into the list, I became infuriated by ads depicting men and women riding in convertibles, obnoxious slogans dripping from graphic banners that ran across the top of the page. In the end, I settled on downtown Denver's parade simply because it was closest. Ignoring politicians had become a national pastime, and I was no stranger to it.

Sipping a glass of wine after a long day of housework, I shifted my thoughts to Brett. And Daniel. Erotic romps consumed my free time, leaving me with little energy for anything else. As my local fling with Brett heated up, I began to wonder if my virtual affair with Daniel had fizzled. Then I received a text from him and held my breath in anticipation,

9:17 PM
DANIEL: Missing u
MAGS: Hi!
DANIEL: ☺
DANIEL: Missing me?
MAGS: Yes, very much
DANIEL: Whatcha been doing, sexy?
MAGS: Cocky jock
DANIEL: Really?!
MAGS: Yes, jealous?
DANIEL: No, horny
MAGS: Not mad?
DANIEL: Mags, I live almost a continent away, of course I'm not mad
I was a little bothered that he wasn't...
MAGS: Okay, good
DANIEL: Was it?
MAGS: Was it what?

DANIEL: Good
MAGS: Very
DANIEL: Care to share?
MAGS: What?
DANIEL: The sordid details
MAGS: Where shall I begin?
DANIEL: At the very beginning, of course
MAGS: May require a call
DANIEL: Dialing now...

Picking up on the first ring, I said, "Hi, Danny Boy."

After some urging, I began describing steamy scenes between Brett and me, shifting my tone from schoolmarm to sex kitten—make that a jungle cat.

"Hey, naughty girl. So tell me, what have you been up to, into, and tell me about what has been into you,"

Daniel's voice coated my body with tingling sensations that felt like pinpricks.

"Cock, lots of cock. And tongue, so much licking and sucking—a delicious blend of cum and pussy juice."

"Yours?"

"All mine, though two pussies would be fun, wouldn't it?"

"Tell me all about it, don't leave out a thing."

It was apparent Daniel wanted me to take over, provide a running monologue of my sexual escapades with Brett so he could sit back, stroke his cock, and cum to images of me fucking some other guy's brains out. Ordinarily not my strong suit, I'd developed quite a flair for storytelling, and it thrilled me I could captivate Daniel. For once, I was in control.

❧

I'd asked Katie to come with me to DIA, an ever-expanding international airport situated east of downtown. Denver had annexed 54 square miles from a neighboring city to develop its vision for a 21st century airport. It was a 30-minute drive from the Denver metro area, unless rush hour had consumed all concrete arteries, making it more like an hour. I didn't mind making the trip alone, actually preferred it. But I was worried the twins would be anxious having flown unaccompanied and might want company; they adored their great-auntie who adored them right back.

Katie's place was a stone's throw from mine. She'd fallen in love with the house Jack and I bought right after we were married and swore she'd find something for herself in the neighborhood. She finally did a few years later, making it a five-minute walk between our houses; less than a minute drive. We'd grown to respect each other's privacy—a good thing, since Brett and I had been seeing each other four or five times a week, usually at my place. However, whenever we scheduled a shopping trip or an excursion to DIA, the quarter-mile trek was most convenient.

I texted Katie when I woke,

> **Today, 6:07 AM**
> MAGS: Morning sunshine
> KATIE: Really? 6 effin oclock? What time is the flight?
> MAGS: Noon
> KATIE: Dammit mags
> MAGS: Just chking to see if u r still on
> KATIE: Better chk to see if u r still sane
> MAGS: LOL, pick u up around 11, k?
> KATIE: Better have my latte waiting for me, going back to bed
> MAGS: Ta-ta
> KATIE: What??
> MAGS: Nothing
> KATIE: U r certifiable – latr

I'd used Daniel's favorite farewell without even thinking. Luckily, Katie was half asleep and didn't call me out for using something she'd never heard before. We were very close as children and knew each other better than anyone else; a slight change in behavior would stand out like an elephant in a petting zoo.

Making my way to the kitchen, I noticed Cody patiently

waiting for his breakfast, so I poured a heaping scoop of kibble. As I thought about what I wanted for breakfast, a pair of panties, lying rumpled on the dining-room table, caught my eye. I smiled, recalling the night before when Brett and I fucked up one side of the house and down the other. I'd made a mental note to go through each room with a fine-tooth comb. My stomach interrupted my thoughts with a loud growl, and I opened the fridge. An increased libido, courtesy of Daniel and Brett, left me less interested in food, which meant I had nothing in my fridge. Slamming the door shut, I headed out for a scone and a latte.

On the way, Brett called, "Hey Mags, excited to pick up the kiddos?"

I was touched he remembered. "Hi Brett. Yeah, I really am! Have the house all squared away and looking forward to two crazy weeks with my rowdy clan. Guess what I found this morning?" I said, giggling softly.

"Dunno, what?"

Suddenly, Brett seemed preoccupied.

"My black lace panties, the pair you so expertly removed when we were in the dining room..." I said coyly, apparently unto deaf ears. "Brett, you there?"

"Hang on just a sec, okay?"

His tone had turned from cheerful to irritated; not with me, but with whatever had stolen his attention. I hadn't experienced this side of Brett before and was perturbed.

Moments later, Brett said, "Sorry Mags, I got distracted with something."

Just then, I heard an angry voice in the distance—a woman's voice.

I felt like I'd been punched in the gut. My mood instantly soured, and I said, "Something or *someone*?"

Stunned, I waited for Brett's reply.

"Mags, it's nothing. An old flame keeps coming around, and she just doesn't get that I'm not interested. That's it, really."

I was struck how swiftly Brett could move from cheerful to angry to...hospitable.

Not sure I wanted to know the answer, I said, "How *old* of a flame, Brett, how long ago did it go out?"

Anger brewing, I waited for his reply.

Shifting smoothly to contrite, Brett said, "I dunno, couple of weeks maybe?"

I quickly did the math and determined his attempt to extinguish the flame occurred after we'd gone out the first time. I was "seeing" Daniel, sure, but a text message was not the same as having someone inside you. *Or was it?*

"For fuck's sake, Brett. Okay, I get it. Wow. Am I a fool or what?"

Completely exasperated, I said goodbye and ended the call. I shut the ringer off too, anticipating an apology call, which came seconds later. Ignoring it, I stuffed the phone into my pocket.

No longer interested in a latte, I went to the market to pick up a few things for breakfast. As I walked through the automated doors, I realized I hadn't thought about filling the fridge for the kids, so my shopping list went from breakfast fixins for me to an inventory any commercial kitchen would envy. I was able to keep thoughts of Brett at bay, at least for the time being, and focused on the fun I'd have cooking for my grandkids.

Several hundred dollars and five shopping bags later, I made my way home. It was 9:30, leaving me a little over an hour to unpack the groceries, shower, dab on a bit of make-up, and pick up Katie. Still, thoughts of Brett crept up every few minutes, but I promptly shoved them back—he didn't deserve better real estate than that.

You're full of shit, Maggie.

Laced with hypocrisy, my reaction to Brett was irrational, and my long-distance secret toyed with my conscience.

"Fuck you, Brett, you motherfucking cocksucker!"

Swearing was the salve I typically applied when I felt hurt or betrayed and, just then, I needed several applications. As I ranted in the shower, I had a sudden, random thought of Daniel. I smiled, thinking about how often Daniel came to mind while showering. Not only was he an instrument for sexual pleasure, but he'd also become an emotional refuge, a place where I could go to avoid pain and suffering. Holy shit, was I an addict?

Knock it off, Mags, no time for this...

I reluctantly stepped out of the shower and moved to the bedroom where I'd laid out clothes, just in case I ran out of time, which I had. Ten minutes later, I was on the road, headed toward Katie's house. Timmy and Lisbeth would be in my arms in a few hours, joy and laugher filling the house once more.

♋

It was the height of the summer travel season and people from all walks of life had flooded the state in search of the best recreation and dining spots. I couldn't wait to leave the mayhem, load the kids into Beater and head home for some much needed R & R.

"Nana! Nana!" Timmy and Lisbeth locked on to me, fleeing the side of the flight attendant who had escorted them to the hand off point.

"Timmy! Lizzy! Oh my goodness, look how you've grown!"

I swooped them from the kind young man, bent down and held them close. I breathed in their scent, hoping to catch a whiff of Michael.

"Nana, look what we got!"

Timmy, the oldest by nine minutes, pulled out plastic captain's wings the airline staff doles out to traveling kids. Lisbeth raised her pin to my eyes, and they both anticipated my response with the kind of enthusiasm Cody displays during a game of fetch.

"I didn't know you guys flew planes? How cool is that!" I said with animation.

They beamed and I grabbed them again, giving even a tighter hug.

"Let's get out of this crazy place, what do you say?"

I stood up, threw my bag over my shoulder, and took Timmy's hand in my left and Lisbeth's in my right. Both were equipped with backpacks, which they slipped on with impressive proficiency.

We took the train to the main terminal to collect their luggage, which might as well have been an amusement-park ride the way they squealed getting on and off the car. I'd decided not to tell them Katie had come along because I knew it would elevate their already super-charged excitement. Instead, she and I had planned a surprise in the baggage area.

"Katie! Katie!"

Lisbeth cried out as she ran to Katie who'd hopped out from behind the over-loaded carousal. Both kids ran into her open arms. I welled with sadness as I watched their reunion. Michael would have loved seeing them like this. I often wondered if I held back because my grandchildren were a constant reminder of my own son, the child I lost. Timmy, the spitting image of Michael, had steel blue eyes and a brilliant shock of black hair. Lisbeth, who had softer features and lighter hair, still managed a resemblance through her eyes and crooked smile. A sharp pang of grief struck me, and I gasped.

"Nana? What's wrong?"

Lisbeth, an intuitive little girl, wasn't fooled.

I looked directly into her sweet face and said, "Oh, honey. I'm just remembering your daddy because you and Timmy look so much like him. It's a good, thing, really. Memories are so good to have, Lizzy. They're like really cool pieces of colored glass you find walking along the beach. You hold each one with care and keep them safe in a pretty jar, so you can always see them."

I kissed her forehead and took her little hand in mine.

"Okay gang, let's go get your luggage and head home," I directed.

We walked to the baggage area and looked for her tangerine-colored case and Timmy's lime green one, bags I'd purchased for their very first trip to Colorado. Originally, I'd picked out the colorful bags to spot them quickly at the airport. Over time, they'd become the twin's signature colors for clothes, furnishings and accessories—at home and at Nana's house.

Katie sat in the front seat while Lisbeth and Timmy goofed around behind us. In the rear, their luggage was stacked on top of several bags of mulch I'd forgotten to unload over the weekend. Traffic wasn't too bad, and we managed to make it to the neighborhood well before rush hour. I dropped Katie off, but not before she invited herself over for dinner, promising to help out in the kitchen and bring a bottle of Prosecco. We blew kisses, knowing she'd be back soon.

Jack and I had put a doggie door in the wall next to the back door when we first brought Cody home. Since then, he'd taken full advantage of his in-and-out privileges. Hearing Beater pull up, Cody sat at the side gate in customary anticipation of me, but when he saw the kids, he romped in circles like a pup.

"Cody! Cody!" Lisbeth called out in her sweet, high-pitched voice.

She was at the latch first and opened the gate. Timmy helped push her through, straining against the lovable, 85-pound pooch. They ran out to the lawn, Cody at their heels, and found the tire swing hanging from my beloved ash tree. Twins don't compete, at least not these two. They climbed into the tire together, and it began moving with perfect coordination. It was breathtaking to watch the twins' connection, and I stopped in my tracks to observe the special moment.

The twins were old enough to be left outside with Cody as their caretaker while I dragged their bags inside. I looked at the clock and was amazed it was already 2:30. Concerned about the heat and altitude, I called the kids inside for a glass of freshly infused honeydew water, gulping a glass of the delicately flavored nectar myself.

I glanced toward my dining room and recalled the exchange I'd had with Brett earlier. I was furious with myself for thinking he and I had potential. Brett was a good time and a great fuck. That's it. I hadn't even found out why he worked at Home Depot after he'd bragged about being a commercial real-estate broker for over 20 years, having done "pretty damn well."

Probably fucked his boss's wife and got dis-brokered.

Straying outside my comfort zone these past few months had exposed emotions I'd avoided for a long time. Mostly, I was angry—angry with Jack for getting sick when we'd planned to grow wrinkled, grumpy and achy together. And I was so damn mad at Michael for joining the friggin military. Jack and I had set up a college fund before he was born. Seeing the way he fixed things and worked in the garage, we knew he'd make an excellent engineer. But he wanted to help rid the world of bad guys. I couldn't get over how the world had lost one helluva good one in the process. Then there was Katie, who lived such a carefree life with little regard for the consequences. It wasn't lost on me that I envied her a little.

As I listed my reasons for being angry, I couldn't stop. I was pissed at my boss for moving on, opening up his position to a real bitch; mad at my neighbor's dog who kept chewing through the fence; furious with my friends who couldn't see I was still quite sane and just happened to be having a thrilling affair with a guy who lived several states to the east. Most of all, I was angry with myself for opening Pandora's Box without knowing how to call back what had escaped.

Maggie's Box. The metaphor leavened my mood and I busied myself with a trivial chore.

৵৵

It took very little time for the twins to get settled, and only slightly longer for me to get accustomed to the goings on of little people. The biggest hurdle was food. Carrie and her parents were health conscious, far as I knew, but I'd found out Timmy and Lisbeth were regulars at McDonalds and Chick-fil-A. My heart went out to their mom, wondering what it must be like raising two babies alone. I imagined she was overwhelmed and filled with a sense of loneliness not unlike my own. Keeping to my no-fast-food rule, I compromised and baked some sweets, stowed several tubs of ice cream in the freezer, too.

The morning of the Fourth of July, I scurried to make a special breakfast: Blueberry pancakes, scrambled eggs, fruit salad and fresh-squeezed orange juice—a favorite in the Garrett household.

Standing at the breakfast bar with a coffee cup in hand, I shared stories about Michael with his children as they kneeled on the barstools. I knew very little of his work in the Navy, so I crafted little stories of heroism to fill in the gaps. They were captivated and I didn't want the moment to end.

We cleaned up the kitchen together and moved to the living room where I'd brought a trunk from the basement. It was Michael's, and the kids knew it. Rummaging through the top shelf, Timmy found a camouflage cap and immediately plopped on his small head, proudly smiling at his effort. Lisbeth slowly pulled a U.S. Navy SEALS bandana from under a stack of books and tied it around her small waist. Both artifacts were permanently affixed for the duration of their stay.

It was getting late, so I ushered the kids out the door. We stopped off to pick up Katie, then took the bus downtown and found a shady spot to watch the parade. I stepped back, allowing

Katie to blaze a trail through the crowds, the twins just steps behind. Timmy and Lisbeth were having a great time, as was I, watching my two adorable grandchildren experience the joy of patriotic music and fanfare.

With a lump in my throat, I whispered, "Michael, we love you and miss you very much."

After the parade and a well-deserved lunch, I herded everyone to the bus stop, making our way home through throngs of cheerful spectators. Katie had plans for the evening, so she said goodbye and walked home after helping me in the house with the kids.

We had a light supper and enjoyed it outside, where the air was beginning to cool and dragonflies swooped around the gardens. Afterward, the three of us crawled into my giant hammock stretched between the ash tree and detached garage. I'd set Pandora to my John Denver station, music flowing softly through the outdoor speakers hanging from the garage soffit.

"Nana, why do you live alone?" Timmy asked.

"Well, I don't now do I? Cody lives with me, the birds, bunnies and squirrels live in my back yard, and Katie comes over and spends the night lots of times. And you two come visit me and stay a long time. I'm lucky to have so many people and animals in my life," I said, nuzzling my grandson.

Timmy continued, "But that's not the same. Granny and Poppy live together, and Mommy and Harry live together, too."

A sharp pain ricocheted through my chest, leaving me struggling for air. A few innocent words spoken from the mouth of my grandson informed me my daughter-in-law had moved on with her life.

When Michael brought Carrie home, Jack and I were thrilled. A lovely girl from a San Diego, she was sweet, bright and most of all, she loved Michael very much. She'd moved to Colorado for college but decided against it when she met Michael; she understood his career would send them all over the world and she wanted nothing more than to make a home for him. He was equally enamored, and they married six months later. Nine months later, she delivered twins—a son and daughter he'd never meet. When he died, Carrie moved back to California with the babies to be with her parents. My pain turned into resentment, though I knew I would have done the same thing. Like two survivors of a car crash where everyone else died, we were bonded by grief, an excruciating awareness that prevented us from facing it together. Instead, Carrie left, leaving me feeling like the sole survivor of the deadly wreck.

"Harry and Carrie," I whispered, hoping the twins wouldn't hear. It sounded preposterous, and the image of their written names was even more so.

Stop it Mags, be happy for her, I urged myself, simultaneously wishing for my own steady stream of happiness.

After some time, Lisbeth chimed in, "Mommy didn't want us to tell you about Harry, but he's so nice and we really like him, Nana. She said it would make you sad. Are you sad, Nana?"

Both sets of eyes locked onto mine, waiting for an answer they surely hoped would support their love of a man who had taken the place of my son.

"You two shouldn't be worried about this kind of stuff. I'm glad your Mommy is happy and I'm glad you two like Harry. He sounds very nice. Now, shush! Let's listen for 'Al the Owl'..."

I pulled them closer, ignoring the tears beginning to well, and told them the story of an old hoot owl that had flown into my yard the day Jack and Michael died. Al, I explained to my attentive audience, perched himself atop my massive ash tree, staking his new claim, and watched over Cody and me year after year.

The temperature had dropped significantly, so we made our way inside where I led the twins through their nighttime routine: a good soak in chocolate-scented bubble bath, two rounds of the alphabet song as they brushed their teeth, and a quick change into jammies. Afterward, we settled into our ritual of bedtime reading. I'd asked Carrie if I could begin the Harry Potter series, and she agreed. Lisbeth devoured books and Timmy, while not as voracious a reader, loved hearing stories read out loud. I wanted to be the one to introduce them to one of Michael's favorite books, and I was thrilled it began that night.

By the time I tucked the twins in, I was exhausted and ready for a cool shower. First, however, I made my way to the kitchen for a much needed glass of wine. Savoring the first sip, I reflected on the day, which wasn't just a celebration of our country's independence; rather, it was a day filled with deep emotions and bittersweet memories. Torn between the warmth of my grandkids' love and the deep desire for uncontrollable passion, I was uncertain if there was a place in my life for a lover; after all, I was a widow, hard-working professional and dutiful Nana—how much more could I give? *Independence, my ass,* I thought, realizing I was more dependent on things *and people* than I'd like.

Just then, my phone went off, clearing my thoughts like the delete button on a keyboard. It was Daniel and I couldn't unlock the screen fast enough,

> **Today, 9:16 PM**
> DANIEL: Rough day?
> MAGS: Sorta
> DANIEL: Thought of you
> MAGS: Me 2, u I mean
> DANIEL: Fun with kids, tho?
> MAGS: Tons of fun, thx for asking...really
> DANIEL: Had a disaster of a date
> MAGS: Real live date?
> DANIEL: In the flesh
> MAGS: Enjoyable flesh?
> DANIEL: No, nope, nada
> MAGS: Wanna talk about it?
> DANIEL: Text okay with you?

I had a flashback of my earlier exchange with Brett and hesitated. I pictured Daniel secretly texting me in bed with a Miss Flesh lying next to him, naked,

> DANIEL: U there?
> MAGS: Ya, just thinking
> DANIEL: About what?
> MAGS: Why text and not a call
> DANIEL: Dunno

Fuck! That stupid word again. Why do men resort to pre-pubescent speak when they feel cornered by a woman?

MAGS: Heard that word today
DANIEL: What word?
MAGS: Dunno
DANIEL: More...
MAGS: Cocky jock's been into more than me
DANIEL: Oh no, mags
MAGS: Ya, and I was having so much fun, really liked the guy
DANIEL: What a let down
MAGS: Ya
DANIEL: So, you worry that I'm into more than just you?
MAGS: U r diff, we know this isn't real
DANIEL: Isn't it?
MAGS: U know what I mean
DANIEL: No, what
MAGS: We do our virtual thing but have real lives
DANIEL: So this isn't real
MAGS: Not in the physical sense
DANIEL: Don't u feel anything physical?

I was beginning to feel interrogated and didn't like it. My head was swirling with images, words, thoughts and feelings about Daniel, Brett...even Bill. I wanted the fling with Daniel to remain simple and easy. His questions opened up an emotional portal I didn't want to access...not now. Was he falling for me?

MAGS: Oh yeah I do
DANIEL: Me 2, so it's real
MAGS: You know what I mean!
DANIEL: Not really, no
MAGS: U fucking with me?
DANIEL: Nope
MAGS: U falling for me?
DANIEL: In a way
MAGS: What way?

DANIEL: No strings, no baggage, nothing to get in the way
MAGS: Kinda like a hooker?
DANIEL: In a good way
MAGS: How can that be good?
DANIEL: Turn it around, Mags, what do u like about it?

I thought about Daniel's question for a minute, drafting a mental note about what I liked about our arrangement: no commitment, no pressure, no love lost...

MAGS: The same kinds of things
DANIEL: So it's real
MAGS: Like vacant lot in a strip mall
DANIEL: Huh?
MAGS: I think of a vacant parking lot when I think of us
DANIEL: Getting philosophical are we?
MAGS: Nope, that's the way my mind works
DANIEL: Vacant lots are open to anything, inviting
MAGS: They collect trash, bird shit and vagrants
DANIEL: Whoa! u r in a mood
MAGS: Ya, prob not the best time to talk
DANIEL: Could be a great time to fuck
MAGS: Text me in 10, gunna finish wine and get naked

Tonight, I'd fill our lot with a Cirque du Soleil tent, overflowing with passionate colors, textures, sounds and sensations. Tomorrow, I'd sweep the trash and shoo the vagrants, leaving the lot as empty as I first found it.

৩৵৶

The two weeks with Timmy and Lisbeth flew by. We played board games, painted birdhouses, hung paper lanterns throughout the yard, and stole a few lazy afternoons, swinging gently on the hammock. We ventured beyond the house, too, enjoying picnic dinners at Wash Park, riding borrowed bikes along the Cherry Creek Path, and hiking a couple of beginners' trails at a nearby state park. Two days before they departed, Katie and I packed a cooler full of goodies and surprised the twins with a day at Water World, a water amusement park just northwest of Denver. We had a blast and came home with rosy cheeks and permanent smiles brushed across our faces. We hung out in the backyard the day before they were scheduled to leave. The twins snuggled with Cody while I read a magazine. I was getting anxious to get back to work, though I'd managed to stay on top of my emails and voice messages after the twins went to bed each night.

A bank of fog—unusual for Denver—descended on the neighborhood the next morning, which intensified the sadness clouding the house. Carrie's new beau, Harry, created a new dynamic in her family, and I feared I would be pushed out. Two or three times a year would probably become once, most likely in summer, so the newlyweds could sneak away to enrich their budding relationship. Still, I was happy my grandkids would have a stepdad. I desperately hoped time would allow me to get over my bitterness and accept the gift of each and every moment with my grandkids, no matter how infrequent.

Getting the house back to normal after the twins left proved to be more work than I'd expected. I decided to leave it until the weekend and opened my laptop to check out what movies were playing at a nearby theater. First, however, I glanced at my email and noticed a few messages from Match.com. Apparently, several men liked my photos and made me their "favorite." I clicked on the link and saw it was all the same guy...holy shit! A 48-year-old was hitting on me. Curious about "Justaguy5280," I read his message,

> Dear MGroadie,
>
> You MUST tell me what your profile name stands for! I'm dying to know... Anyway, you're probably annoyed with my various attempts at getting

your attention. Hoping this old school message works!

I found your profile so refreshing – real pictures, real stories, real life. I wish you knew what your competition's profiles were like. Actually, they aren't your competition – you stand apart from all the rest. I'm sorry about the loss of your husband, but I have to say, you seem so happy and content with life. You must have worked through it with such a positive attitude. Would love to know your secret to happiness!

I have two kids. I started fairly young and they are both in college. Only a year apart—a boy and a girl—they both attend Northwestern. They come home to Colorado periodically, particularly when they need money. Other than that, I have a dog, Fresno, a mutt who is ancient but is still hanging in there. I have my own business, which provides the means to have a little fun on the side. I work out of my house and love it – what can I say? I lucked out, professionally anyway.

I'm an extrovert, can you tell?

I know you're thinking I'm too young, but I would just ask you to consider having dinner. If, after that, you are convinced you can't afford childcare, then we'll shake hands and part ways.

Warmly, Greg

Before I could begin to craft a response, I quickly glanced at his profile,

I'm a pretty down to earth guy. I love the outdoors and feel most at home when I'm enjoying nature. I enjoy white water rafting, camping, biking, rock

climbing, fishing and golf (just learning!)

I enjoy working with my hands around the yard and house, remodeling and landscaping. I'm not a contractor but my dad and uncle taught me well.

Love going to the movies, out for dinner and drinks, dancing, grilling in the back yard definitely with a beer in one hand and my girl in the other – LOL!

I'm hoping to find my best friend and confidant, someone I can share my deepest feelings and fears with, as well as my strengths and aspirations.

I'm not looking for perfection, but I am looking for a woman who can love openly, play fully, and live authentically.

Like me, Greg was a Colorado native. He enjoyed the same things I did, though I realized I hadn't done anything on my list of activities since last fall. I *could* thank Greg for the nice note and leave it at that, but something pressed me to respond further. The last time I contemplated an online relationship was with Daniel, which hadn't turned out too badly. We'd constructed a virtual world insulated from the day-to-day bullshit that hampers "real" relationships. Despite our ups and downs, Daniel and I had managed to become close, thoroughly enjoying our digital time together. I wondered if I could apply the same approach to a local relationship. I answered Greg with more than a polite "thank you," and wrote,

Dear Greg,

I was tempted to send you a "thank you, but" note and decided against it. You had me at "not looking for perfection..." jk! Don't know if you noticed, but we enjoy some of the same activities.

You've reminded me, however, that I haven't been up to the hills since last fall. Movies are my favorite urban activity and, to be honest, I was just thinking about catching one when your message popped up. Haven't been in a while. Would you like to know why? Wait for it... I'm a grandmother and have been spoiling my twin grandkids for the past few weeks. Did you see how I slipped the white elephant in ever so gently?!

Still, I'm going out on a limb by saying "yes" to your suggestion for dinner. Why not cut to the chase, meet for a nice meal, and see if six years really means that much at our age. I'll hold off sharing other factoids about me to ensure crickets don't invade our space at dinner.

BTW, profile name is uneventful: "MG" are my initials and "roadie" signifies my love of road trips.

Warmer than you, Maggie (given name, not short for anything)

Not expecting a reply for at least a day, I opened a new tab and searched Fandango for a nearby movie. I'd heard about "World War Z" and, quite frankly, needed to zone out. There was a showing at 8:20, just five or so minutes away. I didn't have time to shower, so I washed my face, smoothed my tousled curls and grabbed a cardigan. I would barely make it, so I moved quickly out the door and hopped into Beater.

"Bye, buddy boy," I yelled to Cody as I pulled out, noticing I hadn't turned the porch light on.

Luck was on my side; I pulled into a close parking space just as an older couple pulled out. I hurried to the ticket window and held up one finger to the clerk who sat behind a thick slab of glass. I took the stairs two at a time so I could snag a bag of popcorn and fill my water bottle with warm tap water. I wasn't concerned about missing the trailers—I wanted an aisle seat.

The theater was freezing, and I was glad I'd brought a sweater. For the next two hours, I sat transfixed at images of ravenous zombies. Oddly, I could relate to the creatures on the screen: clinically dead, but driven by a diseased, primordial need to suck the vitality out of the living. Is that was I was doing? Was sex a mechanism to breathe life into an otherwise inanimate soul? I brushed those musings away and tossed a Milk Dud in my mouth.

The movie was a good escape, but I was glad to leave the stale air and walk into the cool night breeze. Fatigue was seeping into my body, and I desperately wanted to get home, strip off my clothes, slip into my thin cotton nightie, and hit the sack. As I turned into my driveway, I heard Cody barking, which was odd because, as he eased into old age, his need to bark at things that tickled his senses waned.

I brought Beater to a stop and turned off the ignition. Reaching for the door handle, I jumped when heard a knock on my driver's side window. Looking through the glass, I noticed a hand holding a bottle of beer—it was Brett's.

I considered getting out but saw he was seriously drunk. He staggered back, thinking I was going to get out of the car, which gave me time to think. If I drove off, Cody would be in danger— he was still barking at the side gate. If I stayed, I would be.

Rolling down my window, I said, "Brett, you're drunk. Please leave. Nothing good will come of this."

Simultaneously, I texted Katie and asked her to come over ASAP.

Slurring terribly, Brett managed to get out three words before he fell backward, "Mags, Mags, Mags!" His beer bottle shattered as he hit the ground.

I ignored him, hoping like hell Katie would pull up any time. Seconds later, I saw headlights in my rearview mirror, recognizing Katie's Mini Cooper pulling in behind me. I noticed two silhouettes in the car, one much larger than the other. She'd brought her neighbor, Tyler, a former college ball player whose size meant everything to me now. They both stepped out, Katie hanging back and letting Tyler manage the scene.

"Come on, dude, why don't we get out of here. Called you a

taxi already, we don't want any trouble, okay?"

Tyler had a surprisingly soft voice, and thankfully, it was working.

Brett struggled to get to his feet, and as Tyler walked him to the cab that had just arrived, he yelled out to me, "Love you, babe!"

Katie grabbed my car door and ushered me into the house. I was shaken and needed to sit down. I really didn't think Brett had come to harm me, but drunk as he was, anything was possible.

Protectively, my baby sister said, "Here honey, have some water."

I looked at the glass and asked for wine instead. She fixed two for us then, hearing the door open, she poured a third. Tyler stepped through the door, shaking his head and wringing his hands as if he'd just disposed of a stinking rodent. We sat at the breakfast bar, silently considering a more ominous ending to this peculiar story. Katie and Tyler finished their wine, gave a swift hug and left.

I was drained and glad to finally be alone. I got up to take a hot bath. Soaking in lavender and vanilla salts, I began to cry; wasn't sure why, and I didn't care. I let loose, feeling the strain of the day—and last few years—wash away. After a bit, I pulled myself out of the tepid water, eager to crawl into bed. Before I could turn the light out, a text came through. I looked over at my phone buzzing on my nightstand and saw Daniel's name. I had the strongest urge to respond and didn't hesitate to satisfy it,

> **Today, 11:02 PM**
> DANIEL: U r up!
> MAGS: Ya, bad night
> DANIEL: Bad date?
> MAGS: Can I call?
> DANIEL: Pls do

Daniel answered on the first ring, "Hey Mags, what's going on?"

I couldn't even spit out one work before I started sobbing.

He gently murmured, "It's okay, baby, you don't have to say

a word, just stay on the line with me, I'm here. I'm here…"

I fell asleep with my phone to my ear, listening to Daniel tell stories of his work, flying to exciting cities around the world in search of the sexiest tennis story ever written. I giggled as he spoke, not sure if he was serious or being a joker. It didn't matter; he made me laugh, enticing me into his world, if just for the night. I needed this virtual vacation, and I boarded the plane with no bags of any kind.

CHAPTER 6

August's Embers

August was a blur. I'd packed more into the past four months than I had into the last four years; I needed some serious down time. After the twins went back to California, I spent time catching up at work. The remaining hours were devoted to tending my gardens, guarding them from the scorching summer sun with plenty of water, soil amendments and a generous dose of TLC. I'd buried the incident with Brett in the part of my brain that holds the rest of my demons. How I wished memories were tangible; those of Brett would be stuffed in Cody's dog shit bag and sent off to the landfill with the rest of the city's putrid waste.

Greg wrote me back a few days after the Brett debacle. Funny and sweet, he said,

> Maggie,
>
> Your warmth flows like the rays of our beautiful Colorado sun! (Too sappy?) What movie did you end up seeing? Perhaps your critique can be the icebreaker on our first date... Then you can disclose your factoids (Why, oh why does that word conjure a medical condition not suitable for conversation?)
>
> You bring out my own mischief, Maggie, and I really like that about you. Heck, if you can do that in writing, what can you do in person?
>
> So, shoot me a couple of your favorite places and I'll do the rest. Do you suppose this is a good time

to share personal contact info?

With radical coolness, Greg

p.s. Don't go running off on a road trip without me!

I didn't have any interest in going out with Greg or anyone else, at least for the time being. I wrote him back a few days later,

Hi Greg,

You are too much! I chuckled when I read your message – thanks for a much needed laugh.

Something tells me I can be honest with you, so here it goes... I am beat. My grandkids really took it out of me and then, to boot, I had to do a bunch of catching up at work. I want to take a few weeks for me, myself and I. And, I'm sorry to break this to you: I am hoping to take a road trip with another guy, Cody, who does a terrific job keeping me warm at night. But I'm sure Fresno does the same for you.

Any chance for a rain check? Mid-September maybe?

Equally hip, Maggie

Greg responded later that day with a quick note, saying he'd be happy to take me up on the offer of a rain check; he left it to me to touch base, which I appreciated. He seemed confident and in no hurry to secure a date with me. His postscript, though, sent a small shock wave,

p.s. Cody is the only character allowed in your sleeping bag!

I wondered if Greg was the overprotective type; worse, maybe he'd left an old, new or otherwise messy flame who'd charred his soul.

Tucking away thoughts of Greg came easily; practice with

Brett had paid off. I focused on the much more enticing idea of a road trip. It was as though sharing my desire to hit the road in writing somehow made it real.

So make it real, Mags!

The nice thing about working for the same company for eons was the amount of leave accrued. Several years ago, I had to purge more than 100 hours of vacation time because the new HR rules capped the amount one could bank at 12 weeks. I'd worked like a dog the first 10 years of my career and took only a few long weekends with Jack, including several, magical dive trips. We paid little attention to our valuable free time that escaped like a slow leak in a tire; our careers had become priority one. Even with the two weeks I'd taken in July, my reserve was still in good shape, so I requested another five days off. I'd caught up at work, and my new boss was still trying to scale the learning curve—another vacation request was the least of her worries.

I decided to hit the road the first week in August, counting on low-stress driving conditions. The highways would be full of tourists, though relaxed from enjoyable excursions, most likely heading home. Plus, I planned to head north to Wyoming, long-haul truckers and commuters the bulk of the folks going that way. I knew the route there and back—could probably drive it blindfolded—and looked forward to coasting along, listening to my mega-playlist of music spanning five decades.

It was Friday and I wanted to take off Sunday morning, but Beater needed a tune up. I called my garage and asked if they could squeeze me in, hoping to pick up my resuscitated comrade Saturday afternoon. A friend had recommended Ralph's Imports once I'd earned the "widow" title; Jack had refused to let anyone under the hood of any of our vehicles, leaving me clueless about car repairs. I was on a first-name basis with all the mechanics at Ralph's due, in large part, to my complete lack of mechanical skills. I was in luck; they'd had a cancellation and could fit me in, as long as I came by before they closed.

Leaving Beater in good hands, I walked home; wouldn't be ready until the next afternoon.

Cody knew something was up, so I spent 10 minutes tossing the ball—he and I both needed to work out our jitters. Excited to start organizing my road trip gear, I made my way inside. It took just a few minutes navigating the dusty storage room in the basement to uncover my "ready-bag," one of Michael's old duffels filled with road trip clothes and gear.

Everything looked in order, so I moved on to the first-aid kit, making sure it was fully stocked. Cody's bag received a look-through, too; an old throw, several toys, and a doggie first-aid kit filled it to the brim.

Bags were set, so I went into the garage looking for my road-trip toolbox. My dad had put it together for my first cross-country trek the summer between my junior and senior year of college. I'd taken a short course, leaving four weeks of vacation before another year of brain-numbing textbooks, 30-page papers and grueling exams.

Leaving exactly one hour after my last class ended, I'd taken off for my folks' house, craving familiar surroundings and an abundance of comfort food. After a heaping snack of salami, provolone cheese and tasty crackers, I'd asked Dad to help me look over my old but functioning jalopy, talking him into an oil change. An hour later, he stood up, stretched and, in his typical nonchalant way, suggested I take a few days for myself. By 6:00 the next morning, I'd eaten breakfast, dressed and packed a bag for my first solo trek.

I remember that morning like it was yesterday; tossing my duffle in the back seat, I noticed a box brimming with road trip essentials. Sitting on top was a white envelope, "Magpie" scrolled in Dad's beautiful handwriting.

Unfolding the tattered and yellowed page from a Ziploc baggie, I read Dad's words from a lifetime ago,

> My dearest Magpie, May you marvel at the sights that fill your mind; be eased by the roads you travel; feel peace under the stars; laugh at the stumbles you take, and may you find love for Mother Nature and all Her creations—even in the beautiful black and white scavenger who, in her attempt at survival, clears the paths of weary sojourners. With all my love, Dad

I've updated the box over the years, but the principle remains the same: Be prepared to survive three of four days in the car or wilderness, regardless of the season. Reading Dad's letter made me think about survival; not in the wilderness but the kind I'd strived for the last seven years. I wondered what kind of survival kit I could have rigged to ease my pain. An image of a sleek, solitary magpie crossed my mind.

Had I been scavenging for what was missing in my life? Was I aloof and self-directed by nature?

Without thinking, I began reciting an old rhyme about my totem dad used to whisper as he tucked me in for the night,

One for sorrow,
Two for joy,
Three for a girl,
Four for a boy,
Five for silver,
Six for gold,
Seven for a secret,
Never to be told.

When I was old enough to ask, Dad explained the rhyme— old superstition, really—which foretold one's luck, depending upon the number of magpies seen. For a brief moment, I wondered if I was, somehow, the conveyor of luck, good or bad. Not wanting to dwell on mystical metaphors and prose, I returned on the task at hand, replacing the batteries in the flashlight and making sure my multi-tool knife was in good shape. Everything else looked okay. Finally, I grabbed my camping box that held, among other things, a two-person tent— make that a one-person, one-dog tent—a Coleman stove, and my "kitchen" in case I decided to camp out a few nights.

Wiping my hands on my shorts, I made my way to the front yard. I glanced around, pleased the lush and colorful scenery had survived an unusual heatwave, which was expected to continue. I set the sprinklers for an extra day and piled another layer of mulch on my garden beds. Satisfied with my work, I went inside to call Sean, a neighbor boy who looked after things when I traveled.

"Mrs. G, how are you? I haven't seen you all summer!"

Sean was a good kid and I was glad we'd worked things out.

"I'm well, Sean. Yes, I've been extremely busy this summer. I should have called you over to meet my grandkids, now that I think about it. Oh well, old age is setting in, it seems."

Talking to Sean had a soothing effect on me, not sure why—unless I'd somehow made him Michael's proxy.

"Wondering if you can come by in the morning and talk about looking after my place while I'm gone next week."

"You got it, Mrs. G! Is eight too early? Football practice is at nine sharp," he said, his voice cracking at the end of his question.

I smiled, thinking about the change in Michael's voice and how Jack used to tease him.

"Perfect, Sean, thank you."

Sucking in a deep breath, I placed my phone on the breakfast bar and poured a glass of wine, pondering what sort of dinner I'd fix.

Recollections of meeting Sean for the first time washed over me. A few summers back, I'd heard a loud crash coming from the front yard. Scrambling to my front window, I saw a teenage boy, crumpled on my cherished hostas and ornamental grasses bordering the mailbox. His buddy was bent over his own bike, laughing so hard he could barely catch his breath. Little harm had come to my plants, but the poor kid had a goose egg on his forehead, swelling minute by minute.

My irritation leveled off when I suddenly recognized a terrific opportunity. Changing my tone, I promised Sean I wouldn't tell his parents about the calamity. Relief overcame the youngster until I further explained he'd have to help out around the yard whenever I needed it. After several minutes of serious contemplation, he nodded, shaking my hand to seal the deal. Sean's been my unofficial gardener ever since.

Giggling at the thought of Sean running into my mailbox shook me from my rambling reflection. A wave of excitement washed over me and I cranked my favorite Indigo Girls CD and, completely unrestrained, joined the duo in the last verse of "Galileo,"

But then again it feels like some sort of inspiration
To let the next life off the hook
She'll say look what I had to overcome from my last life
I think I'll write a book...

Scrapping the idea of fixing dinner, I walked to a neighborhood Chinese place and ordered sesame chicken and some lettuce wraps. While I waited, I went next door to grab a six-pack of Stella. I'd make sure to pack what I didn't drink. When I got home, Cody was more excited than usual, circling my legs and jumping up as much as his old legs would allow.

Easing him down, I said, "We're going on a trip, Buddy, and you're coming with me!"

I couldn't imagine traveling without my furry companion; he'd provided unyielding companionship and a sense of security, in spite of his ten-plus years.

Beater was ready by 5:00 the next evening—my gear, loaded by 6:00. I putzed around the house all evening, finishing it off with a hot bath. Still, I couldn't sleep. My night vision was terrible, or I would have left right then and there. Even worse, driver fatigue tended to overcome me like a thick veil—once the sun went down, so did I. TV blaring, I mindlessly scrolled through the channels until I stumbled on one of my favorite movies. I was 11 years old when I first saw *Butch Cassidy and the Sundance Kid*. I think my parents thought it was a typical western, like the Spaghetti Westerns Clint Eastwood made so popular. They allowed me to go to the movie with a couple of girlfriends, all of whom were pre-pubescent, while I was post.

Several years before, Mom had explained all the women in her family matured early, as she handed me a giant box of "feminine napkins." I was ten. I hated how I'd developed so early; it made no sense and left me feeling (and looking) very different from my friends, all of whom thought it was normal to ask to see my boobs and armpit hair.

I never felt more different as the night I saw *Butch Cassidy*. Aside from the schoolgirl crush I had on both Robert Redford and Paul Newman, I was stunned by my physical reaction to the love scene between Redford and Katherine Ross.

My girlfriends giggled and scarfed popcorn, while I questioned the pulsating sensations in my groin. My face

94

flushed, and I had no clue why. Heart racing, I thought I was dying. Literally. I sat completely still throughout the movie. I didn't tell anyone about what happened—I wouldn't have known where to start.

I decided to text Daniel right before that scene, hoping to pique his interest,

> **Today, 9:42 PM**
> MAGS: U up?
> I waited exactly seven minutes for his reply,
> DANIEL: In what way do you mean?
> MAGS: LOL! Okay, awake
> DANIEL: Barely
> MAGS: Sorry!
> DANIEL: Don't be – wassup?
> MAGS: Watching a fav movie
> DANIEL: Porn?
> MAGS: No! I'm serious
> DANIEL: Okay – which one
> MAGS: Butch cassidy
> DANIEL: Classic
> MAGS: I know, right?
> DANIEL: What channel
> MAGS: TCM
> DANIEL: Let's watch together
> MAGS: Okay!
> DANIEL: Going to call
> MAGS: Why?
> DANIEL: Want to hear you
> MAGS: K

He called in under a minute, right when Etta enters her little house, startled to find Kid sitting in a chair. At first, the audience doesn't know about their romance, creating sizzling tension. After having watched the film at least a dozen times, though, I knew theirs was a red-hot affair, and I couldn't wait to get to the part where Kid points his gun at Etta, urging her to unbutton her blouse. Camera closing in, the only thing in view was a string of buttons. The scene was set up to appear as though Kid was taking Etta against her will, until her famous line: "You know what I wish? I wish just once you'd get here on time."

"Do you want me to take you against your will, Maggie?" Daniel said in a smoldering voice.

I was incredibly aroused watching that segment and listening to Daniel's heightened breathing. I pictured him stroking his cock in the dark, lying on his sheets with an air of masculine confidence. His question caught me off guard, and I stopped touching myself.

With hesitation, I responded, "Not sure, Danny, do you?"

Don't overthink this shit, Maggie!

Almost empathetically, Daniel said, "We're just playing, Mags, just go with it, you know me by now. Let's just play this one out."

Ignoring the analytical side of my brain, I allowed myself to fall back into the fantasy. Daniel began to walk me through a scenario much like the one in the film, only modern day. His voice led me through the scene he'd created—my resistance pushing against his insistence. I said nothing, focused only on Daniel's voice and the images dancing in my mind. His orgasm broke my spell, and I came seconds later. His guttural moans reverberated through the phone, making an electronic connection with my whines and whimpers.

"Danny, you drive me wild," I said breathlessly.

How could virtual sex be so incredibly hot?

"You do the same for me, Mags."

Daniel's tone was not as euphoric as mine; sultry tension coated his words.

"I am transfixed, irrationally wooed by your passion. You've cast a spell I can't break away from."

My corny sentiment paled in comparison to how Daniel characterized his feelings. He intrigued me more than ever, yet a flash of panic ripped through me. I was the one who always fell first in relationships; had Daniel upset that pattern?

"I'm tired, Danny, completely spent, courtesy of your vivid imagination," I said, somewhat sincerely.

Needing time to process what he'd just laid on me, I diverted the subject, saying, "By the way, I'm going away."

"What? When?" Daniel said with unexpected concern.

Casually, I answered, "On a road trip...'MGroadie,' remember?"

Half joking, he said, "Ah, yes, I do. Alone I assume?"

What the hell?

Attempting to lighten the mood, I said, "No, I'm taking my man, Cody. He protects me and keeps me warm."

"Will you be in range?"

Fuck if I know.

"Sometimes, though I will be in the wilderness part of the time. Don't worry. I've done this before, I know my way around Wyoming."

Even more annoyed, I wondered if Daniel noticed the shift in my mood.

"I better get some shuteye, I leave at five sharp. Thanks, Danny, for a wild ride tonight."

Dammit, take the bait!

"Okay. Be safe, Mags. I'd say call if you need anything, but I can't really come to your aid, now can I?"

Hook, line and sinker.

Glad the conversation was coming to an end, I said, "I'll shoot you a text every so often. We might be able to squeeze in a date or two, who knows."

"Sounds good, Mags. I really enjoyed tonight. I'll miss you."

The idea of Daniel "missing" me was irksome, but I played into his need for connection.

"G'night Danny, I will too," I said with less conviction.

✎ঙ্ক

I left the house around 5:00 Sunday morning. Heading north on I-25, I took US 287 just past Fort Collins. I made great time, reaching Laramie a few minutes before 7:00, and stopped for a coffee refill at Shari's, a familiar truck stop for anyone traveling this stretch of the Interstate. I didn't travel with a thermos; I scheduled my coffee stops at 24-hour diners and truck stops so I could mingle with the locals—real salt-of-the-earth types. I made sure Cody had a chance to relieve himself and sniff around, something he never tired of.

I jumped on WY 130, which became Snowy Range Road

about 30 miles later. Approaching the tiny town of Centennial at the base of Snowy Range teased my memories, and I deliberated pulling onto an old logging road to find a place to camp. It seemed too early in the day though, so I kept going until I came to the WY 130/WY 230 junction; 230 led to Encampment and 130 to Saratoga, which was home to a dog-friendly hotel, so I turned in that direction.

The hay fields had dried to golden yellow and scattered cattle grazed on meadow grass; the lucky ones sipped along the North Platte River. I pulled into the Riviera Lodge, a large "We Love Dogs" sign hanging above its entrance. It was a few minutes after 9:00 and the front desk clerk was a bit surprised to greet a guest checking in at that hour. Still, there was a room available, and I handed her my credit card. Minutes later, I began unloading Beater.

I was unusually sleepy and stretched out on the worn but neatly made bed. Pulling Cody's throw from his bag, I crumpled it on the floor next to me. Though Cody was invited onto my bed at home, I respected the hotel's policy and kept him off theirs. I snoozed for a little over an hour, waking to memories of Jack, which led to memories of Michael. Tranquility encased me, not profound grief I'd feared would sit shotgun the whole trip. I felt my whole body relax and couldn't wait to get out in the Wyoming air.

My six-day excursion was rejuvenating and provided a much-needed respite from my routine back home. Cody and I hiked rugged trails off Snowy Range Road and strolled along the Platte's banks. Driving through the tiny town of Encampment, I discovered a little diner that served excellent pulled pork sandwiches; I'd leave with a napkin filled with small pieces of the tasty grub for my dear old dog. I spent guiltless mornings on the river's edge, entranced by the ripples caused by stones I tossed with little care.

At the end of each day, I felt restored—physically, mentally and emotionally. I cried very little; instead I smiled, remembering my family's early camping trips in Wyoming. One in particular stood out: The very first time Jack and I took Michael on a rugged hike. He was seven and already competitive—we were amazed at our son's ability to keep up *and* enjoy it. Memories like those fluttered about like the beautiful butterflies flittering around the river's edge.

I woke to a beautiful sunrise the morning I left Saratoga. Staring out my small hotel window, I decided not to call Jack and Michael back. I'd spent seven years hoarding memories of them; as if the massive cache would somehow bring them back to life. I'd come to realize they'd been with me the whole trip—and the last seven years. Accepting they were gone somehow made their presence more *real*. As I loaded the last bag into Beater, I sensed a blanket of love all around, feeling Jack and Michael, knowing they would never leave me entirely. I walked to the North Platte River's edge and silently released them, encouraging a route along the river's bend up to the intersection of the Oregon and Bozeman Trails. I trusted they'd find their way to Montana—a place we loved almost as much as Wyoming.

I'd taken my time driving home, and it was late Friday afternoon by the time I pulled into my driveway. The yard looked the same, maybe even a little better. "Good job, Sean," I said out loud as I got out of Beater, my joints stiff from the hours of driving. Cody made a beeline to the side gate, and, taking the hint, I opened it. Chuckling, I watched him run to his favorite patch of grass and begin to roll around with unfettered joy.

I unpacked the gear, stowing it in the garage. Hauling the duffels inside, I noticed thick, stale air had enveloped every square inch of the house. I dropped the bags in the hallway and, quickly making the rounds, opened all the windows to entice fresh air from outside. I stripped off my nasty clothes and raced to the shower, where I stood for a good 10 minutes, rinsing road trip grime from my skin and hair.

I replenished Cody's water and poured a heaping bowl of kibble—he'd earned it. My thoughtful sister left a note on the breakfast bar,

Hey sis – Left you a present in your super empty fridge (hint: it's white, cold and refreshing!). Drove by the house every day as requested. Apart from the frat party and hooligans ransacking your place, things went just fine. Hope you come back happy, healthy and horny for Greg ... yummy!
Katie

Katie, it seemed of late, had an appetite for the details of my love life. My sister had been single her entire life, and I wondered if she would ever marry. She lived for the chase and, once caught, easily got bored. She'd had a string of boyfriends but none good enough for marriage, or so she claimed.

Our folks had reluctantly accepted the fact that Timmy and Lisbeth would be their only great-grandchildren; since then, they'd focused on their daughters, showering us with love, praise and occasional gifts that, though well intentioned, really didn't suit our tastes. We joyfully accepted them, hoping for re-gifting opportunities along the way.

I cracked open the bottle of wine and poured a glass, making my way outside to the deck. I scanned the yard, hoping Sean had cared for the back as he had the front. Everything looked fabulous, and I silently thanked him. I wiped off my chaise and plopped down. Cody was busy decoding all the new scents along the back fence, and I watched in amazement at how he delighted in the simple things.

Tilting my glass, I said, "Cheers," imagining Jack raising his glass, too.

My official travel itinerary ran through Sunday night; I didn't want people bothering me while I decompressed from my trip. Halfway through my glass of wine, however, Greg came to mind and I wondered if he was still interested in me. Oblivious to the notion I could be bothering him at that hour, I sent a very quick "hello,"

Today, 7:19 PM
MAGS: Howdy stranger

I placed my phone on the table and picked up my glass, not expecting a response anytime soon. A few minutes later, it buzzed,

Today, 7:23 PM
GREG: Hello! How was your trip?
MAGS: Amazing... perfect, actually
GREG That's how trips should be, right?
MAGS: Indeed
GREG: What r u up to?
MAGS: Hangin on my deck, glass of wine
GREG: Jealous!
MAGS: Why?
GREG: Cleaning out my garage
MAGS: So sorry LOL!
GREG: Wanna come help?
MAGS: No way, not for hire
GREG: Dinner included
MAGS: Hmmm – not too hungry
GREG: Tomorrow then?
MAGS: U don't have plans?
GREG: Only finishing the garage
MAGS: Delayed spring cleaning?
GREG: Classic procrastinator, my only flaw
MAGS: Your ONLY one?
GREG: Perhaps u will find more
MAGS: Casual okay?
GREG: The only way to go, for now
MAGS: Where and when?
GREG: Varsity, around 8:00?

Holy shit! The place where Brett and I first met. It didn't feel right at first, but then I decided I didn't want Brett to control where, when and with whom I had dinner.

Fuck it!

> MAGS: Sounds like a plan! Still look like my pics, do u?
> GREG: Yup! Look for jeans and T-shirt
> MAGS: Look for something else
> GREG: Nice – okay! G'nite Mags, sleep peacefully
> MAGS: U 2

I woke early the next morning to birds chirping and the realization I had, indeed, slept peacefully. It was Saturday, and I had chores to do. My backyard beckoned, so I raced through my housework. By 11:00, I was on my way outside. I grabbed a book I'd started before my road trip and fell into my hammock. I wanted to be rested for my date with Greg, so I committed to a relaxing afternoon. I didn't need any more color, either. My days in Wyoming were spent outside, and I'd come home nicely tanned. I opened my book and read for the next couple of hours, falling asleep for a couple more.

Cody's bark woke me, and I saw Katie walking through the gate.

"Living 'La Vida Loca,' I see," she joked.

"Hey, sis. Yes, I am."

I gave her a bear hug, and we walked into the house for a glass of water.

"Meet anyone on the road?" Katie asked.

"Nope, wasn't my plan. But you know what?" I said, eager to share my Wyoming adventure.

Gulping her water, Katie said, "What?"

"I had the coolest experience, Katie. You know how Wyoming makes me thing of Jack and Michael? Usually, I choke back my feelings and memories. I think because I'm afraid I might lose them forever."

My eyes began to water—not with sadness, but tender reflections.

"This time, I really let my feelings out, when I was hiking, resting, sleeping. I wanted to really *feel* my guys. Then, on the last day, I let go. Out loud, I mean."

Full on crying now, I reached out and held Katie's hand.

"I told Jack and Michael I was okay and that they didn't have to be locked up in my head anymore. I told them to follow the river to Montana...and then said goodbye."

Katie walked around the breakfast bar and wrapped her arms around me. She was crying, too, and we stayed locked in a sisterly embrace for several minutes.

Breaking away, she said, "Oh Mags, you deserve to be free. I've been hoping for this, honey. I've watched you try to move on, but I've never seen you let go. I'm happy, sis. I'm sad, too, because I know how much you love and miss them, but you need to live your life. I'll always be here for you, you know that?"

Smiling through tears, Katie found a couple of my curls to play with, like she'd done her whole life. It was such a soothing feeling, one I needed at that exact moment.

Lacing her fingers in mine, I said, "It feels good, Katie, it really does. I have no idea why I'm crying, but I really feel like I've closed a chapter. As silly as this sounds, it's like I'm giving birth to a new me. Does that sound weird?"

I recalled my labor pains followed by the joy of giving birth to Michael and was struck by the similarities.

"By the way," I said, "I have a date tonight..."

ॐॐ

The giddiness that normally accompanied my preparation for a date was surprisingly absent. In its place was a sense of self-assurance, and I walked up the steps of the Varsity Grille with poise. I'd chosen a colorful summer dress and tan, low-wedge sandals. Makeup was minimal, as usual, and my lips were glossy with a light pink tint. I felt every part a lady.

True to his words, Greg was wearing jeans and a T-shirt. Unlike Brett, however, his jeans were European cut, and his T-shirt was a crisp V-neck in a beautiful shade of blue that matched the color of his eyes. I glanced at his shoes and was surprised to see very expensive-looking, closed-toed leather sandals and my mind lingered on glossy images of Italian male models.

"Hi Maggie, it's wonderful to meet you in person," Greg said as he reached to give me a light peck on the check. "We have a table. They normally don't take reservations, but the owner is my neighbor. I called in a favor after watching his dog for a long weekend last month."

I caught my breath as a flash of perfectly aligned teeth shone from a very handsome face. All I could muster was a warm smile.

As we made our way, I blurted, "Tell me again what you do for a living, Greg. Can't recall if your profile mentioned that."

My question came out of left field, and was a tad embarrassed.

Pulling my chair out, Greg responded, "Didn't mention my job on my profile. Don't really think it's who or what I am. It's just what I *do*, you know?"

He sat down, looked at me and, finishing his commentary, said, "You didn't go into detail about your work, either, Maggie. Wondering if it's for the same reason?"

"Probably so. My work is important to me, and I truly enjoy it. But, at the end of the day, you're right, it's not who or what I am, it's what I *do*."

I used his words to create a connection, though I realized it wasn't necessary—the connection had been made, and it was growing like grass in spring.

The food was great, the conversation better, and our goodnight kiss unparalleled. Greg packed more style, grace and good manners into his 48 years than all of my recent dates put together. There was no clumsy post-dinner gab; Greg simply walked me to my car, kissed me on the cheek (again), and thanked me for a wonderful time. Shock waves rippled through my body and I felt dizzy for just a second. I looked up and his eyes pierced mine.

I stood frozen until Greg broke the silence, "I would love to see you again, Maggie. I'm not going to say 'I'll call you' because I know how those three words can be interpreted. So, instead, I'll tell you I will be calling you in the morning to ask you if you'd like to join me for dinner tomorrow night."

"Sounds wonderful, Greg," I said as I scooted into Beater.

I started the ignition and drove off, noticing him wave goodbye in my rearview mirror...confident I'd be watching.

BOOK 3

Fall

CHAPTER 7

Autumn's Chase

Summer's end always brings a sharp wave of sadness. Labor Day, the symbolic ending to the season, closes the gates to neighborhood pools; colors the earth with fading shades of green and emerging shades of gold; flavors farmers' markets with fall-harvest vegetables; and fills football stadiums with pumped-up athletes and adoring fans. For most, these festivities seem to prolong summer's verve; for me, they signal decay.

A day dedicated to the social and economic achievements of American workers, I spend Labor Day working my ass off to "close up" my backyard and prepare my gardens for the harsh days of winter. My routine is simple: I pack up all my yard art, torches and pillows, and stow them in the garage. After pulling the withering annuals from their pots, I toss them into the compost heap. Table and chair covers are placed over my dining set, which remains stacked against the garage wall all winter. Finally, I roll my hammock, stuffing it into a nylon case, and tuck it away in a closet downstairs.

Acknowledging the dormancy of my oasis, I'm filled with resignation, though I know in six months the crocuses would break the hard crust of my garden beds, signaling the first hint of spring. On Labor Day, my heart feels as vacant as my backyard looks.

––

Greg and I'd had a few dates following our first one that, quite frankly, blew my panties off—not literally, though I imagined having sex with him. Was he as smooth in bed as he was when he ordered wine? Did he know how to please a woman like me? Was this the man I would learn to make love to instead of merely romping in the proverbial haystack? Could this throwback gent turn me into a comeback lover?

We'd come close on our third date. After a wonderful dinner and night at the symphony, Greg asked if he could come in as we pulled into the driveway. Hesitating for just a moment, I said yes. Cody greeted us, but was more reserved than usual. Ignoring my buddy, Greg sat at the breakfast bar.

"Would you like a glass of wine?" I said, dumping my bag on the barstool next to his.

Brazenly, Greg said, "Among other things."

He smiled and came around to where I was standing.

"Greg, I'm not sure..."

I was taken aback, and it showed.

"Maggie, lighten up. I'm just trying to be funny. I like you, and I want to get to know you in your own environment. I want to know where you live, how you live and with whom."

He reached down and patted Cody on the head, looking at me, seeking approval—or so it seemed.

"Here, let me open that," he said, reaching for the wine bottle and ushering me to the stool he'd occupied.

Exaggerating a circular glance around my place, I said, "Well, this is it."

I settled back, trying to ignore my heightened nerves.

Greg poured two glasses and walked to the living room. Like a puppy, I followed, sitting next to him on what had been my "single sofa" for the past seven years. We sat in silence for a few minutes, enjoying the crisp, green-apple flavor of the Sauvignon Blanc I'd picked up for myself.

Sounding more like a schoolmarm than schoolgirl, I said, "I like you too, but I don't want to rush things, Greg."

Don't be a prude, Mags...Christ.

Finishing his sip, Greg looked at me, took my glass from my hand and placed it on the side table along with his. Leaning in, he kissed me—a tender, prolonged kiss, which I responded to with unexpected desire.

Sitting back, he said, "I have no intention to, Maggie."

He kissed me once more and got up, making his way to the

kitchen where he'd left his coat.

I trailed him, asking if he wanted another glass.

"Maggie, I've had a fantastic time. Thank you for inviting me in—I knew it was risky for you. I'm glad you trust me. I will, indeed, call you in the morning."

Another sweet kiss and he left, leaving me flushed.

I'm not sure why, but I was suspicious of Greg; it was hard to believe a man like *him* was interested in *me*. My biggest hang-up was his age—more likely mine. I'd grown comfortable with my position in life; my career, hobbies, friends and family all created a sense of contentment. On occasion, I considered whether I could live the rest of my life alone and be completely satisfied.

Nevertheless, he aroused my curiosity; spending cold days (and even colder nights) in the arms of a mysterious man lessened my dread of winter's short, lifeless months I'd normally spend futzing with indoor projects. I used to quilt and sew throughout the frosty season; baby clothes, home adornments and occasional shower gifts kept me busy. Nowadays, I attend more funerals than weddings.

Labor Day dwindled into a cool evening, a transition I observed on a single piece of outdoor furniture I left out year round: a deeply weathered Adirondack chair Jack and I had acquired from a specialty store in Cherry Creek the year we married. We could only afford one, so we'd often race to see who'd get dibs on it after a long day working in the yard. Teak didn't require much care, though Jack had preferred to lightly sand and oil it to maintain a smooth, honey-colored appearance. Lately, the chair's texture had become rough and silver gray, making it even more appealing—for me, anyway. I'd often wonder if I'd age like that, impervious to anyone with an opinion about it.

I curled up in my favorite quilt, a patchwork piece I made for our king-sized bed, now reserved for outdoor bundling. I cracked a nice bottle of Pinot Noir and, sipping idly, reflected on the past three months that roller-coasted by. By May, my virtual affair with Daniel had spiked to a record temperature; I'd had more sex in the month of June than I'd had in almost a decade, on Brett's bike, among other places; I was blessed with the gift of my grandchildren in July, who reminded me how important it is to play *and* rest; August arrived on a blanket of hot dry air, the cool mountains of Wyoming calling me away; and, like a dash of chipotle, Greg added just the right amount of spice to wrap up the most spellbinding summer I'd ever had.

I felt a wet nose on my arm and looked down at a pair of loving brown eyes.

"Hey there buddy, time for bed, is it?"

Cody grounded me. Whether I was fuming about work, annoyed with Katie, or intoxicated with lust, he stood (played, ate and slept) by me, offering his unconditional love. I gathered up the quilt, scooped up my glass and headed inside with Cody at my heels.

I'd left my phone on the nightstand plugged into its charger. I looked at the screen, and there wasn't a single notice. Not one call or text message, not even a calendar alert. My phone had taken on the personality of my bleak backyard—creepy. I changed into new jammies I'd picked up on sale and went to the bathroom to clean up for bed. As I made my way, I heard my phone buzz. Was the device reading my mind?

"You watch way too much Sci-Fi, Mags," I said under my breath as I dotted my toothbrush with mint-green goo.

Until recently, I hadn't been motivated to race to my phone the instant I heard a text come through. Greg preferred to talk on the phone, and Daniel, it seemed, had moved on. I felt relieved actually, as long as the reason for our waning relationship was distance. Thinking about Daniel in the arms of another woman fueled my jealousy, even from afar.

Staring at my reflection in the mirror, I tried to coax the sensations Daniel so easily could. I imagined his voice, felt his breath on my skin, his fingers probing my swollen pussy, his tongue licking and sucking my nipples. I felt a bolt of heat race through my body and ignite my groin. My eyes remained locked onto my reflection, hoping to get a glimpse of the passion my lover's observed...and quenched. In a flash, I became self-conscious, lowering my eyes to avoid the image of a middle-aged woman in roomy lavender flannel pajamas, a dribble of toothpaste running from the corner of her mouth. The hot, pulsating bolt was doused with the splash of self-criticism, and I made my way to my bedroom.

The text was from Daniel. Funny, I'd sensed it. I settled into bed before entering my passcode. It was one of the longest texts I'd ever received from him,

> **Today, 8:41 PM**
> DANIEL: I've missed u, Mags. I know u r prob expecting a "fuck" text, but I have to get something off my chest. I know distance keeps us apart, but I can't stop thinking about u. The countless dates this summer (ok, not countless) never came close to what happens when u and I talk and text. U prob think it's only about the sex, but it's not. I really care about u.

"Holy shit," I said out loud, my surprise waking Cody from his slumber.

I stared at the screen and didn't know what to do. I wasn't about to respond to his message. Not after that. He was most likely drunk or sad over a recent breakup and wanting advice from a love expert, which I wasn't—not the kind he was after anyway. I mentally drafted a message to Abigail Van Buren on Daniel's behalf,

> *DEAR ABBY:*
>
> *I've never done this before, but here it goes. I'm 56 years old and I have a 13-year-old daughter and two ex-wives. I've always thought I had my act together, particularly in the love life arena. You may question that, given I was twice married, unsuccessfully. But "my mamma raised me right," as they say. I treat women well, enjoy their company, and they enjoy mine, so it seems. My problem is I can't find a woman where I live. I find plenty of dates but just can't find "The One." As a result, I've resorted to long distance (even virtual)*

love affairs that have no promise of a future, just some physical gratification now and then. What can I do to change things so I can find true and lasting love?

BAFFLED

I had to sit for a moment, trying to channel Ms. Van Buren. She was a tough cookie and rarely doted on the lovelorn. How would this queen of advice respond? Closing my eyes and crunching up my face a bit, I called to her; a few moments later, she responded,

DEAR BAFFLED:

Grow up, man! Your matrimonial mishaps leave the clue from which you must take a cue: Decide to commit and commit to longevity. "The One" only exists in your mind, which can be a far greater barrier than the miles you accuse of sabotaging potential relationships.

I quickly shut down my imaginary exercise, fearing I'd seriously invoke the spirit of Ms. Van Buren who would most assuredly rip me an even bigger one than she would Daniel. It occurred to me I'd been distracting myself from the real issue. I was scared to death Daniel was falling for me. Ironically, I'd fallen for him soon after the twins returned to California. Like a hormonal teenager, I was thrilled a man I'd never met aroused me like he had. Certain our passion meant *something*, I tried connecting the dots but only came up with one word that made sense: Fantasy. Going from teenager to middle-ager in a matter of months, I concluded our cooling-off period was emotional menopause.

I reread his message, pondering it for a moment. If I'd laid out my guts to Daniel, I'd expect an answer. And so I began,

Today, 9:04 PM
MAGS: Sorta blown away here

I could almost hear the minutes tick away on my silent

phone. Glancing at the nightstand, I became hypnotized by the steady change of the glowing numbers: 9:05, 9:06, 9:07, 9:08...

Today, 9:09 PM
DANIEL: Was afraid of that
MAGS: I read it twice
DANIEL: Figured that
MAGS: Why now, Danny?
DANIEL: What do u mean?
MAGS: Things have slowed down for us, I thought u found someone, I kinda have
DANIEL: I thought I did too, about 7 times
MAGS: What do we do?
DANIEL: Talk?
MAGS: I cant, not now, sorry
DANIEL: Too much?
MAGS: Too much, need to think
DANIEL: I understand, pls don't be angry
MAGS: Nothing to be mad bout, just need to think – fair?
DANIEL: Fair
MAGS: Sleep well
DANIEL: Wanna fuck?
MAGS: Hmm – interesting offer, no strings?
DANIEL: Unless u r into that
MAGS: Ha! Why not

⚮

Fitful hardly described the way I slept the night Daniel dropped his text bomb. Though we'd had amazing restitution sex, I couldn't get the taste of his emotional vomit out of my mouth.

I was pissed, too. His decree had opened a floodgate of feelings I'd carefully stowed months ago. Now, they ran loose like a horde of gluttonous marauders hungry for any titillating morsel remaining from our languishing fling.

My alarm ringtone forced me out of my contemplative

state…and out of bed.

The Tuesday following Labor Day was pivotal for my department at work. It marked the end of summer, an unhurried season that allowed time for a good deal of rest (for some) and recreation (for most). The folks who worked for me were incredibly driven and thrived on managing really big ideas. Their work was not highly technical; rather, my team's creativity manifested in their ability to ensure the realization of technological innovations—otherwise known as project management, a field many believe to be drab and uninspiring. I knew otherwise.

For the next three months, I would pour myself into my work, leading my team through demanding projects designed for our company's continued success, which meant long days, short weekends and too many meetings. Chewing over my situation at work, I wondered if I should dust off the list I'd started last spring that included, among other life-changers, a new job.

Before starting my workday, however, I went for a morning jog—a no-fee alternative to trendy and over-priced gym memberships. Washington Park was a mile away, so I warmed up with a brisk walk then picked up the pace when I reached the three-mile jogging trail that wound through Denver's most popular playground. Heading home, I slowed to a walk so I'd be cooled down by the time I walked through the door.

I was greeted by a drooling brown dog and promptly poured his kibble, adding a slice of butter just for the heck of it. Although I walked him regularly, jogging was too much for the old guy. Now a solo activity, I often listened to music to pass the time, allowing my mind to wander freely. Nonsense like what color to paint the house, whether I should dig out a new garden in the back yard, or how to carve out more time with my folks comprised the remainder of my cranial space. That morning, though, I thought about Daniel…and Greg.

My shower felt unusually good after my run, probably because I couldn't get Greg out of my mind. I wondered what his chest looked like, what his back felt like. I mentally scrolled down and imagined a line of pubic hair forming right below his navel, leading to a perfectly proportioned cock, tracing his muscular thighs, the foundation of his Adonis-like frame. Sucking in deep breath, I rinsed my hair with my left hand and found my throbbing pussy with my right, realizing I was surprisingly close to orgasm. Rubbing hard and fast, I came within seconds. I stood under the flow of hot water as a smile crossed my face.

"I could fuck you right now, Greg," I whispered as I grabbed the towel off the rack.

My smile turned impish, recalling a similar declaration a few weeks back; made, of course, on Daniel's behalf.

Once dressed, I grabbed my phone off the nightstand, unplugged it from the charger, and unlocked the screen. I had several text messages, including one from Tony,

> **Today, 6:24 AM**
> TONY: Mags, Steve's had an accident, can't come in today

After 18 years together, they'd finally agreed to marry. Vermont was the spot; not only was it Steve's birthplace, but also an ideal location for a Christmas wedding inspired by the 1942 classic, *Holiday Inn*.

I quickly responded,

> **Today, 7:18 AM**
> MAGS: What happened?
> TONY: Bike accident
> MAGS: How bad?
> TONY: Concussion, waiting on tests
> MAGS: What hosp? OMW

Steve had just turned 60, almost 20 years older than Tony. Both were in great shape, gym rats who worked out five or six times a week. Year-round cyclists, they'd toured much of the U.S. and Canada. Safety was always a concern, so their routes often included back roads and highways. I was stunned and couldn't shake my nerves.

I called my third in command at work, Stephanie, who took over operations with unwavering dedication. My team was a loyal bunch of folks who supported each other in good times and bad. How could I possibly think about leaving this team just because my boss was a horse's ass? I made a mental note to burn the silly list I'd been reworking for months.

Tony's text interrupted my contemplation. Steve was at Swedish, a well-respected hospital with a strong reputation in neuroscience, which made me think "critical head injury."

Messages like Tony's sent me reeling to the worst possible scenario, a dramatic trait I'd acquired since losing Jack and Michael, and one I'd gladly surrender if given the opportunity.

Heading south on Downing Street for several miles, I found on-street parking fairly close to the hospital. My phone buzzed with a voice message—I hadn't even heard the phone ring. I hurried to the main entrance while listening to Greg's voice.

Normally, he avoided texting, relying on it for emergencies or quick check-ins. My voice mailbox was nearly full; I'd saved all of Greg's messages for no other reason than to listen to the sound of his voice. Each message was different and captured his various moods. Luckily, there was capacity for one more message. Greg wanted to know if I was interested in seeing a play on Saturday night. Not just any play, but *Wicked*, a show I'd wanted to see for years. I'd made it to the elevator, sure I wouldn't be able to place a call in the steel carriage, and I sent a quick text,

Today, 7:47 AM
MAGS: Friend in the hosp, will call when I can
GREG: Sorry Mags, prayers going out your way
MAGS: Thx

I was glad he didn't ask if there was anything he could do, or worse, ask what had happened. Greg had style, no doubt.

Steve was not in his room; he'd been taken away for another scan of some sort. Tony sat in a comfortable recliner all rooms were equipped with. He stared out at nothing in particular; his face gray and his posture stiff—he resembled a zombie character from a movie, but he wasn't acting.

I quietly walked toward him and said, "Hey, Tony, I'm here. What do you need? Coffee?"

There is very little one can do in a situation like this—I know firsthand. He said nothing, obviously needing his space. I pulled up a chair and held his hand.

About 45 minutes later, a nurse wheeled Steve into the room. He was hooked up to lots of equipment, but one machine in particular stood out: a ventilator.

Tony stood up, weak-kneed, and asked the nurse, "How is he? Why is he plugged into all this stuff? Why is there a tube down his throat?"

With each question, Tony's voice raised an octave. He was panicking, and the nurse was not able to give him the information he was so desperately seeking.

"Please, Mr. Carras, the doctor will be in shortly. Please try to calm down."

I knew exactly what Tony felt the minute she told to calm down, so I stepped forward and said, "Thank you. Can you tell us Steve's doctor's name and specialty?"

My question seemed to redirect the conversation. Tony relaxed and waited for the answer.

"Certainly, it's Dr. Henny, Joseph Henny. He's our chief neurologist. Steve is in great hands."

I wasn't comforted and I knew Tony wasn't either. Until we met Dr. Henny, we'd be just as in the dark as before, but it bought me a few minutes to figure out how to manage the situation. Meanwhile, Tony pulled a chair next to Steve's side, keeping vigil for 20 minutes until the good doctor walked in—a slight man, about 50, with thick salt and pepper hair. His eyes were a brilliant shade of blue, and his smile seemed genuine.

"Mr. Carras, I'm Dr. Henny, but you can call me Joe if that works for you."

He extended his hand toward Tony's.

"It's Tony, doctor. Please tell me what's going on," my friend said, his hands now shaking in rhythm with his voice.

"Ok, Tony, I believe in telling it like it is, and that's what I'm going to do in Steve's case, okay?"

Eyes fixed on Tony's, he went on, "Steve has suffered a severe brain injury. His other injuries are superficial in comparison and will be taken care of in due time. For now, we're concerned about the swelling of his brain."

Patiently, Doctor Henny continued, but Tony couldn't absorb anything he was saying.

Politely interrupting, I said, "Can you explain why Steve looks the way he does and what all the tubes are for?"

I knew lay-speak was difficult for some doctors; prodding was often the key to unlocking it. Within 15 minutes, we'd been informed Steve was in a medically induced coma to better monitor the swelling in his brain. Until he was brought out of it, the doctors wouldn't know the full extent of the damage. Tony couldn't take in any more details, so I gathered as much information as possible, hoping to relay it later.

Suddenly coming out of his own coma of sorts, Tony asked, "Is he going to live?"

With a sliver of optimism, Dr. Henny said, "Yes, we feel very good about that. However, we can't say for certain what the extent of the damage is until we take him off the ventilator and run more tests. I'm sorry we can't tell you more right now."

After he left, Tony eased back into his chair and began to cry. I kneeled next to him and took his hand in mine, silently crying with him.

By 11:00, several of the couple's friends had made their way to the neurology floor's waiting area with armfuls of flowers and food. I greeted them, provided an update, and made my way back to Steve's room to say goodbye. Tony's head rested on the side of Steve's bed, his hand gently on top of Steve's arm. He'd fallen asleep, and I didn't want to wake him. I left a note on the food tray, saying I'd be back later, which was a white lie; I wasn't sure if I could return. Since Jack's illness, hospitals and all the sounds, smells and medical paraphernalia made me queasy and claustrophobic.

Minutes later and in a daze, I combed the neighboring streets looking for Beater until I finally stumbled across him. I opened the door, got in and buckled my seat belt, frozen in thought until my phone rang.

"Hello?" I answered in an unfamiliar monotone.

Tenderly, Greg said, "Hi Mags. You've been on my mind. I'm calling to see how you and your friend are doing."

"I don't know where to begin, really," I said flatly. "My friend, Tony, is my admin at work. He's been with me for years. His partner, Steve, was in a biking accident. I just don't know what to think," I said, feeling a lump building in the back of my throat. "I'm sorry, Greg, it's just so much to take in. Any chance we can talk later?"

But I wanted to see him more than ever, and I silently cursed myself for cutting him off.

"Mags," Greg said evenly, "Why don't I come over, bring some tea and make you some toast. I don't think you really want to be alone, do you?"

How could he have known?

Giving in, I said, "I'd like that Greg, I really would. You'll have to forgive my state, I'm a complete mess right now."

Forever apologizing...Jesus, will I ever stop?

Not taking my bait, Greg simply said, "I'll see you in about an hour. I want to run to the market. Please drive safely, Mags."

When I arrived home, Cody sensed my sadness and kept out of my way as I headed straight for the bathroom. I barely made it to the toilet before heaving what little was in my stomach. I was so sad for Tony and Steve and their future; once again, I was pissed at God, demanding to know why bad things happen to good people. I didn't expect an answer, but it felt good to curse Him.

I ran a hot bath. Greg wouldn't arrive for another 30 minutes, and I longed for a much-needed soak in steaming water and lavender oil. It was early afternoon, and it felt odd being home in the middle of a workday. The neighborhood was quiet, and I was grateful for the solitude.

Closing my red, swollen eyes, I listened to a playlist brimming with my favorite female artists. The haunting voice of Joan Baez was lamenting "Diamonds and Rust" when I heard Cody bark.

I'll be damned; here comes your ghost again...

"Cody, come here boy," I shouted, but he kept at it.

"Cody! Don't make me have to get out of this bath!"

I was just about to hoist my tired ass out of the tub, when I heard a voice, "Hey there, I remember you." It was a male voice, obscured by the music and the span of the hallway.

"Hello?" I shouted, not feeling particularly frightened because it dawned on me it was most likely Greg, recalling I'd left the door unlocked.

I remember your eyes were bluer than robin's eggs...

"Mags, it's just me, Greg. Your door was partially open, not just unlocked. Are you okay?"

I said with a sense of familiarity, "Yeah, all good here. Still soaking. Is Cody behaving?"

Nerves began to get the best of me—what if he decided to bring me something? I had Harpo hair, mascara dripping down my face, and my legs, underarms and bikini line were certainly unsuitable for viewing.

Another shout from the kitchen, "Just making some tea. Brought over some *Tomme Estaing*, I get it from *Fromage*. I think you'll like it. I'll toast the baguette," he said casually like we'd been doing this sort of thing for a long time.

We know what memories can bring, they bring diamonds and rust...

"You brought over what?"

I had no idea what he was talking about, and I frantically washed my face then wrestled to find my razor. Like I'd been hit by a brick, I slouched back into the tub; I needed to let it go—not of the cloth, but my crazy way of trying to be exactly what was expected of me...or so I thought.

"Cheese! Give me just a second," Greg said with a focused tone.

Well you burst on the scene, already a legend...

I gave him a second, and then some. I sank into the water, closing my eyes, feeling the sensations of water and sound...

I heard footsteps and then his voice, "Mags, here's your tea."

Opening my eyes, I stared into Greg's piercing blue ones. He'd found one of my Italian ceramic serving trays and loaded it with a steaming cup of chamomile tea, English biscuits and a semicircle of cheese and toasted baguette rounds. He'd crafted a tantalizing arrangement—something I'm not sure I could do.

The light was dim, a few candles burning on the edge of the tub. I looked up and saw Greg looking at me, my body wet with lavender water. I caught my breath and said thank you, but before I could go on, Greg said, "Maggie, you are lovely, truly lovely."

I couldn't escape his eyes, and as much as I wanted to turn away, I couldn't. I said nothing as I reached for my tea. No one—not even Jack—had offered me anything while I soaked in the tub. My bath time was off limits to kids, husbands and dogs. And yet, Greg had managed to penetrate my sanctuary with such ease.

Greg kneeled beside the tub and kissed my cheek. I closed my eyes and took in a deep breath. His right hand traced my face, my neck, and stopped at the curve of my breasts. His left hand then stroked my head, moving to my neck with gentle pressure.

Our breath comes out white clouds, mingles and hangs in the air, speaking strictly for me, we both could have died then and there...

I stayed there, not wanting to move, think or act. I let Greg explore my body, my breasts, belly, and thighs. He kissed my neck while he gently probed between my legs. I let out a slight gasp as he fingered my swollen lips with one hand and squeezed my left nipple with his other. I couldn't move, could barely breathe.

I came in less than a minute, which left me feeling despondent over the immediacy of my orgasm. With my eyes still shut, I drove out the criticisms forming in my head. Hadn't this summer been one of renewal? Hadn't I vowed to move on and let go of old habits...and ghosts? A few moments passed when I finally opened my eyes. Greg was sitting on the tub's edge, making gentle circles in the water with his right hand; the other held a glass of wine, which he offered to me before easing me out of the water. He softly patted me dry then led me to the bedroom where I crawled under the covers while he effortlessly undressed. It was like slow motion, watching every part of his body move. I wanted him so badly, I moaned in anticipation.

Greg slid under the covers and leaned in to kiss me. Passion unleashed, my mouth met his and he kissed me harder. My hand groped for his cock, and I began rubbing against his thigh, letting him know how much I wanted it...wanted him. Sliding on top of me, he spread my legs with his and held my wrists down while he moved to find my wet and willing pussy.

Greg was breathing hard, almost grunting as he began to pump; slow at first, then harder. My hips moved to his rhythm, leading him faster. It was like nothing I'd felt before—wild, raging, uncontrollable.

We came together in an almost orchestrated way, though

nothing about our lovemaking was scripted. All the day's suffering and sadness was exorcized right then, replaced by a sexual tranquility foreign to me. I hadn't felt completely satisfied in ages, and I smiled to myself. After lying on top of me to catch his breath, Greg slid off to one side. The light was streaming through the window, and I noticed the outline of the muscles in his back, highlighted by the sweat coating his skin. Thick hair fell over his face, which he'd buried between my breasts. I lay still, my breath slowing with each exhale. Minutes passed before he looked up, kissed me lightly, and said, "You are most irresistible, Mags."

Smiling, I slipped away to get some much-needed water for both of us. It was already 4:00, so I fed Cody, grabbed a few more snacks, and sauntered back down the hallway. Greg leaned up on one arm and watched me walk into the room. Surprisingly, I didn't feel self-conscious, and I asked him if he wanted water and something to eat. Nodding like a schoolboy, he said yes, and I placed the tray of goodies on the bed.

"I feel like I have to say something," I said with a more formal tone than I'd wanted.

Greg popped a strawberry in his mouth then said, "Don't."

We spent the rest of the day in bed, making love several more times and napping in between. Falling asleep came naturally; his arms tenderly wrapped around me. I didn't dream that night, nor did I toss and turn. I woke early, cocooned by strong arms. Moments passed before I felt Greg's hard cock pressed against my back, provoking an instantaneous and extremely wet reaction in me.

"Good morning, beautiful," Greg said, as he maneuvered on top of me.

"Good morning, handsome," I said, "What's for breakfast?"

CHAPTER 8

Wicked Times

It snowed on September 19th. Eleven days later, the temperature soared to 82 degrees. I was looking forward to less erratic weather patterns, which October refused to supply. The harvest month reported temperatures ranging from a balmy 79 degrees on the 8th to a frigid 27 degrees mid-month. Denver reported its first measurable snowfall of 1.4 inches on October 18th. The city's news channels loved this time of year because climate fluctuations were big business in the ratings game. Denverites began to text, tweet and post images of autumn sunbathers at Wash Park then a week later, shared pictures of unique snowmen decked out in retired winter gear. I didn't stow my warm-weather clothes until late November.

Greg and I had fun incorporating unpredictable weather into our plans. I played hooky one afternoon and we drove to Boulder, strolling the Pearl Street Mall in search of Ben & Jerry's ice cream. Later, we settled on a cozy Irish pub for dinner, tucked just a stone's throw from straggling tourists and rowdy college students. I had tasty fish and chips, while Greg devoured a heaping shepherd's pie. When the temperature plummeted, I played hooky again, hiding out at Greg's house where we enjoyed his outdoor hot tub...and indoor California king.

I'd been to Greg's home on a few occasions for dinner or a nightcap but hadn't really seen much of it except his masculine, yet incredibly comfortable den. The day the thermometer wasn't supposed to go beyond 30 degrees, I didn't leave Greg's house at all. I explored every nook and cranny, beginning with his gourmet kitchen (where we fucked on the center island); moving on to his impressive home office (this time, on his sleek leather sofa); meandering through his vast closet (where he licked my pussy until I screamed in ecstasy beneath endless racks of fine men's clothes), finally winding up in his lavish bedroom, where we stayed through the night.

It was Saturday, the day after Greg and I exhausted ourselves fucking like teenagers in every room of his house, I went to work on my kitchen pantry: Consolidating duplicate containers of breadcrumbs; getting rid of near-empty spice bottles; and wiping small trays that held a wide variety of oils and vinegars. I was expecting a large crowd for Thanksgiving and probably the same number for Christmas Eve. To top it off, Steve had managed to make a full recovery from his accident; I intended to celebrate the holidays with panache, well seasoned with love and joy. It was only mid-October, but they'd sneak up on me, so I dedicated the next few weeks to preparing the house—especially the kitchen—for the merrymaking.

Coffee on, Cody fed, I stood at my back door, glancing at the empty bird feeder hanging from the bare ash. Reaching for my jacket, I heard the phone buzz; it was Daniel. I hadn't heard from him in weeks. We'd stopped talking altogether and only texted late at night when we (mostly him) needed a good virtual fuck. I couldn't get past the emotionally charged text that exposed his feelings for me—feelings I'd had earlier on, but were eventually dowsed after realizing how much easier things were between us with no strings attached. I went outside to fill the feeder and empty my head.

I could smell the coffee before I opened the back door. It wasn't as cold outside as it looked, and I was glad to shed my jacket once inside. Grabbing my green mug, I poured a steaming cup and looked at the phone. Three more texts had come in, all from Daniel.

What the fuck. I unlocked the screen, hit the text bubble and opened Daniel's string,

> **Today, 8:19 AM**
> DANIEL: Hey
>
> **Today, 8:21 AM**
> DANIEL: Hey?

DANIEL: U up?

Today, 8:25 AM
DANIEL: U even there??

There was something very unappealing about his desperate tone. Still, I didn't want to string him along by way of digital avoidance, so I responded,

MAGS: Was outside, what's up?
DANIEL: Not me, anymore that is
MAGS: Seriously
DANIEL: Lighten up!
MAGS: Just bsy today
DANIEL: Oh okay, we haven't talked lately
MAGS: Ya, bsy at work 2
DANIEL: Mags, what is it?

I knew this time would come, I just didn't expect it—or want it—to be today,

MAGS: I've met someone
DANIEL: So? Me 2!
MAGS: Really like him, its good
DANIEL: Tell me more
MAGS: I don't want to Danny, it's special
DANIEL: What else r u saying?
MAGS: This could be it for me
DANIEL: How long have u known him?
MAGS: No, I mean it for u and me

Daniel didn't reply for some time. He could have received a call or become distracted with work. He did tell me once his best writing happened on the weekends. Hell, I didn't have time to contemplate Daniel's feelings; I had a pantry to clean out.

My phone buzzed as "Maggie May" played on my iPod,
I know I keep you amused, but I feel I'm being used...
I hesitated to look because I just didn't want to deal with the Daniel dilemma. Relief washed over me as I read the screen: One missed call from Greg. I quickly unlocked the phone and

listened,

Sorry I missed you, Mags. Been on my mind all morning. Missing my green-eyed lady with golden skin and crazy hair. Call me back if you get a chance. Greg.

I hit the call back button and listened for a ring, but Greg picked up before a single tone sounded.

"Hey you! I was just going to try you one more time in hopes of securing a 'yes.'" Greg's excitement was contagious.

"What kind of 'yes'?" I said, fidgeting on the bar stool like a schoolgirl waiting to be asked to dance.

With heightened enthusiasm, Greg said, "Okay, so remember when I asked you to go see *Wicked* with me last month, but Steve was in an accident and you had to cancel?" He didn't wait for my answer and, interrupting my train of thought, continued, "You know, I sold the tickets and figured we'd wait until the next time it came around. But the waiting is over."

Confused, I said, "What are you taking about?"

"Mags, this year marks the show's tenth anniversary. It's playing on Broadway in less than two weeks, October 30th, to be exact." Greg's enthusiasm was adorable, but it still wasn't clicking.

"Greg, please slow down. I don't understand." I was trying to sound rational, but I probably came off like more of a fuddy-duddy.

"Mags, I want to take you to New York to see *Wicked.* It's a Wednesday, but that shouldn't be a problem... should it?"

Greg paused, waiting for an eager, "yes."

"I have to work. I think you know that," I said, shooting him down with a perfectly aimed missile. "As much as I appreciate your proposal, I can't just take off mid-week."

Now, let's talk about lunch, I almost said, but was interrupted.

Puzzled, he said, "You're joking, right? You told me you had tons of saved personal time. You told me you couldn't wait to see *Wicked.* You told me you loved how spontaneously I lived my life, Mags. What was that all about?"

"Greg, I don't even know how to process this. I don't live like that. I have a job, I have a dog, I have..."

For the second time, Greg interrupted me and said

emphatically, "All of which can go on without you for a couple of days! Mags, I'm not talking about a week. I'm talking about 36 friggin hours spent in The Big Apple enjoying fabulous food and a show you've been dying to see for years!"

"How can you just take off? I mean, you have a job, too, right?"

Fuddy-duddy to the nth degree, but I couldn't stop my rational strong arm from striking down Greg's thoughtful and exciting plan. I'd never done anything so impulsive with someone else; spontaneity had been reserved for my solo adventures. Would his enthusiasm prevail? Would I let it?

"Mags, remember when you didn't want me to come over after you'd spent the morning with Tony and Steve in the hospital? Do you remember how glad you were when I insisted?"

Yes, I do.

"Trust me, this could be the best time we've had together and the start of something fantastic for us."

Greg's confidence was beginning to chip away at my skepticism.

"I really don't want to be a 'Debbie downer,' but this is a biggie for me, you have to know that about me by now. I just can't take off with you like this..."

Interrupting me for the third time, Greg said, "Here's what I know, Mags. I know you feel stuck. I know you feel stressed. You'd have a blast, Maggie, and I know I'd have one with you. Thirty-six hours, Mags. A day and a half, that's all I'm talking about."

Stubbornly, I added, "We haven't even talked about the cost of the trip, Greg."

"That's ridiculous, and you know it. You're being childish now. I'm asking you out on a date. He who asketh, payeth!" Greg was teasing me now, which meant he believed he'd won this battle.

Playing into his victory, I said, "What shall one weareth?!

"Oh, m'lady, now we're talkin!"

I had Colorado clothes in my closet, not attire fit for New

York City dining and theatre. In a panic, I texted Katie,

> **Today, 1:22 PM**
> MAGS: Need u sis!
> KATIE: Really?!
> MAGS: Ya, usually the other way, right
> KATIE: Whats up?
> MAGS: Clothes dilemma
> KATIE: What, where and when?
> MAGS: Dinner and a play, NYC, soon
> KATIE: WTF?!
> MAGS: Ya
> KATIE: OMW – better have wine

Katie barged through the door like a wild boar, "Okay, pour me a glass, and tell me everything!" She was grinning from ear to ear, seemingly waiting for this moment.

I opened a simple California white and broke out some veggies and dip. I had a few ripe avocados, so I whipped up some guacamole and found a not-yet-stale bag of chips.

Katie sat on the edge of the barstool, so she could reach the guac. She scooped up a good-sized dollop and shoved it in her mouth, washing it down with a gulp of wine. Clearing her throat she said, "Okay, start from the beginning, Mags."

Katie knew I'd been dating Greg for a while, but I'd shared few details. Tonight however, I opened up and told her *almost* everything there was to tell. She chuckled at his age, drooled at his pictures, questioned what his job really was, and probed a little too much into our sex life.

"Katie! Really, some things are off limits," I said as color filled my cheeks.

"Oh, Jesus, Mags, we're sisters! We're supposed to know everything, like how big is his cock?"

She had always been more open to talking about her sexual escapades and I got a kick out of listening to the way her voice lowered the more she delved into her lusty tales. We hadn't had a heart-to-heart "sister" talk in some time and I missed it suddenly.

No longer sipping my wine, I took a generous swig and said,

"Okay, okay! But be patient, you know this is much harder for me than for you."

I started with the day Steve had his accident and Katie's questions immediately followed.

"He just walked into your house? He didn't knock?" she said, wearing a look like a kid listening to one of Andersen's fairy tales for the first time.

I explained he'd noticed the door ajar, and wanting to make sure I was okay, he walked in without my invitation. I went on to explain Greg made himself at home, preparing a wonderful tea tray he brought to me as I soaked in the tub. Then, the details—how he touched and kissed me, making me feel like there was no one else in the world but the two of us. Transfixed, Katie strained over the bar, and this time she wasn't after guacamole.

"You'll never guess what was playing when Greg came over: 'Diamonds and Rust.'"

Staring into my glass of wine, I replayed the afternoon in my head, pairing Greg's persona with Baez's lyrics.

Piercing my day dream, Katie said, "Holy shit, Mags, I hope it's not an omen. Dylan treated Baez like shit!"

Spell broken, I shoved a guacamole-covered chip into my mouth.

I hesitated divulging details of the snow day I spent at Greg's house, exploring each other's erotic desires, curiosities and limits. I choked at the thought of having to describe the fuckfest we'd had because Katie didn't know that side of me. She'd been an integral part of my family since Jack and I married, witnessing all the joyous moments then standing by me through all the tragedies. She'd marveled at our unconditional love for Michael and how easily the two of us became three. I wondered if my baby sister's perception of me as a wife and mother would keep her from knowing me as another man's lover. Not really sure how she would react, I skipped to the time Greg and I, completely spent from our ravenous lovemaking, slept like babies, waking in the same spot where we'd dozed off the night before.

Twenty minutes of filler passed before I revealed Greg's invitation, requiring another bottle of wine.

"So, he just asked to you go see *Wicked* in New York, just like that? What the hell does he do again, Mags?"

Katie's innocent nosiness shifted to an ever-growing sisterly suspicion.

I hesitated a few seconds before answering Katie because, quite honestly, I didn't know precisely what Greg did.

"He dabbles in the stock market," I said with enough confidence to satisfy my nosy sister, or so I hoped.

Katie wrinkled her face and said, "What does that mean exactly?"

I let out a little harrumph and began, "Well, I know he doesn't trade. He says he buys and holds companies that seem promising, financially I mean."

I obviously lacked any authority on the matter, fueling my sister's tirade.

Arching her eyebrows for emphasis, she said, "What does *that* mean exactly?"

Exacerbated, I barked, "I don't know Katie, you'll have to ask Greg!"

"I'd love to, Mags. When do I get to meet the mysterious market manipulator?"

I didn't like the way my sister was taking jabs and I wanted it to stop.

"Come on, Katie, it's not like he's a mobster. Shit. Do I know everything about the ass wipes you date?"

I stomped off to go to the bathroom. I was pissed. Sitting on the john, I scrutinized Katie's question: *What does that mean exactly?* I had no fucking clue.

I heard my sister rustling around in the kitchen, and when I came out of the bathroom, she'd already put on her coat.

"Oh for Christ's sake, Katie. Really? Don't leave. You just triggered something in me that's been festering all morning. Please stay. *Please?*"

I rarely pleaded with Katie, but I wanted to walk through a few things with her. I needed a sounding board now that Greg's shadowy career had moved to the forefront.

Katie dropped her purse and, plopping back down on the barstool, said, "I worry about you, Mags. You haven't been dating long, and there are creeps out there."

So Tina says...

"Yeah, I know. And I appreciate it, sis, I really do."

I reached for my laptop and opened it so both of us could see the screen. I Googled "dabble in stock market" and was surprised to see the volume of sites listed. I scrolled to see if there was a more formal looking site, rather than the ehow.com or answers.yahoo.com types.

"Hey, hit that one," Katie said with a much perkier voice than before.

She pointed to a blog written by a 37-year-old guy who appeared to be successful, or so his picture suggested. He'd written an article outlining criteria for buying companies. The article highlighted topics like purchasing strategies, goals and methods. The content was way over my head, but its seeming legitimacy bolstered my confidence in Greg.

Reassured, I said, "See, it's a real business. This guy has done very well for himself!"

"It's a blog, Mags. He could have written anything. It's not like it's a *Wall Street Journal* article vetted by layers of editors." Before I could protest, she went on, "But I'm okay with it for now. I'm going to dig a little deeper when I get home and talk to a few buddies at work, just to be safe."

"Deal," I said as I poured two more glasses of wine, polishing off the second bottle.

୬୧

I went shopping with Katie the next day for some clothes appropriate for New York theatre—hell, New York in general. I was struck by the holiday apparel and accessories draping emaciated mannequins in all the major department stores; it wasn't even Halloween yet. I despised shopping malls, and my sister knew it. She, on the other hand, could roam the endless stretches of polished tile, peering into shop windows as if she were in a museum.

As promised, I'd prepared a list of "must haves," which was scribed next to a list of "can't stands." Katie inspected it, grabbed my arm, and we headed toward Nordstrom.

I dreaded trying on fancy dresses. The sales ladies (rarely men) groped and prodded almost as intimately as my gynecologist. What kind of person considers a career that requires manipulating women's breasts for ideal positioning in an overpriced garment made in China?

Like a mother hen, Katie scolded me when I protested such dressing room antics. "Mags, stop it with the faces. You have to go through this to find the right dress, okay? Let her feel you up, it'll make your time with Greg that much better."

Shirley, a stout grey-haired woman who looked to be my mom's age, brought in several choices, but my eyes closed in on a simple, black sheath dress with a cut-out yolk, stopping just above the knee. I tried it on and fell in love with it. Both Shirley and my bossy sibling insisted I try on more, but I knew this was the one. I paid for the dress, and we drifted to the shoe department, where I found a simple pair of heeled sandals with an ankle strap; I was betting on motorized transportation, not strolls through New York's bitter cold. We rounded our shopping adventure at a specialty shop that sold interesting and unique accessories. Looking for a wrap, my eyes landed on a gorgeous turquoise and gold jacquard shawl. This treasure would bring out my eyes, making me stand out in an otherwise sea of back dresses.

Pleased with my goodies, Katie and I stopped at *California Kitchen* for a quick salad before heading home. My excitement stirred, and I silently imagined what it was going to be like traveling with Greg to one of the most cosmopolitan cities in the world.

ৎৡৣ৶

I woke early Sunday to the buzzing of my phone. It was Daniel; he'd never texted at this hour and I was curious,

Today, 3:02 AM
DANIEL: I know it's late
MAGS: Early
DANIEL: Thinking bout your pussy, so much sweeter than the one I fucked tonite

Funny, Daniel could always wake my libido, regardless of the hour. A shot of guilt ripped through me knowing I'd be on a plane with Greg in a few days. Oh, what the hell...

> MAGS: You don't know that – she any good?
> DANIEL: Sorta
> MAGS: Trying to make me jealous
> DANIEL: No, just horny, wanna fuck u 2
> MAGS: Gotta lick me first
> DANIEL: With pleasure
> MAGS: Squeeze my tits
> DANIEL: My cock is rock hard, need u to suck me off
> MAGS: God I want to 69 with you, ur entire cock in my mouth while u suck my clit
> DANIEL: Baby, I hate to say it but im gunna cum!
> MAGS: me 2! cum for me - oh fuck, of fuck, oh fuck!

I dropped my phone and came hard, screaming unabashedly. Normally, Daniel took great pleasure in hearing me cum; then I'd tease him through his orgasm, savoring his guttural moans. Our near simultaneous climax tonight was one of the best I'd had with Daniel—it dismantled the emotional barrier I'd carefully constructed. Was sex better with Daniel when we were detached from each other? Had Daniel become an emotional vibrator I could manipulate according to my own selfish desires?

"Shut the hell up, Mags," I said with resignation and turned to pick up my phone.

Two texts from Daniel,

> **Today, 3:19 AM**
> DANIEL: Amazing
> MAGS: Ya
> DANIEL: For u 2?
> MAGS: For me 2+
> DANIEL: ??
> MAGS: Really good

DANIEL: Worried u had someone there

MAGS: Ha! He wouldn't get us

DANIEL: Does he know?

MAGS: About u?

DANIEL: Ya

MAGS: No

DANIEL: Why?

MAGS: Not sure, don't want to mess it up

DANIEL: That's not nice!

MAGS: U know what I mean

DANIEL: Yes, sadly

MAGS: ??

DANIEL: Sometimes I hate the distance

MAGS: I know, me 2, wonder what u and I would be like together

DANIEL: Really?

MAGS: Really

DANIEL: But it's not real

MAGS: No it's not

DANIEL: This has been a good night

MAGS: Morning

DANIEL: LOL, okay morning

MAGS: It has

DANIEL: Really?

MAGS: Really

DANIEL: I gotta go to work

MAGS: Ugh, me too

DANIEL: Sorry I woke you

MAGS: I'm not

DANIEL: Ta-ta

MAGS: ☺

∞∞

Greg booked two first class tickets on United for the evening of October 29th. I was able to get a decent amount of work done before noon, and per Katie's recommendation, I'd packed the weekend before. I was ready and full of childlike anticipation when a town car pulled up in front of my house at 4:00. The driver stood by the open trunk, while Greg collected my bags and escorted me to the car.

Handing the bags to the older man who afforded VIP-like courtesy, Greg said, "Here you go, Edward."

A string of questions formed in my head, when Greg asked with genuine interest, "How was your day?"

Successfully distracted, I replied, "Good. I got a lot done, actually."

Fully situated in the car, I looked around the interior and noticed leather—lots of it. Other than that, it looked like any other sedan I'd been in, except for the wooden console in the front, revealing high-tech navigation and audio equipment. I wondered, had Greg hired this car?

Casually, I said, "Is this *your* car, Greg?"

"No, it's not. Not really. It's my company's car. We all use it."

For the first time since I'd met Greg, he struggled to get his words out. I flashed back to my conversation with Katie, and heat briefly rose in my face.

"Oh," I said, taken aback by his nonchalant manner.

"Mags, I'm a successful businessman, that's all."

No shit.

"I see that," I said, not intending the sarcastic inflection.

"Here's the deal, Mags, we can do this, quarrel over the specifics of my work and why we're headed to DIA in a town car. Or we can enjoy the ride, metaphorically *and* literally," Greg said with a serious tone I'd not experienced before, and it caught me off guard.

Forcing myself to cheer up, I agreed, "Of course. Yes, let's enjoy the ride."

I wondered if the commercial flight (albeit first class) was just a smokescreen to give Greg time to introduce me to his private jet.

I sat back and enjoyed the rest of our comfortable ride to the airport. By 5:00, I'd surrendered and was appreciative of our first-class security screening. When we were finally called to board the enormous Boeing 777, I delighted with our first class "pods." The flight alone could have been a vacation for anyone in my crowd. Apparently, this was business as usual for Greg.

We took off around 7:00, but before we even started moving, a handsome flight attendant offered us a drink. I asked for white wine, and Greg had a Maker's Mark, neat. His social rank becoming more apparent, I squirmed, my self-consciousness rising like bile.

Sensing my mood, Greg said, "You good, Mags?"

"Yeah, just get a little nervous taking off."

I lied. I had nerves of steel—when it came to flying, anyhow.

Greg took my hand, laced his fingers in mine, and closed his eyes as he sipped his bourbon.

I slept most of the flight; Greg having to rouse me so we could collect our things and deplane before the main cabin did. We didn't say much to each other—I was tired and so was he. This time, I asked no questions when we got into a waiting town car that ushered us to our hotel. I was pleased when we didn't pull up to the Ritz; rather, the sign read "The Greenwich Hotel," a simple red brick building just blocks from the Hudson River.

The lobby was fashioned with comfortable leather sofas and plush velvet chairs. The subdued lighting played off the buff-colored walls with seductive warmth. Dark wood framed the windows and doorways, and I felt like I'd been transported to an entirely new world; one in which people lived cheerful, carefree lives and never had to pick up dog shit themselves.

Greg checked us in as I gazed wide-eyed at my home for the next few days. I hadn't noticed, but our bags had been taken to our rooms as if by magic. Greg took my arm, and we walked—luggage free—to the elevators. He pushed the "PH" button, and it took me a second or two to figure out what the two letters meant.

We walked into a suite that looked like something you'd find in Europe, or so I imagined; I've never been. Thirty-foot atelier windows framed a fantastic view as we made our way to the sitting room, a handsome brick fireplace off to one side. Behind us, a fully stocked kitchen stood next to an open dining room facing the City's skyline. I left Greg in search of the bathroom and came to a dead stop when I stumbled across it. Marble slabs covered the walls, and the floor was tiled in delicate white squares of the same stone. A giant tub cut from a solid piece—all white with veins of light gray—called out to me. Lovely brass fixtures and towel racks added much-needed warmth to the room, though I wasn't complaining. I turned the nobs on the monolithic basin and ran a steamy bath; I couldn't think of anything I wanted more. The whole room was simply exquisite.

While soaking, I was treated to a nice cup of herbal tea and a small tray of cheese and crackers—clearly not Kraft or Nabisco. Greg didn't stay, however. He dropped the tray on the tub's ledge and left to catch up on a few emails, his frosty demeanor annoying the hell out of me. All this fancy shit didn't mean anything if a cold shoulder was the only flesh I'd experience for the rest of the trip.

Initially, memories of my first bath encounter with Greg flooded my mind, but were quickly doused with his acerbic demeanor. "Fuck it," I said, as I sank deeper into the still steaming water, closing my eyes, hoping to close out the world.

An hour later, I grudgingly pulled myself out of the water. I found a plush robe hanging on the back of the door and wrapped myself in it. Stepping out of the bathroom, I found Greg sitting on the bed in a T-shirt and gym shorts, reading something on his laptop that captured his entire attention.

"Thanks for the tea and snacks, they were very nice," I said.

Not looking up, Greg said, "Sure, glad you enjoyed it."

Pensively, I said, "What are you reading?"

"Work stuff."

"Oh," I murmured, taking the clue nothing of the carnal sort would be taking place in our extravagant penthouse bed.

I quickly changed into a pretty nightie I picked up last minute and crawled under a delightful, lightweight duvet.

What a waste.

I grabbed my readers and a book I'd packed for the trip, flipping to page one. I didn't expect to be reading on our getaway, so I'd snatched something from Katie's stack of tattered paperbacks, paying no attention to the title, author or genre, for that matter. Nevertheless, I wore my engrossed face and slogged through a really bad novel.

About 15 minutes later, Greg shut his laptop, placed it on the nightstand, turned to me and said, "Mags, I have something to say and I need you to just listen, okay?"

"Okay."

"I've been single a while, now. I've dated a lot, Mags. Some good, mostly not so good. My kids are very important to me, but they live in Chicago, near their mom. I don't see them much, which saddens me, but life goes on," Greg said, his eyes brimmed with tears he quickly blinked away.

"The majority of women I meet want a sugar daddy. It's pretty disgusting, really. You wouldn't believe the women who crawl out of online dating sites. I've been approached by a 74-year-old, for Christ's sake! I considered signing up with one of those 'million dollar matchmaker' clubs because, Mags, I make a good deal of money. The romantic boy in me, though, wanted to find a sweet girl. I finally found her, and it's you Mags. You didn't even Google me, which would have revealed to you who I am and what I do. We've had a blast, and I've enjoyed every tender, sexy and simple moment together."

Greg stopped to take a sip of water. Though he left an opening for me to say something, I didn't; I wanted him to finish.

"You accepted me 100 percent until I showed up at your door this morning. In a fucking car, Mags, that's all it was, a car. I wasn't quizzed on the flight, so you must have enjoyed flying first class. And clearly, you loved your bath. I clocked you at 53 minutes. But you have this air about you now, like you are sitting in judgment, like you disapprove of the apparent overindulgence of this trip I planned just for you."

Another sip of water and an even longer pause; respecting his wishes, I said nothing, though it was becoming increasingly difficult not to interrupt and defend myself.

"I just wanted you to have a really nice time, stay at a wonderful hotel, eat great food and see a Broadway musical *on Broadway*. I'd hoped to take you away from your life, for just a few days, and show you what things could be like. I'm not talking about a continuous stream of five-star hotels and first-class flights, but maybe *sometimes*, we could enjoy it," he said, followed by a very deep breath.

"I love you, Mags."

I never knew why books and movies depicted shock as one's jaw dropping, but mine did when Greg uttered those few words. I couldn't come up with anything to say, so I bought a few seconds by taking a sip of sparkling water Greg had poured and left for me on my nightstand.

Gathering my thoughts, I began, "Greg, I don't know where to start. First, I care about you, a great deal, actually." Bypassing the obvious, I continued, "But what I can't ignore is this need to defend myself. I do feel bad for giving you the third degree about the car. I've *never* been exposed to this kind of living, travel— whatever you call it. I was childish the way I handled my surprise and curiosity. I'm sorry. You're right. I did enjoy and appreciate the ride to DIA and flying first class. And this hotel is spectacular, truly. I could *live* in this penthouse!"

I was trying to lighten things up, but the look on Greg's face said I was failing miserably.

"Greg, you and I live completely different lives. I feel guilty when I spend over 200 dollars at Home Depot on annuals that will last maybe four months. I don't buy anything full price and get excited when spring comes around so I can peruse yard sales. I live a tidy life, and you know that, you've seen my place and me in it. I've grown accustomed to my routine, which, I must say, is more comforting these days than constricting."

I paused for more water, gulping this time.

"I'm sorry I came off so critical. I've relished every moment, really. Please know you're dealing with a small town girl. Denver's not really small though, is it? Let's say a 'cow town girl.'"

He added, "I'm a Colorado native, too, Mags."

"Yeah, but how much time have you really spent in Colorado?"

More interrogation, Mags?

"I didn't mean it that way, Greg, what I meant was you're *worldly*, I'm not. It's that simple."

Fuck I want this to be over!

Defensively, Greg said, "I see, so I don't have what it takes to understand anything outside of my *grandiose lifestyle*?"

Greg's earlier treatise didn't pack the punch his caustic question had.

"I want to say something now, and please just listen."

It was my turn, and I wanted the entire floor.

138

"I don't want to argue about lifestyle, income, career choice, family status or anything that will draw a line between you and me. All I want to say is you and I have known each other just a couple of months. Really, really good months, Greg. But anything different from the norm—things, places *and* people—give me pause. It's who I am. I just need time to get used to all this."

I underscored my point by glancing around the lavishly adorned bedroom, returning to meet his icy blue stare.

"When you meet my sister Katie, she'll tell you how giddy I was when we went shopping for a dress for *Wicked* tomorrow night..."

"You went shopping for a new dress?" he said, his eyes lighting up hearing my preparative tidbit.

Smiling, I insisted, "Don't interrupt! Yes, I did because I wanted to look and feel fantastic—for me *and* for you. I've never experienced anything like this, and I can't tell you how much I appreciate all of it, Greg."

I reached over to kiss him, and he met me with an even more eager one.

Taking in a deep breath, I continued, "I'm tired and I'm sure you are, too. Can we just agree we got off to a bad start, but it's over and tomorrow—er today, is a new day?"

More questions swirled around my mind, like dried leaves scattered by a spiffy coupe racing along a country road at 90 miles an hour. In the end, I brushed them off, wanting to absorb every ounce of our upper-crust jaunt.

"Agreed, Mags, and I'm sorry for the lecture. My feelings were hurt, if you can believe a man like me has feelings," he said, jokingly.

Make-up sex can be ridiculously mind-blowing. That night, it was even better. Our heightened emotions manifested in primal maneuvers, competing for the dominant position. I rolled on top of him and began to fuck him hard, my ass slapping against his balls while his engorged cock filled my drenched pussy perfectly. In a flash, Greg flipped me over and pulled my ass into the air and slammed his cock deep into me while groping my tits and biting my back. Our power fuck lasted only a few minutes; Greg cumming first, letting me take his still-rock-hard cock in my hand and rubbing it angrily against my clit, sending a subliminal message I am still a fiercely independent woman.

～～

A text buzzed several hours later. My phone was plugged into an outlet imbedded in the bedside lamp, close enough for Greg to hear it. I quickly picked it up and saw Daniel's name.

"Who's Daniel?"

The tone had apparently woken Greg, who was now leaning over looking at my phone.

Squirming just a little, I answered, "Oh, just a friend."

"A friend who texts at...what time is it? Five in the morning?"

Greg sounded suspicious, and I was too groggy to get into it with him. This trip was, indeed, off to a bad start.

"He works weird hours."

I had no idea how I came up with such a lame reason, and I felt foolish saying it.

"What does that have to do with texting you at the crack of dawn, which would be, what, three Denver time, by the way."

He got up and went to the bathroom.

"Oh fuck," I said into my pillow.

When Greg came out, he fetched a pair of boxers out of the dresser and moved into the kitchen, presumably to make coffee. Clearing my head of irrational crap, I threw on my robe, and met him in the kitchen.

He'd put the coffee on, and I said, "Wow, the coffee smells terrific!"

"Who is he, Mags? You've never mentioned Daniel before."

He fussed with the creamer, sugar and mugs as he asked me about Daniel, avoiding my eyes.

"Greg, Daniel is a friend. He lives in Atlanta, so there is nothing to worry about. Seriously!" Guilt seeped between my words, and Greg sensed it.

Still futzing in the kitchen, Greg said, "How'd you meet? Is he an old college buddy or something?"

There were times when I could pull off a lie pretty darn well; this wasn't one of them. I hadn't planned on building a relationship on a foundation of lies, but I'd already fibbed about being a nervous flier. Still, I didn't want white lies—or any kind for that matter—to become the norm. Could I somehow soften the blow? *Probably.*

"I met Daniel online. Geez, Greg, you and I met online. When I found out he lived in Atlanta, I realized it wasn't going to amount to anything; we agreed to stay friends. It's no big deal."

Hell, I was convinced!

"I have lots of female friends, Mags. It's not about that. None of them text me in the middle of the night."

Greg's eyes landed on mine. They burned like daggers, and I looked away.

"Greg, he's a friend. That's all."

My stomach churned; I didn't know where this was going, until his next question.

"Can I see your phone, Mags?"

"No, Greg, you can't. But not for the reason you are thinking. I won't stoop to this. You either trust me, or you don't. It's that simple."

I stomped off to the bathroom, feeling bile rise with each step.

Daniel was a friend, dammit! We'd never had *real* sex. We'd never been on a *real* date. I don't know what he smells like, what his cock feels like or what he eats for breakfast, for fuck's sake! I hadn't been unfaithful to Greg. Daniel was like porn—couples from all walks mess around with smut. Still, why did I feel so guilty? Strangely, I felt equally as bad for Daniel as I did for Greg; I'd shoved him into my box of sex toys to justify dating other men—local men, who I could see, touch and fuck.

How the hell could anyone be in love with a phantom?

I walked to my phone and unlocked the screen,

Today, 5:04 AM
DANIEL: You fuck him yet?
MAGS: We have to talk, not now, when I get home
DANIEL: Uh oh
MAGS: Please don't
DANIEL: U okay?
MAGS: Ya, just need a couple days then we can

talk
DANIEL: Mad at me?
MAGS: No
DANIEL: Okay take care
MAGS: Will try

Greg walked in just as I put the phone back down on the nightstand. Ignoring my movements, he said with a hint of contempt, "Let's go get breakfast, Maggie, just the two of us, please."

ೂಲ

Greg and I moved past the Daniel fiasco fairly well. The instant we walked outside, the soul of New York City grabbed our attention and refused to let go. We had breakfast at *Bubby's*, an eclectic, out-of-the-way place that served everything from scratch. Because our breakfast was so filling, we passed on lunch and snacked back at the hotel. Lying back to back, we napped for a little over an hour.

Reservations for dinner had been made well in advance at *Gramercy Tavern*, not far from the Theatre District. Our table was in the Dining Room, not the Tavern, and I wondered if Greg knew someone to get into a place like this with such short notice. Our server announced the menus were seasonal as he expertly handed them to us, along with a massive wine list. I expected higher prices—I'd paid more in some of Denver's fine-dining establishments. In the end, I kept all my observations to myself and enjoyed an evening of great food and wine, enjoyable conversation, and lots of people watching.

After dinner, Greg and I jumped into our car, which swept us along the "Great White Way" and dropped us at the Gershwin Theatre. Ticket holders eagerly made their way inside while paparazzi buzzed about, waiting for the perfect shot of somebody famous—they never seemed to care who as long as the subject was drunk, stumbling, or kissing someone other than their spouse. We found our seats just in the nick of time; the music started as Greg helped me with my wrap.

Wicked was electric, to put it mildly. I sat at the edge of my seat the entire show and giggled with delight after every musical number. I caught Greg's glance several times, and he seemed pleased I was so enthralled. After the third encore, I kissed Greg passionately and whispered a very sincere, "Thank you."

We made love more tenderly that night, lingering on sweet kisses and gentle touches. I fell asleep in Greg's arms and woke to his hand exploring between my legs. I rolled over and let him kiss and lick every square inch of my body.

҂ѻ҂

Our trip home was effortless, at least for me. I let Greg take the lead while I sat back, enjoying the carefree experience. He managed our bags, called our town car, and navigated the airport with the expertise of a world traveler—after all, he was one. There was Wi-Fi on the flight, and Greg spent much of the time online. I chose to close my eyes and doze, which was easy in first class. Edward picked us up at DIA, and we headed to my house, saying very little along the way.

Shortly before turning into my neighborhood, Greg said, "I had a great time, Mags. I hope you did too."

"You're kidding, right? Oh my God, Greg, it was fantastic! The whole trip was like a dream, a *very* good dream."

I did, indeed, speak the truth this time.

"I'm glad, Mags. I'm hoping we can pick up where we left off."

He'd turned serious, and I wasn't sure how to take it.

"Where we left off? What do you mean?"

"I told you I loved you, Mags, and I meant it. I'd like to know how you feel about me."

Greg's comment came out of left field and I was not prepared to respond.

"Sure, we can talk Greg but not now. Why don't we get together this weekend? Trust me, I want to talk about this," I said, trying to buy time so I could sort my feelings for him.

"That sounds like a plan," Greg said flatly as we arrived at my house.

Edward unloaded my bags and took them to the front porch.

In step behind his driver, Greg walked me to the door and said, "Thanks, Mags. I look forward to this weekend. I'll call with details."

Smiling, I said, "Oh Greg, thank you. I'll never forget these past two days."

Not returning my smile, Greg said, "Oh, and Maggie? Lose your fucking friend."

Speechless, I stood on my porch, keys in hand, and watched Greg walk back to the car, never turning back before the black sedan drove off.

CHAPTER 9

Rebounds Abound

Today, 1:36 AM
MAGS: U up?
DANIEL: Am now
MAGS: I woke u?
DANIEL: Naw, watching porn
MAGS: Ugh!
DANIEL: Jk, whassup?
MAGS: My trip went south
DANIEL: That why u wanted to talk?
MAGS: That was for another reason, doesn't matter now
DANIEL: ??
MAGS: Can we talk?
DANIEL: Sure, gimme 5
MAGS: Me 2

I hadn't been able to sleep. The last couple of days had been a whirlwind, rage hovering in the eye of the cyclone. Normally, I blame myself for relationship failures. With Greg, I dug a little deeper and noticed red flags rippling behind his good looks and charm. Not caring to know what he did for a living was the brightest one; I knew better.

It wasn't so much *what* he did but where, for how long, and with whom...not to mention whether it was legitimate—Katie's greatest concern. Beyond his work, Greg's control issues came to light the day he walked away from my front steps after our tumultuous trip. In retrospect, I should have paid attention to the sense of foreboding I felt when, after one of our first dates, he insisted on coming inside. Instead, I fell headfirst into a pool of seductive overindulgence.

I'd been in a contemplative mood since walking through my door the day Greg dropped me off, refusing to go out. Wanting to purge the asshole from my life, I avoided all distractions. Luckily, I'd taken a vacation day Friday, so no need to call in. It was early Saturday morning, and I was restless. And the person I most wanted to talk to was Daniel.

"Hey, you," Daniel answered cheerfully. I wasn't sure if he was always so chipper in the wee hours of the morning or if he was scrambling to rouse good cheer in me.

"Hi, Danny. Thanks for taking my call."

I made a weak attempt to mask my troubles: one quarter feigned cheer and three quarters authentic angst.

Concerned, Daniel asked, "Mags, you don't sound like yourself. What happened in New York?"

"It's not what happened in New York; it's what happened afterward," and so began the tale of my wicked adventure.

I provided a little history, too. I told him what I knew of Greg's work and how he delighted in showing me a first class time. I shared a good deal about our sex life, explaining it was some of the best sex I'd ever had. Hearing it out loud, I began to understand how I could feel so torn.

When I got around to our trip to New York, Daniel cut in, "Wait a second, Mags. I think I know you pretty well, and I know you like your routine, your schedule—your life in order. How could this guy convince you to take off, mid-week, to New York?"

Good question, my friend.

"I kinda thought you'd ask that. My sister was concerned about that, too. But I figured *because* of my friggin tight-assed life, I needed to live a little, break out of my mold, you know?"

I hated clichés but the image of me stuck in "Mag's mold" was stark, illustrating how I felt about my life and how I'd chosen to live it since losing my husband and son.

"Mags, you have to know I love how confident you are. You live your life according to your own terms and it's sexy as hell. You are one of the most self-assured women I know, at least virtually, anyway."

I was struck by Daniel's sense of me. I really didn't expect it, and tears began to well.

He went on, "Baby, I know you think we're just fuck buddies, but I care deeply about you and what goes on in your life. This guy—what's the asshole's name? He's not good for you. I know he seduced you with a glamorous few days, but, Mags, that's not you."

I'd always loved Daniel's smooth voice. Over the past six months, it coaxed my long-buried passion, lured me to sweet, uninterrupted sleep and made me guffaw until my sides hurt. Tonight was different, though. For the first time, Daniel's words were comforting, almost nurturing. In my experience, only close friends and family supported me through difficult times. How the hell could a man I'd never met know me so well? How could he be *exactly* what I needed in this *exact* moment?

Choking back tears, I said, "You make me feel so secure—not in an overprotective sense, but secure in my own skin, if that makes sense. You live thousands of miles away, and yet, it feels like you're right here with me...What do I do now?"

"I'm not going to *tell* you what to do, Mags. I can't do that. I won't. You already know anyway, you just have to accept it and carry it out. Maggie, you'll get through this."

He was right. I did know, but I didn't have the foggiest idea how to do it. I was sure Greg was not the kind of guy who went down easily—I'd have to really think it through.

"Danny?"

"Yeah, baby..."

"Tell me a funny story, I don't care if you make it up. I just need to laugh," I said, fluffing my pillow and settling in for a bedtime story.

"Oh, Mags, this is *not* fiction, seriously! You won't believe what happened at the U.S. Open last month..."

❦

Daniel's story was hilarious, easing me into a deep sleep where I stayed until almost 10:00 the next morning. I felt extremely rested, thankfully. The morning's chill was gone, and it looked to be a beautiful autumn day. I'd planned to start my Thanksgiving menu but decided to go for a much-needed jog. I hadn't been very active lately, and my body protested with stiff muscles and achy joints. Cody knew my solo drill and moped back to his bed, refusing the kibble I'd just poured.

My heart hurting, I followed him into my room and said, "Cody, I wish I could take you, buddy. You just wouldn't make it." I bent down and gave my dear friend a bear hug.

Scratching behind his ears with both hands, I said, "Tell you what, let's take a drive when I get back!"

My inflection stirred Cody's enthusiasm, and he forgot his brooding and dove for his food.

November weather in Colorado is anyone's guess, including the well-dressed and overpaid local meteorologists. The beginning of the month was downright frigid, like the day ahead was forecast to be. I hated jogging in the cold; it hurt my lungs and made me grumpy. Still, I needed it, so off I went. My "Kick Ass Women" playlist was streaming through my headphones, helping me find my rhythm, which didn't take long. Despite the cold, lots of folks were out jogging, cycling and walking their dogs. I felt a pang of guilt every time I passed a human-canine couple. I missed Cody's youth and swore a ride in Beater later on would include a hot dog and an ice cream cone just for him.

As always, I felt great by the time I got home. Why don't I remember *that* feeling when I vacillate on my exercise regimen? I made my usual breakfast even though it was closer to lunchtime. While my oats simmered, I jumped in the shower, dissecting my conversation with Daniel the night before. My feelings for him had intensified, confusing the hell out of me. It wasn't like I was falling in love with Daniel, but I was drawn to his kindness, humor, intelligence and, yes, his irresistible sensuality—all of which he expressed so easily from 1600 miles away. I cared a great deal for my Atlanta phantom and wished like hell I could snuff those feelings.

"Why can't you find a regular guy within 10 fucking miles, Maggie?" I said, nagging the only person within earshot: me.

Cold Saturdays meant yoga pants, a turtleneck and whatever sweatshirt was in reach. I grabbed my favorite, a worn gray treasure with "GEORGETOWN" spread across the front. I'd dreamed of going to law school there, and a friend had sent it to me on her first day of classes. It wasn't fit to wear in public, so I kept it for lounging around the house, or a quick jaunt to Katie's.

I poured a cup of coffee and tossed some nuts and dried fruit into a small bowl of oatmeal. Sitting at the breakfast bar, enjoying my morning ritual, I heard my phone go off. *Shit.* Greg had sent a text, which was something he rarely did. I wanted this day to be Cody's and mine. Still, the pull was too great, so I unlocked my phone and read his message,

Today, 11:32 AM
GREG: Can we talk?

What a fucking pantywaist. "*I* can talk, asshole, but can *you*?" I blurted out.

Heck, it might just be fun toying with Greg, who was apparently feeling uneasy,

MAGS: Bout what?
GREG: I think u know
MAGS: Nope, I don't
GREG: Can I call?
MAGS: Can't, leaving for the day
GREG: Later then?
MAGS: Prob can
GREG: Have a great time, whatever u r doing
MAGS: I will, thanks!

I didn't enjoy playing games, but meeting Greg at his level seemed to be the best approach to ending it with him; wasn't interested in patching things up—ever. The sinister side of me wanted him to stew.

Serves him right.

I took my dishes to the sink and gave them a quick rinse; I'd wash them when I got back. Grabbing my daypack from the hall closet, I stuffed it with a few Cliff Bars and Milk-Bones. Scooping up the gallon jug of water near the side door along with a collapsible water dish, I made my way to the garage to start Beater. I'd pick up a large bottle of coconut water for me on the way. When I came back into the house to get Cody and the rest of my hiking gear, I noticed another text message. It was from Daniel, wishing me a fantastic day and urging me to forget about Greg. Smiling, I stuffed my phone into my bag and headed out for a fabulous afternoon with my favorite boyfriend.

An hour later, we'd found a trailhead in Elk Meadow Park, situated just outside of Evergreen, a delightful mountain town about 15 miles west of Denver. Jack and I used to hike the area with Michael. Due to poor planning leaving us with just a few hours of daylight, Cody and I took a shorter route, avoiding the summit of Bergen Peak. Instead, we hiked a lower elevation trail, hugging the base of the mountain. About an hour and a half into it, we chowed our snacks and, with the light fading quickly, headed back to Beater.

Cody plopped in the rear seat and, within a few minutes, loud snoring filled the cab. My legs were burning, more from my earlier jog than our easy hike. I was daydreaming about a hot soak in the tub when I heard my phone. I took it out of my bag and noticed a call had gone to voicemail. It was Greg.

"Fuck!" I shouted, interrupting Cody from his delicious dream, surely involving a never-ending rabbit chase.

"Sorry, buddy. Go back to sleep," I said, I as slammed my phone into the passenger seat.

I vowed to ignore Greg for the rest of the ride home and played Crosby-Stills-Nash & Young's Déjà Vu CD, singing loudly to "Carry On."

Cody and I walked into the house like we'd trekked Everest. I could barely lug the last of the gear past the doorway. Cody was beat, too; he barely ate his kibble before collapsing on his bed. I hadn't heard from Greg—a good thing, for sure—and ran a bath.

Not hungry, I downed two glasses of melon-infused water before the tub was full. A very tasty Malbec in hand, I eased into a bubbly concoction of vanilla mineral bath and a splash of lavender oil. I'd brought my phone into the bathroom and, glancing at it, wished I'd left it in my bag.

Just then, it buzzed with a text. It was Daniel. Questioning my teenage-like addiction to the device, I hesitated. Still, my curiosity won, and I unlocked the screen and read his text,

Today, 6:19 PM
DANIEL: It's freezing here!
MAGS: U don't know freezing
DANIEL: Our roads are covered in ice

MAGS: Ya, right
DANIEL: Was stuck in traffic 4 hrs today!
MAGS: Cuz of a little ice?
DANIEL: We have no road equipment, ms mountain mama!
MAGS: Can't believe u called me that!
DANIEL: Can't believe u don't feel pity ☹
MAGS: Poor baby
DANIEL: More like it
MAGS: Need to relax?
DANIEL: The purpose of my text, sexy
MAGS: What if I told you I was soaking, naked, in a tub of vanilla and lavender bubbles...
DANIEL: I'd say, nice, very nice
MAGS: What if I told you I was extremely wet
DANIEL: I'd say u r making me hard
MAGS: What if I told you my pussy was really swollen
DANIEL: I'd say how badly I want to lick it, suck that plump cherry
MAGS: What if I told you I want to fuck you
DANIEL: I'd say how badly I want to fuck you from behind
MAGS: What if I told you I'm fingering my pussy, so swollen, wanting to cum
DANIEL: I'd say that I'm stroking my cock, ready to explode with cum I'd rather pump into your dripping pussy
MAGS: What if I told you I want u to cum all over my tits
DANIEL: I'd comply, cumming wherever you want, your tits, your ass, your face
MAGS: Cumming, hang on...
DANIEL: Me 2

I threw the phone down and came hard, splashing water

over the edge of the tub. I screamed with uninhibited passion and, when I finally caught my breath, reached back for the phone,

> MAGS: What if I told you that I came so fucking hard
> DANIEL: I'd say so did I, hard
> A few moments passed, then I wrote,
> MAGS: How can it be so damn good with you, Danny?!
> DANIEL: Dunno, duz it matter?
> MAGS: No, just thinking
> DANIEL: Don't
> MAGS: Greg called
> DANIEL: Tell him to fuck off?
> MAGS: Didn't talk, didn't want to
> DANIEL: U have to some time
> MAGS: I know
> DANIEL: Mags?
> MAGS: Ya?
> DANIEL: I had a great time tonite
> MAGS: Me 2
> DANIEL: Better go
> MAGS: Really?
> DANIEL: Ya, have plans
> MAGS: With a girl?
> DANIEL: Ya
> MAGS: Why did we do this?!
> DANIEL: Cuz its nice
> MAGS: Feels icky now
> DANIEL: Stop it Mags, it's our way
> MAGS: I know
> DANIEL: We good?
> MAGS: Ya, thanks Danny, I needed tonite

Semi-conscious of our arrangement, I reminded myself we both dated other people and lived our lives independent of each other. Still, it stung just a little to think a few hours after our bathtub frolic, he'd be out on the town with another woman. I wasn't jealous, just a little dejected. Physically, I felt really good. Fatigue induced by an incredible orgasm and a day of exercise meant sound slumber, and I couldn't wait to crawl under my heavy duvet and crash.

It was still dark when I woke the next morning. My spirits were high, and I nearly skipped to the kitchen to make a pot of coffee. Cody was feeling sprightly, too, and gobbled up his kibble as I sat at the breakfast bar, reading the rest of the terrible novel I'd started in New York. I was fascinated how—and why—such books were ever published.

Twenty minutes and two cups of coffee later, I finished the book. I was pretty hungry, so I put on some oats. Something tickled my memory, recalling I'd planned on sketching out my Thanksgiving menu. My mood moved up a notch higher thinking of my favorite holiday.

"Cody, it's going to be the best Thanksgiving yet!" I said to my goofy-looking pal who was peacefully lying on his back with all four feet splayed in every direction.

His ridiculously long tongue drooped from one side of his mouth, which embodied his lack of interest in my excited state.

Not quite admonishing my friend, I said, "I see this is of great concern to you, buddy boy," and opened my laptop, logging onto one of my favorite foodie sites.

Several hours later, I got up to stretch and longingly gazed outside. I yearned for my outdoor paradise, especially during Colorado's cold, lifeless winter months, so I'd developed a ritual: Standing at my back door, looking through its good-sized window, I'd call forth Lady Spring and all the new life she'd bear, often losing track of the time. I suspected my routine might be a symptom of dementia and moved away from the door, returning to my incomplete Thanksgiving menu.

Just then, my phone rang. It was Bill...hadn't heard from him since spring. I wasn't sure if I was excited or annoyed. Our last date was unexpectedly enjoyable, but I hadn't heard from the man since.

"How strange is this," I said out loud.

Another symptom? I wondered.

I decided to pick it up, "Hello?"

"Maggie, so glad I caught you," he said, in an awkwardly jovial tone that made me wince.

Miffed, I said, "Hi Bill. Long time no talk."

"Yes, it has been a while, hasn't it? Do you have a moment, Maggie, to talk I mean?"

Pensiveness replaced Bill's good humor, and I became curious.

With my "good pal" voice, I said, "Sure, Bill. What's up?"

"Well Maggie, I have to say I've been thinking of you quite a bit. In fact, I've never stopped."

Uh huh...

"But something happened to me soon after our date, which knocked me over and it's taken this long to get back up. Though I'm not fully together yet."

Bill's voice began to quiver, but he continued, "I don't know where to begin, actually. I suppose I'll get right to it. I lost my son, my only child, in early June. He was a sailor. He enlisted right after high school..."

Frozen, I no longer heard Bill's words. Thoughts of Michael swirled like seagulls, their loud squawks drowning out whatever Bill was saying.

" ... And they came to my door, two sailors in their sharp dress uniforms, and I didn't really understand because I hadn't seen my son in over 10 years and..."

I vividly remembered opening my own door but can't recall a thing afterward, except waking up to Katie's soft crying as she rubbed my head.

" ...You have to know I just fell apart, totally and completely. I'm just now coming out of a black pit of anguish, Maggie. I'm still terribly sad, but I can get dressed now and go to work, and I've begun to live again...sort of. Maggie? You there?"

Quietly, I said, "Oh, Bill, I am deeply sorry for your loss. I don't have many words right now, but I am so, so sorry."

Shaking my head, I came 'round and gently nudged Michael's ghost aside. I wasn't sure if I'd told Bill about my son. How could I offer support—or whatever in the hell he was looking for—to a parent who'd lost a son much like I did, when I wasn't entirely over my own loss?

Crying through his words, he said, "I just didn't know who else to call. My friends and family have been great. But, to tell you the truth, none of them have kids in the military, let experience with losing a child. I remembered you mentioning losing your only son in the Middle East and I thought...Oh hell, I don't know what I thought. I was drawn to you, that's all, Maggie."

Bill sounded resigned, almost as if he expected me to end the call.

With a hint of distain, I replied, "I don't remember telling you. Hell, I don't remember a lot of things about Michael since his death. Bill, I wish I had the answers you're looking for. I wish I had the magic words to ease your pain. But I don't. I just don't."

Painfully recalling the few months after Jack and Michael died, I idled on how miserably I lived, later resigned to a constricted life—emotionally and physically. It was like I operated on autopilot by day, losing all control at night; weeping turned into sobbing, which turned into immeasurable despair. I drank too much, tossing and turning 12 hours a night. My free time spent on my sofa, crying uncontrollably; when I ran out of tears, I'd gaze out in a zombie-like trance.

Awkwardly, Bill said, "Do you think we could get together and just talk? Would you be up for something casual? I know you never get over losing a child—at least that's what the books say—and I'm sure you're still hurt over your son, but I need to talk to someone who get's it, Maggie."

I'd always hated the idea of support groups. Many were recommended after I lost my family in one day; I refused each and every one. I imagined a circle of people sitting in hard plastic chairs holding Styrofoam cups full of stale coffee, bowing their heads as one member relived his terrible tale, shredding other members' already ragged wounds.

Bill, it seemed, was offering membership in his two-member group, and I hesitated doing something I'd sworn off years ago. Friends and family told me I was in denial; I simply knew I was trying to move on as best as I knew how.

I mustered as much empathy as I could, and said, "Bill, I know what you are going through, trust me. Yes, we now belong to the same wretched club. We share the same loss, but I don't have any interest in reliving mine. I am sorry for how this may come across, but I've moved on. I really suggest you do the same. It's what worked for me all this time, anyhow

What came out of my mouth was not what I'd intended; it was cold and arrogant, and I instantly regretted saying anything.

"Ok, Maggie, I just thought..."

"Wait! That did *not* come out as I'd hoped. Please forgive me, Bill. You really threw me. I'm trying to figure it all out as we speak, but I don't think I've done a good job. Let me propose this. Let's meet for coffee, promise not to go too deep, and see where things go. Does that sound fair?"

Relief in his voice, Bill said, "It does. Thank you. How about tonight?"

Gimme a break!

"Well, gee, let me think for a minute."

I had absolutely nothing planned, but I wasn't sure if I wanted to meet him so soon.

Plodding through my own bullshit I said, "Sure, Bill. I insist on casual, though, or the deal's off."

Adnan's coffee house closed at 4:00 on Sundays, and I didn't feel like meeting at Starbucks surrounded by perky baristas and not-so-hip hipsters. I Googled, "coffee shops" and included my zip code. A couple of them seemed okay, but noticing the hour, I decided a place with real food was a better idea. I didn't dare recommend Varsity Grille, but I knew of a trendy hamburger joint that served beer and wine, just in case. I texted Bill the name and location of Burger-Miester, just a couple blocks from my house.

No real preparation went into my burger date with Bill. I managed to swap jeans for my yoga pants and a dark green pullover sweater for my sweatshirt. Other than that, I went "as is."

Stepping into the narrow joint, I was surprised to see there was a wait. I gave my name and sat down on a surprisingly comfortable plastic retro-looking chair. A few minutes later, Bill arrived. I was glad to see he'd put as much time into getting ready as I had. He wore faded jeans, bright white sneakers and a light gray wool sweater, drawing attention to his hair and still moist eyes.

"Hey there!" I said a bit too enthusiastically, leaving me feeling silly for trying so hard.

Bill approached and gave me a tight hug. Pulling back, he said, "Thanks for meeting me, Maggie. It means a lot, you know?"

"I suppose I do, yes."

I had no idea what else to say; suffering through a few more awkward moments, a waif-like hostess finally called my name.

"That's us," I said, avoiding Bill's eyes.

We were escorted to a small table, tucked in a corner with a soft pendant light hanging above.

"Perfect," Bill and I said simultaneously. We chuckled and sat down facing each other, providing a nice buffer—for me, anyway.

Not sure why, but I felt apprehensive. Our last date was superficial and easy to fall into. It was very different this time; the rawness of our emotions outweighed any urge to impress.

How strange is that?

"Are you hungry?" Bill asked kindly.

"A little, yeah," I said as I glanced over the menu.

Just then, our waiter approached and asked what we wanted to drink.

"I'll take a Stella and, Maggie? What would you like?"

My favorite beer, hmmm...

"I'll have the same, thanks."

Relaxing just a bit, I explained I rarely drank beer, but when I did, it was Stella. He met my smile and went on about the various beers he enjoyed depending upon the various and, in my opinion, arbitrary reasons upon which beer aficionados choose their suds. His boyishness captivated me and, leaning in, I propped my elbows on the table and laced my fingers, signaling to Bill I was honestly interested.

Out of nowhere, Bill said, "You look great, Maggie."

Mid-swig, I choked and gurgled a polite, "Thank you."

I was confident in my own skin, yes, but I also knew when my look was "Second Hand Rose."

"What I meant was I know you're not all dolled up, but I like you natural, no makeup, jeans, you know? It's appealing."

Jack used to say the same thing, though I'd shrug it off as something couples said after years of marriage, when everything about each other is known, accepted and loved. Bill and I, on the other hand, didn't have that kind of history, and I squirmed a little in my chair.

"You look nice too, Bill. I like you casual. It's more approachable."

"Approachable?" Geez, Mags.

Smiling, Bill said, "Is that a compliment, Maggie?"

I nodded, scrunching up my face with embarrassment.

"It's okay, I know what you meant. I can see through you, Mags, in a good way. You are so real. God, if you only *knew* how awful and fake women can be!"

I chuckled, thinking about my boss.

Bill looked at me inquisitively, and I said, "I think I do. I work for one of 'em."

We shared a laugh and, for just a moment, I looked deep into Bill's eyes. I could see his pain, and a lump formed in my throat. I wondered if I could get through the night, after all.

Bill sensed the shift and asked if I was okay. I nodded and we ordered a couple of burgers; he wanted regular fries, I chose a side salad.

We talked through our meal and a couple more beers. After a while, our waiter interrupted and said they were closing in a few minutes. I looked at the time and inhaled sharply after calculating we'd been there over three hours. Bill was equally shocked and quickly asked for the check—I'd learned not to offer.

Standing up to leave, Bill helped with my coat and asked, "Want to take a drive?"

"Where?"

As if it mattered.

"It's such a clear night, why don't we head west, along 285. There's no snow on the roads; it'll be nice. I have satellite radio and can find a station that suits you."

We were already walking in the direction of his car, when I gave in and said, "Oh, sure, why not?"

As soon as I laid eyes on Bill's car, I understood why he wanted to go for a long drive. He owned a new carbon black BMW 650i Gran Coupe with an interior I would have chosen; black trim with off-white Merino-leather seats and side panels.

It was beautiful, and I sunk into the passenger seat with a newfound joy and interest in sports cars.

"Wow, Bill, this is very nice," I said.

We drove in silence for a good half hour listening to a smooth jazz station. I didn't want to be tempted by lyrics that would regrettably expose Bill to my unpleasant warbling. Leaning my seat back, I stared through the sunroof, feeling calm and carefree. Glancing at Bill, I let go of my need to comfort him, thinking instead about how I'd grown fond of him over a few short hours and a shared tragedy. His face had changed since I last saw him. Haunting memories had etched new lines around his eyes and mouth; his eyes, dull and sunken. I wondered if I'd developed such a look in the months after losing Jack and Michael.

Thinking out loud, I rambled, "When I was young—I mean like *way* back in high school—I was so uncomfortable with silence, the kind that keeps a girl from getting to know a boy. A few minutes would pass before I couldn't stand it any longer, asking my date, 'What are you thinking about?' I'd impatiently wait for his answer, which was almost always, 'Oh, nothing.'"

Randomly, I said, "What about the passage of time changes that?"

Expecting no answer, I soaked in the stars, Bill's smooth driving lulling me into a meditative mood.

Bill smiled and added, "I remember the same thing. And guess what? I was one of those boys who said, 'nothing.' But, Maggie, that wasn't the truth. I bet I can speak for the boys you dated and tell you their nerves kept them from saying anything more. Boys back then—heck, probably today—didn't know how to give a simple kiss or offer a sweet compliment. Silence scared us to death."

We both chuckled then, becoming more serious, Bill said, "When I first met you, Maggie, I felt the same way. You are so striking, so damn different from the rest of the man-eating pack. I stuttered and stammered my way through our first conversation. You probably didn't notice, but I was sweating like crazy!"

Bill and I travelled memory lane like we'd been together for eons. It felt so...familiar.

Small talk kept the mood light; there wasn't a need to talk about our dead sons. I hadn't realized Bill had turned around until I saw Denver's amber glow above the shrinking hills. About 15 minutes before we pulled up to Burger-Miester where I'd left my car, he reached over and took my hand in his, lacing his fingers through mine. I didn't protest, gladly accepting the gesture.

Bill pulled up right behind Beater, slid a high-tech gearshift into "P" and left the car running.

Angling my body to face him more directly, I said with utmost sincerity, "Thanks for dinner and the drive, Bill. I know I was hesitant to go out with you tonight, but you have to know how much I've enjoyed every minute of it."

"Me too, Maggie. Not the part about being hesitant, but how I've enjoyed the drive. I've missed you, strange as that sounds—we only went out a couple of times," he said, clutching my hand with no apparent plans of letting go.

"Well, I guess it's time to head home," I said, trying release his hand so I could open my door.

Sensing my tension, Bill let go of my hand and jumped out to catch my door before I'd completely opened it.

"Oh thanks, not sure if I'll ever get used to that," I said jokingly.

With a youthful sort of vigor, though not completely masking his underlying pain and sadness, Bill said, "You better, my dear! You deserve every courtesy a man has to offer. Oh, and Maggie, can we do this again sometime soon?"

"I'd like that Bill, I really would."

I meant every word.

Though I didn't look in my rearview mirror to confirm it, I knew Bill watched me drive off. Before I made it home, he called, saying he wanted to make sure I'd made it home safely. I said I hadn't because I wasn't there yet. We laughed, and as I pulled into my driveway, I confirmed I had, indeed, made it home in one piece. We laughed even harder, and then I asked him a question.

"Would you like to come to my house for Thanksgiving?"

ഇൾ

Bill and I went out a few more times before the third Thursday of November. We'd agreed on simple dates, allowing us to get to know each other in a more authentic way. We joked, listened to music and found solace in the silence between us. We laughed a lot—just a few times, we cried. Work, politics, religion and other sensitive topics were left alone because they just didn't matter.

Bill was actually a bit of a "softy. He cared deeply for animals and was a member of ASPCA. I was amazed to discover he volunteered at a local shelter that fed and housed the chronically homeless in Denver. Each time we got together, I discovered something new about this man I once wrote off as a "clueless chump."

My earlier perception of Bill was based on nothing more than faulty assumptions. Forgetting dating could be awkward, I'd rushed to judgment. When he invited me to dinner in May, I'd dragged my bag of assumptions along, keeping it tucked snugly at my side, easily accessible. In truth, my bag was an emotional saber kept sharp with fear and pain, keeping at bay anyone who had the potential of hurting—or worse, leaving—me.

Even though I'd enjoyed our dinner date, I hadn't really given Bill a chance, and I felt bad about it. I hoped like hell I was making up for it, not just by helping him through his grief but being open to *all* of him, revealing much of me at the same time. I shared my recent dating disasters but not my long distance affair with Daniel. It was difficult to explain, even to myself. I had little doubt I'd figure out a way to weave it into our conversation at some point.

The week of Thanksgiving was cyclonic—I cleaned the house on Monday and shopped all day Tuesday, stopping first at Tony's Meats for the turkey, then a giant discount liquor store for the booze, ending at a local market for the rest of the fixings. Before I headed home, I picked up several bunches of fresh-cut flowers from Lucy's, a lovely flower shop set in a tiny bungalow a stone's throw from mine.

By Tuesday night, I was dead tired but pleased I'd gotten

everything done. I smiled in anticipation of the next day then realized I hadn't thought about what to wear. Causal most of the time, I took the role of "hostess" very seriously and usually dressed to the nines. Perhaps I'd break with tradition and don something comfortable. I was pretty sure my guests would accept me in just about anything, so I closed the debate on the matter of attire and went to bed.

Bill arrived at 9:00 the next morning, excited to spend a day in my kitchen, listening to music, sipping Prosecco and creating epicurean delights that would later delight dear friends and family. I'd been up for several hours, having prepared the kitchen for our culinary marathon. A silly mood overcame me, and I pulled out a dated Christmas sweater, hoping to encourage the spirit of the season. Knowing the kitchen would become too hot for a sweater, I hung a crisp white blouse on the door handle to my bedroom for a quick change.

Arms brimming with brown paper bags and a huge bunch of flowers, Bill struggled through the door. I grabbed a few things and ushered him into the house, immediately going to work unloading the bounty. The flowers were nothing short of spectacular; I'd have to rethink where to place mine. One bag contained three bottles of wine and another held several brightly wrapped packages.

"What's this?"

"Oh those? Just a little something for Cody," he joked as I moved in to slug his arm. "Ouch! What was that for?"

I stepped in a little closer and kissed him on the cheek—an apology of sorts. He held my chin and stared into my eyes for what seemed like an eternity. Saying nothing, his kissed me on the mouth with a mixture of heat and tenderness.

Slow to release his kiss, I said, "Wow, what was *that* for?"

"Does a simple boy need a reason to kiss a beautiful girl?"

Bill turned on his heels and put the bag of presents on the dining table. He stacked the wine on a small artsy rack Tina had given me a few years back.

"Have any coffee?"

I was miffed by the way he brushed off the beautiful kiss we shared, but I quickly decided not to dwell on it. Overthinking had always gotten me into trouble, and I wasn't going to let it spoil the day.

"Of course I do, I'm a java junky."

Passing over my green mug, I grabbed one from my earthenware set and poured him an almost full cup. I knew he took cream and sugar and left enough room for his liking.

The breakfast bar had been transformed into a Thanksgiving War Room, holding the primary menu, with a scattering of recipes from foodie websites I'd printed out the week before.

"Holy cow, Mags," he said, obviously impressed.

I smiled, having conquered the first of many prep day battles.

After relishing a steaming cup and a bagel piled high with cream cheese, I mixed a couple of mimosas, adding interest with a splash of pomegranate liqueur and topping the concoction with plump blackberries.

Clinking our glasses, we said in unison, "Cheers!"

⤳⤲

Bill and I didn't stop until the last dish was dried and put away. We'd done very well for a day's work and had completed everything on my list: A perfectly executed vat of butternut squash soup; 12 baked sweet potatoes, twice baked and properly dressed tomorrow; roasted red and yellow beets, the main ingredient for an arugula, goat cheese and roasted beet salad; two dozen honey-glazed whole-wheat dinner rolls (from scratch, of course); and a huge loaf of bread we left out to dry for the stuffing we'd prepare tomorrow. Bill demonstrated his expertise with a knife and chopped all the remaining vegetables, storing them in plastic containers for the final product the following day.

Satisfied with our work, we plopped on the sofa; herbal tea had replaced Prosecco, and we sipped in silence. I hadn't noticed Bill was holding my free hand until I got up to feed Cody.

Groggily, Bill said, "Where you off to, honey?"

"Poor Cody has been drooling over the smells coming out of the kitchen all day; if I don't feed him soon, he'll really begin to protest, probably aimed at you," I kidded.

After pouring a healthy amount of kibble in Cody's dish, I

noticed Bill was up from the sofa, looking for his coat.

"Oh no you don't! Sit back down, we haven't discussed the contents of the bag that's been sitting in full view of me all evening."

"Mags, I'm afraid if I stay, I won't be able to control myself. Seriously, the time we spent in the kitchen today might as well have been time spent in the bedroom. If I may say so...I've been horny as hell since walking through your front door."

Bill was more animated than usual, and I sensed an intensity I hadn't before.

A slow sigh escaped my mouth as I recalled how we navigated the small kitchen, pressing against each other as we slipped by to get to the other side. I closed my eyes, visualizing our hands kneading the bread dough, and inhaled deeply.

Shaking me from my suggestive trance, Bill said, "Is everything okay?"

"Yes, everything's fine. I just hate awkward moments like these."

I moved to fetch Bill's coat when he took my arm and pulled me back. He kissed me hard, and I returned it. We stayed locked right where we stood, kissing deeply and exploring each other's bodies, as much as we could through our heavy clothes.

Pulling back just a bit, I murmured, "Stay, Bill, please."

With no further words, Bill led me to the bedroom, where he slowly began undressing me. I'd wanted to shower after a hot and sweaty day in the kitchen, but the urge to remain in Bill's arms outweighed anything else.

Devouring my naked body with his eyes, he began to undressed himself. I attempted to unbutton his shirt, but he moved me to the bed, standing over me while removing the rest of his clothes. The full moon shining through my window, I traced his muscular body with my eyes. Bill was exceptionally handsome and, as expected, built to perfection. He moved confidently and gently eased himself on top of me.

Lost in the moment, we kissed softly, exploring each other. Bill's mouth moved from my neck to my breasts, tickling my nipples with his tongue. Moaning and twisting, I was unable to hold back. His tongue traced a line to my navel and continued in a straight line to my very wet and swollen pussy. I spread my legs with anticipation and lost all control when he found my throbbing clit. With amazing proficiency, he flicked, sucked and licked me until I came with a ferocity rarely experienced. I shuddered with a mixture of ecstasy and pleasure, verging on pain. Before I could catch my breath, his stretched cock found me, moving with a masculine grace I'd never experienced.

Bill's orgasm mirrored how he made love—assertive and to a degree, refined. Our relationship transformed that night: Formerly agreeable companions, we'd turned a crucial corner, converting to red-hot lovers.

A few minutes passed when he leaned up and smiled, saying nothing. I smiled back and, in one swift move, flipped me over, so I was sitting on top of him. Still wet with his cum, I rubbed against his spent cock, slowly at first, feeling it harden with each motion. He made no attempt to move; he was my sex toy, and I played freely. I came for a second time, collapsing on top of him. Moments later, I slid off to one side and lay there, extremely satisfied—sexually and emotionally.

Stroking my hair, he instinctively began twisting a few curls, and whispered, "Good night, beautiful Maggie."

I nuzzled into his chest and said, "It has been, hasn't it?"

My feelings of appreciation and affection welling, I remembered it was the day before we'd be celebrating Thanksgiving with the people who mattered most and I shivered with delight.

BOOK 4

Winter

CHAPTER 10

Winter's Solace

As children, Katie and I drove our folks crazy for the month between Thanksgiving and Christmas. Their tolerance for our restless antics withered like December's daylight. By the time winter break rolled around, Mom and Dad had given up on any semblance of household structure and played along with our childish enthusiasm. We drove around surrounding neighborhoods every night in search of the best Christmas lights and front-lawn decorations. When they dried up, Dad trolled country roads looking for old barns outlined in soft, off-white lights and brightly lit Christmas trees framed by large farmhouse windows.

Katie and I anticipated the end of those outings almost as much as Christmas morning. Mom made hot cocoa and topped each mug with mini marshmallows, while Dad set out to decorate our own house, and though we never won any prizes, we delighted in his creations. Looking back, Norman Rockwell could have found his inspiration for his holiday art from our small, Western Slope town and all the genuine people who enriched its charm.

When Jack and I were married, I attempted to replicate my childhood Christmases by bringing out some of the old decorations my parents divvied up between Katie and me. I followed Mom's recipes to a T and made a beautiful Christmas quilt designed after my grandmother's that won First Prize at the Saint Mark's Catholic Church Holiday Bazaar shortly after World War II. I played Christmas carols sung by the likes of Gene Autry, Andy Williams, Perry Como and Doris Day. But it wasn't until Michael was born when Christmas took on a whole new meaning in the Garrett household.

Jack and I'd kept some of the old decorations, but made it a point to create new ones each year. Cranberry and popcorn garland draped our old oak handrail; silver and gold snowflake cut outs dotted our windows; and tree ornaments—made from anything and everything—cluttered every branch of our fresh-cut tree.

One year, Katie gave us a Christmas cookie cookbook, a familiar fixture on the kitchen counter from Thanksgiving to New Year's Day. Plopping Michael on the counter, I'd begin the ritual of making cookies for every member of our family...and then some. I'd find cute tins on sale at various shops throughout the year, but it was the goodies inside the containers our relatives longed for. Over time, Michael took the lead and developed a few recipes of his own. By the time he was 12, I'd backed off altogether and assumed the role of dishwasher, but mostly head taster. Torn and tattered, my treasured book was no longer usable, yet I couldn't bear to throw it away.

Year after year, love and laughter engulfed the Garrett holidays; moments held together with unbreakable family ties. When Jack and Michael died, so did our holiday traditions— paraphernalia forever stowed in plastic storage boxes in the farthest corner of the basement; memories tucked nearly as far.

ৡৡ৶ঌ

Three weeks before Christmas, Carrie called. She and her new husband had originally planned a Christmas holiday at Disney World, which had cut into my winter break with Timmy and Lisbeth. I accepted their plans with resignation, fearing the Garrett connection to Michael's family was, indeed, fading. Carrie's call made me wince and, before I answered, I braced myself. I didn't expect what I heard and secretly rejoiced as she asked if I were willing to watch the twins for a week while they honeymooned in Mexico. The conversation was awkward, but we moved through it; I needed time to deal with their new arrangement.

My grandkids were scheduled to arrive in less than a month, leaving me full of joy and giddy with anticipation. I made three frantic loops around my house before I was able to stop and think about what needed to be done in the upcoming weeks. The first thing I did was make a list:

Tree—real or fake?
Decorations—buy new?
Cookies—find the cookbook and fix it!
Xmas eve get together—call Katie!!

I hadn't celebrated Christmas in my home since Jack and Michael died. I either drove to Mom and Dad's, weather permitting, or hung out at Katie's with her friends. The first few years I stayed at home, not wanting to see anyone who'd be tempted to say, "Don't worry, it'll get better over time."

How the fuck would any of you know?

After seven years though, I missed it—Christmas music blaring throughout the house, smells of pumpkin bread wafting from my kitchen, and decorations adorning every square inch of my home. I was determined to bring Christmas back with gusto.

Having a little over two weeks to get the house in order didn't make me flinch one bit. Any other time, hives would have broken out over 50 percent of my body. I knew Katie would be on board with planning a Christmas Eve gathering and wouldn't balk at shopping for gifts ordinarily impossible (or too expensive) to ship to California, giving me added comfort. Playing it safe, however, I took the day off so I could get a head start.

It was the first Friday in December; three and four-day weekends were common around the office. I opened my laptop to logon to my work's private network and quickly drafted an email to my boss, letting her know I'd be taking a personal day. A second request for five vacation days over Christmas followed, and I tossed in the fact my grandkids would be visiting, hoping to cajole a little empathy. I didn't expect a personal response; she'd approve my request electronically and ask about their holiday visit sometime in late January.

I made a mental note to re-insert "look for new job" on my crumpled list I'd tacked to the kitchen bulletin board after retrieving it from the trash, more than once I recalled. The need to move on professionally no longer was driven by fluctuating conditions (or emotions); I'd hit a wall under her leadership and

I knew it was time to make a change.

Next, I called Katie. It was a little after 10:00 and I hoped she was still awake. Surprisingly, the late sleeper picked up on the first ring and, before she could say anything, I yelled, "Guess who's coming for Christmas?"

"Hmmm—a boyfriend?" Katie said in a teasing sort of way.

"Nope! One more try."

"Well, in that case... the twins?"

"You got it! I was sure the twins would never come for Christmas, but Carrie and her new husband are taking a honeymoon. Totally works for me!" I was pacing my kitchen floor and could hardly contain my excitement.

Katie piped in, "So, what's the plan, sis?"

ço～ço

I couldn't sleep. I didn't want to bother Bill this late, so I texted Daniel,

> **Today, 11:07 PM**
> MAGS: U up?
> DANIEL: Ya, reading, what's up?
> MAGS: Great news! gkids coming for xmas!
> DANIEL: I'm so happy for you! i know u miss them
> MAGS: Ya, I'm so excited I can't sleep
> DANIEL: Hmm...
> MAGS: Hmm indeed

Daniel and I hadn't exchanged texts, calls or emails recently. He'd met a wonderful woman online, and I'd been dating Bill exclusively since the night of our drive to the hills. Still, it warmed me to connect with him. Aside from well-needed orgasm, I missed Danny's voice and way with words—sexual and otherwise. I considered him to be a good friend, and I didn't want to lose track. I felt a pang of guilt after sexting with him.

For a man who'd never laid eyes or hands on me—hell, who'd never laid me—Daniel was a master. We'd stopped swapping pictures months ago yet I was able to easily recall his cock while listening to him describe kissing and licking me all over. I came hard and so did he. We said our goodbyes, and as I turned over on my side, I pulled my duvet up under my chin to keep the December chill out and Daniel's heat in.

I woke to Cody's hot breath in my face. Year after year, he'd pounce on the bed with puppy-like enthusiasm, rousing us early in the morning, which amused Jack more than me. Silly canine antics slowed after our bed for two became a setting for one, and I often wondered if Cody sensed it would hurt me too much to keep it up. Anthropomorphizing our dog used to make Jack laugh; now it just makes me wonder if I'm losing my mind.

"Cody, get your stinky breath away from me!"

I pushed his face gently away and sat up, scanning the floor for my slippers.

"What's all this about, buddy?"

We made our way into the kitchen and, horrified, I realized I'd forgotten to feed him last night. All the commotion of the twin's trip for Christmas interrupted my routine and poor Cody was the unsuspecting victim.

"I have no excuse, buddy, I'm a terrible mom! I am going to make you eggs for breakfast, maybe even some bacon! Does that sound like a plan?"

Words meant nothing to Cody; my inflection, on the other hand, made him and jump and twirl as if he were a pup.

I figured I'd break my routine of eating oats and join Cody. I scrambled four eggs and fried four slices of thick cut bacon causing Cody to drool uncontrollably; I kept my excess saliva in check. Just as I sat down to enjoy the scrumptious concoction, my phone buzzed with a call. It was Bill, and my heart leaped. I'd grown so fond of him.

We decided to let our relationship develop slowly. We didn't force anything and took our time getting to know each other. Bill and I talked openly about our past lives, yet I hadn't disclosed my virtual relationship with Daniel. There were a few opportunities early on, but I just didn't know how to explain it. I held this secret very close and I didn't share it with anyone, even my sister.

Exuberantly, I answered, "Hey you, how are you this fine wintery morning?"

"Wow! What did you put in your coffee?" Bill said jokingly.

"What do you mean? I'm always this chipper."

I was grinning from ear to ear, waiting for the chance to tell him about the twins.

"I will admit you are a cheerful gal, but there is something going on and I want in."

"Bill, I am so excited, my grandkids, the twins, are coming for Christmas. I got a call from their mom yesterday, and I haven't been able think straight since, I am ecstatic!"

Sensing my growing excitement, Bill interjected, "Hey, slow down! Tell you what, why don't I bring you a latte, and you can tell me everything in person? Maybe I can keep you from falling off the barstool."

We laughed together, and I asked him to give me 30 minutes.

Thirty-three minutes later, Bill knocked at the side door. After the first night we spent together, an ease set in, eliminating the need for his front door calling. I waved him in, and he gave me a big hug and a sweet peck on the check.

"Morning, sunshine," he said as he fluffed my tousled hair. Patting my ass as I moved passed, he mumbled, "Mmm, love your bum, it's so...round."

"My 'bum' is off limits and my hair doesn't need any more volume, thank you very much. And I hope, for your sake, 'round' is a compliment," I kidded. "Thanks for the latte, by the way."

"Oh, but it is..." This time, he squeezed my ass with purpose.

Offering another peck, I said, "Off limits...for now, mister. So here's the list I've made so far."

I went right into planning mode, which tickled Bill, and he leaned in with genuine interest.

I ran through my list as we savored our lattes. I shared my childhood memories of Christmas and how Jack and I created new ones, especially after Michael was born. Bill talked about his childhood, and though not as idyllic as mine, he had a few funny stories of Christmas morning with his rambunctious younger brothers.

More painful memories followed. His father was an alcoholic who abused his mother and Bill, the eldest of five boys. He and the next oldest drew the majority of the beatings and tried like hell to protect their younger brothers. As soon as he graduated from high school, he joined the Navy. The Vietnam War was over and the military was not well favored by most Americans, yet he saw it as a way to pay for college. Once back home, he earned a business degree at Edinboro University, which was close enough to Pittsburgh to check in with his mother and younger brothers, but far enough away from his father to avoid his wrath. Bill graduated summa cum laude and went on to earn his MBA at Harvard after receiving a partial scholarship, something he didn't seem particularly proud of.

Until that moment, Bill had only talked about his life after Harvard. He thrived professionally, and it never occurred to me he, a successful entrepreneur, came from such meager and painful beginnings. I was in awe of his accomplishments and wondered why he so casually skimmed over his grad school years. I insisted on hearing more, and as he spoke, it was clear he'd rarely shared his achievements with anyone.

My guess was his dad was too drunk to care, and his mom was too paralyzed by fear to understand. His ex only seemed concerned about the health of their accounts, which allowed a lifestyle she still enjoys thanks to his generosity and willingness to keep the courts out of their settlement. Though we never discussed it, I'd guessed he was making up for what his father failed to do for his family.

When Bill stopped talking, I looked into his eyes, which revealed his profound suffering. Though I was curious about his marriage and why he hadn't seen his son in 10 years, I decided to leave that for another time.

Giving him a sweet peck, I said, "Hey, how 'bout a walk around Wash Park?"

"Was wondering when you'd get around to asking!" Bill was up and reaching for his coat before he finished his comment.

Like a kid, he urged me to hurry up and grabbed Cody's leash. We began our trek that would take up the rest of the morning—I couldn't have been happier, as was the case for both boys.

Cody was more excitable than usual, and I struggled to control him. Bill took the leash and he kept on talking as naturally as if we'd been doing this very thing for years. I smiled and continued to listen to his story of sailing from San Diego to

Costa Rica in his sailboat, which he proudly identified as a Jeanneau Sun Odyssey 43DS, which meant nothing to me but I didn't let it show. I fantasized about sailing with Bill, lying on the deck of a sleek yacht, not missing my past life at all. Bill didn't flaunt his affluence like Greg had; I treasured his humble maturity and wondered if I could find love with Bill.

We made it home several hours later—cold, happy and hungry. We stripped off our coats and made a beeline for the kitchen. I pulled out a small saucepan to start the hot cocoa, while Bill rummaged through the fridge looking for sandwich fixings.

Disgruntled, Bill said, "Maggie, you don't have a whole lot of *anything* in here."

"I know, I know. I was planning on going to the market this weekend."

I hadn't planned on Bill stopping by and I made no apologies. Heck, I always managed to put something together for a meal, even if it meant a bowl of cereal. I suggested we order pizza. Bill agreed but offered to go pick it up from a real pizzeria that happened to be next to a liquor store.

Bill stood, made his way to the door and said, "Gotta have beer with pizza, Maggie. I don't have many, but this is one rule I live by."

I took full advantage of the time Bill was out and took a hot shower, shaved my pits and legs and afterward, smoothed on some coconut body butter. I wasn't going for anything romantic; I simply wanted to be clean and comfortable. I slipped into black fleece pants with a hunter green pullover. I didn't own a pair of decent looking slippers; wool socks would have to do. My hat hair needed work, though not much, and I ended my aesthetic workout with a little blush and lip gloss.

Satisfied with my reflection in the hall mirror, I made my way back to the kitchen just in time to open the door for Bill, whose hands were brimming with bags.

Helping him in, I said, "Did you bring me any presents like the last time?"

The gifts Bill had brought over the day before Thanksgiving remained unwrapped until the day after our houseful of friends and family devoured a delectable holiday spread Bill and I lovingly put together. Bill had spent the night, too tired to make it home; the matter of the trinkets coming to light after we'd had several cups of coffee the next morning. I'd opened each with care, laughing at the rawhide bone for Cody and delighting over the red toile oven mitt and matching tea towel. Opening the last gift—a bright pink box tied with a mint green ribbon made out of a delicate strip of organza—I'd gulped a deep breath, holding it in while I stared at a bottle of Après L'Ondée Eau de Toilette. It was a fragrance I'd mentioned weeks earlier merely as a side note to a story I couldn't recall. As much as I'd loved the perfume, his thoughtfulness warmed me from my heart to the tips of my fingers and toes.

"Yes, as a matter of fact I did."

Bill's voice brought me back, as he pulled out a bottle of whole peppercorns and handed it to me, a mischievous grin erupting across his face.

Half pouting, I said, "That's not what I meant. By the way, clever boy, I have pepper."

"Honey, you have *boring* pepper. This is the *spicy* kind, laced with cayenne pepper. You may just get me to stay forever if you keep this in stock," he said, laughing at himself—the side I first perceived as arrogance but now I knew was just his way.

"I don't like spicy food, you know that. Why would I keep it in the house?"

I began unpacking the rest of the bags, when Bill took my arm and pulled me into him.

"All joking aside, Maggie, I like spending time with you, here, in your home. I like how well we get along doing simple, ordinary things. Don't get me wrong, I love the fun and exciting stuff. But Maggie, honey, I love this more."

Bill kissed me before I could say anything. I went limp in his arms, and we stood in the middle of my kitchen, kissing for what felt like hours.

Pulling back just a bit, we locked eyes. I cared for this man. Deeply. Lately, I wondered what life with him would be like. It didn't occur to me, however, he'd be thinking the same thing.

Moving awkwardly toward the breakfast bar, I busied myself with place settings beer and pizza really didn't require.

"Well?"

"Well What?"

I knew exactly what Bill was asking, but didn't have the guts to tackle it.

"Maggie, do you ever think about us, our future, what it would be like to be together... permanently?"

Bill's voice quivered, and I empathized. He must be feeling vulnerable, I thought. This can't be easy for him.

"Yes, Bill, I have. A lot. I am head over heels for you, if you must know the truth. But all this scares me because, well, I don't know, really. It just does."

Place settings set, I began unloading the dishwasher. My heart was racing, and I couldn't remember the last time I felt so confused.

Bill moved over to me and, pulling me closer, said, "Maggie, it's okay. We don't have to talk about this anymore. It's a big deal, I know. But honey, Maggie, I'm head over heels for you, too."

He kissed me softly and grabbed two beers, pouring them into the ice-cold steins I kept in the freezer. I smiled flipping open the square flat box that held an extra-large, hand-tossed pepperoni pie.

ॐ

A week before the twins were scheduled to arrive, I'd invited Katie over for dinner so she could help me plan the festivities. Bill had been spending more time at my place so it was no surprise when he'd opened the door. She'd brought a salad and a very nice bottle of wine. Once we sat at the table, conversation was easy and fun, including a few really bad jokes, courtesy of Bill.

The remainder of the evening had included a thorough review of my Christmas to-do list before the twins' arrival; posing questions about what kind of tree to buy; how many decorations I needed to pull out of the basement; and what kind of a Christmas Eve we should plan. Michael's cookie cookbook was intentionally left out of the conversation—I knew I'd have to figure that out on my own.

Surprisingly, we'd unanimously agreed on a fresh-cut tree, counting on the twins to dress it with traditional and contemporary decorations framed by newfangled, LED lights. We'd struggled finding common ground on Christmas Eve, however. Both Katie and Bill had proposed a casual open house; I wanted a more formal gathering, as was my inclination for almost everything I hosted. In the end, they won. Surrender hadn't been too difficult when they reminded me I had less than two weeks.

Smiling, I recalled the conversation with my sister as Bill cleaned up the kitchen,

Mags, I like him. I mean, I really like him.

I do too, Katie. I mean I really do!

Maggie, you look happy. You and Bill are so good together. I'm not suggesting anything crazy here, but just know you have my blessing.

Bill had finished up in the kitchen and broke our sisterly exchange as he plopped between us on the tiny sofa and said, "Okay, okay, what's going on over here?"

He pulled us all together, kissing me on the forehead and patting Katie on the knee. It had felt so good to have family around—old and new. I'd shed a few tears that night, but concealed them; hadn't wanted them to be misconstrued for sadness.

Glancing at the clock, I realized I'd been daydreaming for close to 30 minutes. I didn't have time to waste on sentimental slop so I gathered my thoughts. Even though there were no chores to do or errands to run, I wanted to make sure everything was perfect for Timmy and Lisbeth. I walked through the house one last time before slugging through Christmas traffic. Katie couldn't join me; she had an office party to attend and, though he kindly offered, I didn't think it wise to bring Bill along. Not yet. I did, however, manage to clear out the back of Beater, stuffing Cody's giant memory foam bed, which filled the entire cavity. He would be a wonderful surprise for the kiddos, especially after a hectic day of holiday travel.

As anticipated, traffic was incredibly slow. Thankfully, the weather cooperated. Though cold, the snow hadn't made it to Denver yet. It didn't look like it was going to snow on Christmas, but the forecast for later in the day and tomorrow suggested a thick blanket of the white stuff throughout the twin's stay. For the first time in close to 10 years, a snowman would stand tall and proud, welcoming my guests Christmas Eve.

I gave myself ample time to get to the airport. I dressed comfortably and made sure to stop at Adnan's for a steaming latte that would get me through the drive's rough spots. Latte in hand, I jumped back into Beater and heard my phone buzz. Daniel had just texted me, and I responded with a brief text saying I was on my way to pick up the twins from the airport. He asked if we could chat for a minute and I agreed; my blue tooth was still functioning—sort of.

Pulling out of the parking lot, I answered, "Hey Danny, long time no talk!"

"I know Mags, it's been too long. How are you? I'm thrilled about your time with your grand kids. Perfect timing, no doubt," he said, trying very hard to conceal his dark mood.

"Danny, what's wrong?"

I pulled onto University Boulevard, heading north for I-25.

Cutting in, Daniel said, "Are you sure you have a minute? I know you are driving."

"Yes, I'm hands-free right now. Please tell me, what's going on."

I navigated onto I-25 easily and noticed traffic, though heavy, was flowing well. I stayed in the middle lane, knowing my turn onto I-70 was only 10 minutes away.

Close to tears, Daniel said, "Mags, my ex is moving. She's taking Sami. They're moving to Germany." Taking a deep breath, he went on to say, "She married a banker who works with one of 'the big four,' a fucking term she threw at me as if I'd be impressed. She went on to tell me the bank, *like I fucking care*, is headquartered in Frankfurt. Who the fuck takes their kid to Germany? Who fucking does that, Maggie?"

He was full on crying now, and I felt bad for not being able to give him all my attention.

"Jesus, Danny, I am *floored*. This is unbelievable! Aren't there laws to protect fathers' rights? Have you talked to an attorney yet?"

I slowed and got in the right lane; I-70 was a few miles away.

"Yeah, I did. She said at Sami's age, courts put a lot of weight on the child's preferences. Guess what? Sami is on cloud nine about the move. She thinks it'll be 'cool' and can't wait to meet German 'dudes'. What kid wouldn't think moving to Europe is cool? Fuck, Mags. Fuck me…"

I took the I-70 exit and merged into lighter traffic than I expected. I would be at DIA in 20 minutes at this rate, leaving little time to talk to Daniel.

"Look, Danny, I have zero words right now. It fucking sucks, I get it. But you have to hear me on this, really. You will get through it. You'll cry, scream and hate your ex. You'll miss the shit out of Sami, but you'll get through it."

I felt cheap spewing crappy clichés.

"Danny, I'm getting close to the airport, but I promise you this. Tonight, after the kids go to bed, I'll call you, okay? You've been there for me through some pretty dark times and, as your friend, I want to be there for you, okay?"

Seconds ticked by, then, "Mags, I think ordinarily I'd say never mind, but I want to take you up on that. I need to hear your voice, if nothing else."

No longer crying but still incredibly sad, Daniel hung up. My heart was heavy for my friend, but I didn't want his grief to taint my joy, so I blared my favorite Christmas carol playlist, singing unabashedly to "Let it Snow, Let it Snow, Let it Snow."

Amazingly, I found a parking space close to the terminal; I knew the kids would be tired and a shorter walk to the car would make all the difference. So far, this trip had been a piece of cake. Smiling, I looked up and quietly thanked Jack for looking out for me. Told him to give Michael a hug and kiss, too.

Picking up Timmy and Lisbeth was a breeze and we made it back to Beater in no time.

"Cody! You brought Cody! Come here, boy!" Timmy reached his small hand through the gate that kept Cody from accosting the twins with his giant, wet tongue.

"Nana, Can I sit back there with him?"

Timmy and Cody had a special bond, and their reunions were incredibly touching.

Heaving a bag into Cody's space, I said, "No, honey, I wish I could. It wouldn't be safe, but we'll be home soon, okay?"

I finished loading the bags and pulled out of the parking lot when Lisbeth screamed, "It's snowing! Nana, it's snowing!"

She rolled down her window and stuck her face out much like Cody would have done had he occupied her seat. Timmy followed suit, and I cranked up the carols (and the heat), thanking Jack once more.

తోళ

Somehow, I managed to power through getting home, unpacking, fixing dinner and getting the twins ready for bed. By the time I closed their door for the night, I was ready to hit the sack myself; it was only 8:30.

I called Bill to let him know we'd made it and the twins were all settled in. He wished me a good night, and I kissed him through the airwaves.

My phone's battery read "4%," so I plugged it into the charger and made my way into the bathroom to wash my face and brush my teeth. With a mouth full of green foam, I gasped remembering I told Daniel I'd call him. I spit into the sink, rinsed my mouth and wiped it with the sleeve of my robe. Reaching for my phone, I noticed a text from Daniel,

Today, 8:43 PM
DANIEL: Hey, u gunna call?

I didn't bother texting back.

I dialed Daniel's number, and he answered on the first tone, "Mags, I thought you forgot."

"I did, but only for a second. You don't sound so good, Danny. Talk to me."

I fluffed my pillows and sank into my bed, wishing I'd made a cup of tea before making the call.

"There's nothing new to say, really. I'm just so fucking pissed at my ex and kinda mad at Sami for not hearing me out. She's so blinded by the idea of Germany, but she hasn't even considered what leaving her friends would mean, not to mention school, and all the things she loves to do… "

His voice drifted off with resounding resignation.

"I am so sorry, Danny. I know how much you love Sami and wanted to be there for her through high school. And girls need their fathers so much at that age. What can I say? I feel so helpless right now."

It was true. I didn't know what to say or do for my friend. All I could do was listen—from 1600 miles away.

"You know, Mags, I have friends and family, even a girlfriend. But all I want right now is to hear your voice. You may not believe this, but I like you a hell of a lot. We've been through a lifetime it seems, you and me. It's so strange to me we haven't ever really met, you know? It just feels like we have… "

I understood his need to babble; it was one of the best ways I dodged pain, too.

We talked for over an hour. Nothing erotic this time, just honest conversation and sharing a few laughs. I cared deeply for Daniel. For months, I'd struggled with my feelings for him. It was hard to put a finger on something so illusory, even though it felt so incredibly real. Everything I knew about Daniel I'd learned through technology. We'd never sat face-to-face, held hands or kissed. Our passion was entirely manufactured, becoming experts at long-distance lovemaking enhanced by erotic images, sounds and fantasies. How the hell do you fall for a ghost?

He wished me a good night, and I wished him a good night's sleep. "I love you" was stuck in my throat, the need to be straight with my feelings becoming more salient. Fear took over, however, driving those three words back down somewhere out of reach.

⋘⋙

Morning came early, with two small children pouncing on my bed demanding I wake to see all the snow that had fallen during the night. Cody joined in, leaving me no other choice but to acquiesce.

"Okay! Okay! Let's go!"

We hurried out of my room toward the back door and peered out the window. Cody slipped by us and shot through the doggie door, making a deep trail through the powdery snow blanketing every surface of my back yard.

"Nana! Can we go outside? Please?" Timmy said, jumping up and down while Lisbeth squealed with delight.

"Of course you can. Your mom is so smart! She packed snow pants *and* boots *and* hats *and* mittens—just for you guys. Let's go find them. But guys, let me make my coffee first."

They ran, side by side to their room and began to rummage through their bags. I quickly ground my beans and started a full pot.

It was Sunday, the second half of the last weekend before Christmas, and I was pleased as punch my shopping was done. I wanted to do things with my grandkids I so fondly remembered as a child. A few days ago, Bill and I drove around my neighborhood, scouting the best lights and decorations. We thumbed through the paper deciding which holiday event we'd attend, knowing he and I would have the energy for only one. It wasn't a difficult decision and Bill purchased six tickets to Denver's *Zoo Lights* for later that week—four for us and a couple for Katie and her "Plus 1."

The day was cold and, by the time the sun went down, the temperature read 26 degrees. The kids spent less than an hour outside building a snow owl, hoping to hear a hoot or two from Al. Calling them inside, I noticed a light dusting had coated the old snow, and made the trees and shrubs glisten, stirring memories of old.

While Timmy and Lisbeth organized pieces to a *Harry Potter* puzzle on the coffee table, I gathered all the ingredients for cookies and hot cocoa. I'd repaired my cherished relic as much as I could, covering each page with a thin clear adhesive that didn't exist when I packed it away with Michael's other childhood keepsakes. Thrilled to think our baking tradition would live on, I would make certain Michael's children would experience what he had. I felt at peace; there was no need for tears on this joyous day. Perhaps tears were a thing of the past.

Katie came by just as I turned on the oven—she'd insisted on helping my personal pâtissier and pâtissière, sampling their goodies along the way.

"Holy cow, sis, you pulled out all the stops," she said as she smeared goat cheese on a delicate cracker I'd set out, along with other adult treats.

Laughing, I said, "Would you have expected anything less? Oh, look at this..."

I showed her the cookie cookbook I'd repaired.

"Mags, this is fantastic! But you said it was ruined," she said, carefully leafing through it, lingering on a few of our favorite recipes.

Looking over her shoulder, I said, "I decided to take a stab at restoring it. Came out pretty good, I think. Want a glass of Prosecco, sis?"

"You have to ask?" she said, taking two flutes out of the cabinet.

Later that evening, we delighted at the sight of the carefully arranged and not-so-expertly decorated cookies displayed across the breakfast bar. Permanent cocoa mustaches rested under the twin's noses, cookie crumbs dotting their sweaters. Bing Crosby crooned, "I'll be Home for Christmas," while we gobbled more confections.

"Simply magical," Katie announced, sneaking a gingerbread angel piped with red icing and heavily coated with silver sprinkles.

The kids giggled, watching her stuff the entire heavenly creature in her mouth, mumbling, "Mmmm—yummy!" as she washed it down with hot cocoa.

"Hey sis, got anything to spice this up?"

Pouring a healthy slug of Bailey's into Katie's cup, I proclaimed, "Tis the season!"

ᔔᓫ

The events leading up to Christmas Eve were picture perfect. I'd made a game of deciding which was the best-decorated house in the neighborhood, and the kids presented the lucky winner with a tin of their homemade cookies. The next day, Bill had prepared a delicious snack pack for our excursion to Zoo Lights, which turned out to be a wonderful outing for kids who'd rarely experienced snow, especially 12 inches of it. We'd bring each evening to a close with hot cocoa, cookies and stories of Christmas's when Michael was young, embellishing just a smidge to tickle the kids.

Early Christmas Eve morning, I'd tempted my sleepy cherubs out of bed with fresh-out-of-the-oven cinnamon rolls. My plan involved picking up a tree I'd ordered from a nearby nursery, accompanied by my squirmy duo. I'd selected a Fraser Fir not only for its deep-green color and rich pine fragrance, but also because it was more slender than most, making it perfect for my snug living room.

I'd had no other errands, so we'd made it home by the time Katie and Bill arrived. My sis had volunteered to make most of the food while Bill had assumed the role of bar manager, requiring a refresher course in kids' drinks. Dessert was covered—there were enough Christmas cookies to last well past New Year's. Meanwhile, I'd taken on the main course, going for a maple-glazed ham; easy-peasy and a real crowd-pleaser.

My Christmas Eve guest list had been pared to about a dozen people, including Katie's boyfriend, Kevin, who rounded our number to six. The other half included three of my favorite couples: Tony and Steve, Tina and Trish, and my best-kept secret—Mom and Dad. They hadn't been to Denver in well over a year and hadn't seen their great grandchildren in close to two. The Western Slope was as dry as a bone, hopefully making the first half of their trip uneventful. Dad was an expert driver and Mom knew well enough to keep quiet, so navigating snowy roads east of the Eisenhower Tunnel would be a piece of cake, Dad would later claim. Nevertheless, I kept my fingers crossed until I saw them pull up unscathed...physically anyway.

Lisbeth, who had drifted toward a table loaded with bright red Poinsettias, squealed with delight, "Nana! Nana! Can we get pointsetters, too?"

Shaken out of a cloud of thoughts, I smiled at my sweet granddaughter. I didn't want to disappoint, but I didn't like having these holiday favorites in the house. My hesitation wasn't because of their rumored toxicity (they are only mildly toxic to dogs); Poinsettias simply don't last long and their red petals leave terrible stains.

I offered Lisbeth another option and said, "I tell you what Lizzy, I am going to give you something very special, something you can take home that will bloom year after year and it will remind you of this very special Christmas."

"What, Nana? What are you going to get me?"

Lisbeth's curiosity reminded so much of Michael. A twinge of sadness crept up and I quickly choked it back down.

Her tiny hand in mine, we made our way to another table, and I said, "Let's go over here."

Bending down so my head was level with Lisbeth's, I said, "Lizzy, this is an 'Amaryllis.' I'll show you how to take care of it so it blooms every year, just like in the picture here."

She squealed with delight and I took the box that held one very special bulb to the counter and added it to my order.

A young man who didn't seem to mind the bitter cold helped load the tree atop Beater and waved an enthusiastic goodbye as we pulled out of the parking lot. Minutes later, Katie and Bill rushed out of the house as we pulled into the driveway and began untying the tree before I'd shifted to "park."

"Katie, guess what? Nana got me a murillus! Look, it's going to bloom every year! I got a red one cuz it's Christmas, and red is a Christmas color! See, look..."

Katie bent down to look inside the paper bag while Timmy shadowed Bill as he carefully loosened the twine around the tree.

"Hey Timmy, can you hold this end for me?"

Bill was so natural with kids. It suddenly occurred to me this was his first Christmas without his son. Even though Bill hadn't seen him in 10 years, it still must hurt like hell. I wondered if he was experiencing any sadness at all. If he was, it didn't show.

I pulled out sandwich fixings while Katie busied herself in the kitchen. The ham wouldn't take long, and I'd set the tables the night before.

Only one task remained; the tree stood bare, demanding to be embellished with decorations and ornaments that had lain dormant for too many years. As Timmy and Lisbeth danced about, singing unabashedly to "Rudolph," I stacked the boxes of Christmas doodads in front of the tree. I worried my emotions might overcome me so I joined them, amplifying my voice to elicit some giggles and keep a few ghosts at bay.

Bill looked up and noticed a pained look washing across my face. He put down the half case of wine and walked over to me. Taking my hand in his, he bent down to open one of the boxes. The kids were eager to see what was inside, and before I could say anything, Timmy spotted a bright red container of Styrofoam balls covered in cotton, felt and beads, the faces of Santa, Mrs. Claus and a couple of elves staring back. They were a Christmas gift Michael had made in fifth grade, and I smiled remembering the day he brought them home. The cheery Christmas characters had always been the first on the tree and last off, and Timmy zeroed right onto them.

Michael, are you here with us? Please stay...

With Bill by my side, I welcomed this new tradition and family set-up, unexpected as it was.

Just a few minutes into stringing the lights on the tree, Kevin, Katie's boyfriend, came through the side door carrying several large loaves of crusty bread. He dropped the bag, kissed Katie and trotted over to check out our work. He shook Bill's hand and gave me a bear hug. Then, he rumpled the twins' hair and plopped on the sofa.

"Hey wench, where's my beer?" He jokingly shouted to Katie.

Katie wasted no time and said, "Ask the barmaid, her name is 'Bill.'"

Laughing, Kevin pulled himself up and asked Bill if he'd like one. I reminded Kevin I, too, enjoy a beer now and then and Katie echoed the same sentiment. The twins were busy placing ornaments on the tree, while Bill worked around them with the popcorn and cranberry garland. It felt like I was looking through a plate glass window in front of Macy's smack dab in the middle of New York City.

Reflecting silently, I toasted Jack and Michael, thanking them for their love and the joy we shared. Though I wasn't really sure they had anything to do with it, I thanked them for giving me the time and space I needed to surrender to their passing.

Finally, I whispered, "I love you" to both, embracing the moment with gratitude.

While everyone worked on the tree, I ducked out to shower. I wanted to be ready when Mom and Dad walked through the door, surprising everyone, especially their great grandkids.

I stopped in my room to grab my robe when I noticed a text from Daniel,

Today, 2:03 PM
DANIEL: Merry x-mas, mags
MAGS: Hey Danny, merry x-mas to u 2! U okay?

DANIEL: Ya, with my bro, its all good

MAGS: Really?

DANIEL: Really – wanted u 2 know that I'm so
grateful we r friends, Mags

MAGS: Same here, Danny, really – who knew
we would make it this far? If I ever get married
again, you're invited

DANIEL: You get a front row seat at mine –
you'll always be in my heart, Mags

MAGS: Same to you, friend, same to you

DANIEL: Bye then, Mags, I hope u r having the
time of your life with your babies

MAGS: I am, Danny, thx. I wish you happiness
these next few days, u deserve so much of it.
Merry x-mas my friend

I sat on the edge of my bed, realizing Daniel and I had said goodbye. It wasn't a hard stop, really; there was no mutual ending to our relationship. Still, what we once had was gone, and I didn't think we'd ever get it back. I was so tired of grieving. I needed—no, I *wanted*—happiness to flood my life. I longed to shower under endless streams of joy, peppered by moments of ecstasy and contentment. Seven years was enough. From now on, I would celebrate my life, not try to renovate it.

"It's my time, damn it!" I said slightly louder than intended, hoping the ruckus in the living room prevented anyone from hearing my proclamation.

I marched into the bathroom and took a long, hot shower. I wanted to thoroughly wash away my emotional grime, which took a bit longer than the other kind.

Standing under a heavy spray of hot water, I said, more softly this time, "It's my time, Mags. It's my time."

CHAPTER 11

New Years—Recurring Tears

A calm washed over me as the year expired. It reminded me of the time I ate magic mushrooms someone had given me at a party in high school. Within minutes, I was *feeling* colors I'd never seen before; the room was spinning and my thoughts vacillated between reality (fantasy?) and fantasy (reality?); my mind, body and spirit separated, floating up and away from each other like soft, summer clouds. And then the fragments came together as I descending from one helluva trip. Lucky for me, I'd found a quiet bedroom in the midst of a frenzied party and was able to come down gently.

My adolescent curiosity around drugs yielded this single experience, yet I recall it vividly; the end of my trip felt like my mind, body and spirit had reconnected, perfectly aligned like a space shuttle exacting its position with the dock of the mother ship. I'd been given access to an alternate world that forever changed my perspective, or so it felt. Like my one and only psychedelic trip, the holidays revealed a new perspective; intense sensations, colors and emotions swirled, encasing me like a warm cocoon.

I pledged to live each moment in the present, spurred by watching my grandkids do it so effortlessly. They reminded me how to find magic in everyday things, like inventing new Christmas cookies and building snow animals instead of an old, tired snowman.

Finally, peace and serenity had begun to set in.

Our Christmas Eve open house had exceeded all my expectations. My folks' presence aroused good cheer, as did the twins' exuberance. We saved the tree topper for Dad to place—

a crocheted snowflake, somewhat yellowed and floppy from the degraded starch used to stiffen it decades ago.

As soon as Mom shed her coat, she'd stormed into the kitchen to check on the food, lifting lids and sniffing the contents, looking through the glass window of my oven to see if the ham was on schedule—an annoying behavior I've learned to ignore...sort of.

A few hours later, the rest of the guests had arrived, which enhanced the already festive atmosphere in the house. The evening had been perfect; the food was delicious and the company, enjoyable.

Spirits still high, Christmas morning had been intoxicating. I'd kicked the twins out of the guest room for a couple of nights so my folks wouldn't have to sleep on the pull-out in the den. Timmy and Lisbeth made no objection, particularly since Cody squeezed nicely between the two. Of course, they were the first to wake and had squealed with delight over the colorful packages Santa had quietly laid at the foot of our spectacular tree. Mom and Dad, thrilled to wake to the commotion stirred by the twins, had cherished having the family together for Christmas.

There'd been no room for Katie and Kevin to stay the night, but they'd promised to return bright an early, which they did with a basket full of pastries. Arriving a short time later, Bill made a beeline into the kitchen to start a pot of coffee. I'd put on my robe, a new Pendleton with a tartan plaid in hues of deep blue and green. (I'd vowed never to get rid of the red robe Jack gave me, but it was time to retire it.) He'd grabbed me as I made my way through the commotion and kissed me square on the mouth. Mustering as much stealth as I could, I scanned the living room hoping no eyes had found mine, when I spotted my parents' gaze boring straight through me. My face had burned with embarrassment, I recalled, positive it wore a color to match the heat.

To my surprise, Mom had smiled sweetly, followed by a classic wink from Dad, as if to say, "You caught a good one, Magpie, don't let 'em go!"

Sifting through Christmas memories brought a smile to my face. Remembering was an exercise with which I'd developed great proficiency.

Sending the twins back home wasn't a sad event, nor was saying goodbye to my folks, for that matter. For the first time in years, I knew I'd be seeing them again. The fear of loss—the permanent kind—was losing its grip on my soul, and I had no intention of baiting it back. I was glad to have the house back in order (kind of) and equally pleased to be alone. The stillness of my home in early January reminded me of snowshoeing in the forest; deafening silence and exquisite scenery stirring self-reflection. Like a perennial that appears dead at the first hint of spring, I'd given myself a little more time before declaring my life over; new growth had begun to bud, roots tickling life back into my emaciated soul.

It was very different for Bill. The holidays provided a sort of sensory shield from his devastating loss, but as soon as New Year's Day came to a close, his wounds reopened—shredded and bloodied. Attempts to console him were met with emotional barriers I was unable to overcome. At first, I tried to reach him with stories about Michael, hoping familiarity would be the soothing balm needed to accelerate his healing. The blockade only grew thicker, though, so I backed off, avoiding the topic altogether. Instead, I put on a cheerful face and suggested fun activities, hoping things would return as they had been just weeks before.

Regrettably, sorcery was not a skill I possessed, and we coasted a bit longer, then slowly—almost deliberately—my lover and I drifted apart. There was no sunset, no crescendo; our break up was as unremarkable as our first date.

Typically, January is one of my least favorite months. Returning to school after Christmas break was torture, even in college. Likewise, tearing down decorations, stowing cherished knickknacks and hacking up a dried up Christmas tree was something I resisted, even as a child; it was like going to a funeral, painful memories the only thing connecting sad onlookers.

This year, however, I decided to take a different approach. The tree stayed put, as did the decorations. I piled the nativity set, an ancient and somewhat dilapidated *Christmas Town* and other seasonal adornments on the dining table, and studied them one at a time. After a tranquil jaunt down memory lane, I carefully swathed each curio in bubble wrap, placing them in assigned plastic bins easily accessible for the next holiday season.

Memories of Bill received the same handling; gentle recollection not efficient archiving like I'd ordinarily do. Sadness and grief had set the tone of our last exchange—a mixture of my own and Bill's,

Why can't you share more about Nathan? What happened, Bill?

For Christ's sake, Maggie, can't you leave it alone? I don't want to talk about him, ever.

No, Bill, I can't. It's getting in the way of us, are you okay with that? There are lots of things I don't want to talk about, by the way. I lost a son, too.

You lost a hero.

What is that supposed to mean?

I lost a pathetic excuse for a human being.

Bill, what are you talking about?

My son, Nathan. He was a criminal. Sold drugs. He died in prison, after being beaten by a gang of thugs who first raped the hell out of him. He was always a small kid, picked on at school, didn't like sports.

But you said he was in the Navy! You told me officers came to your front door, holding a letter just like they had with me. You made me think we shared an awful experience, Bill.

We did, Maggie. That's the truth. He enlisted but was discharged, dishonorably. I lied about the officers at the door. I was and still am so damn embarrassed. We grew apart after that. My son didn't fit the mold and we both paid a price. After Nathan was convicted, I shook his hand, said goodbye, and never saw him again. I killed my son 10 years before those fucking assholes did.

Bill stood up from my sofa that day, dropped his coffee mug in the sink and left through the side door. He didn't say a word on his way out. Surprisingly, I had no urge to chase after him. He needed space, as did I. His grief was insurmountable. As much as I hated to admit it, I didn't feel like joining him on his journey, he'd have to go solo.

Katie's call interrupted my flashback, "Hey, sis, whatcha up to?"

"Just putting Christmas stuff away. Actually, I've decided to leave the tree up for a bit, just wrapping all the little stuff up. I think I'll keep it all handy for next year, though. I could get used to a holiday season like this last one."

"Me too, Mags, me too. Hey, do you have a minute?"

Katie's pensive voice irritated me. She could be so impulsive and I braced myself for anything.

"Sure, what's up?"

Please, God, make it be just one minute.

Katie squealed, "Kevin and I are getting married!"

A few too many seconds ticked by and Katie asked, "Mags, you there? Did you cut out?"

"No, I'm here. Sorry, I cut my finger on an ornament."

In reality, I'd choked on a sip of coffee just as she announced her engagement, forcing me to mute the phone to conceal my reaction.

"Wow, that's great Katie. When did he propose?"

"You sound as excited as a dead horse...Sorry, I know you like horses. Can you be a little more happy for me, Mags?"

"Katie, come on, I *am* happy. You just have a way of crash-landing news onto me. It takes time to soak it all in, honey, that's all. Of course I'm happy!" This time I meant it. I would have thought a man would have scooped her up years ago—Katie intoxicated everyone with her veracity, quirky character and simple beauty. "Can you stop by? I want to hear everything."

"Really? You have time?"

"Of course! Just bring me a bagel with loads of cream cheese."

A quick sprucing up before Katie arrived was in order, which took all of 10 minutes. The coffee pot was half full and still warm. Cody was resting and the house looked fine, so why the hell was I pacing the floor? Before I could stop myself, I texted Daniel,

Today, 10:12 AM
MAGS: Happy new year!

I stared at my phone as if I had the power to call forth Daniel's reply. Unbelievably, it worked and he texted back in seconds,

DANIEL: U 2, Mags! How the hell r u?
MAGS: Good, Danny, u?
DANIEL: Getting used to life alone
MAGS: I'm so sorry, when did Sami leave?
DANIEL: Before x-mas, needless to say the holidays sucked
MAGS: Can you go there to visit? Don't they play tennis in Germany? U could write the trip off
DANIEL: Funny you should say that, I'm leaving in feb to cover a tournament in Dubai, followed by another tourney – lots of travel, ugh
MAGS: What?? Dubai? Okay, u have no idea what image just came to mind!
DANIEL: Players volleying in thawbs?
MAGS: Ed zachery!
DANIEL: What??
MAGS: Goofy thing my sis says for "exactly"
DANIEL: Oh! LOL
MAGS: Speaking of my sis, she's getting married
DANIEL: That's good, right? Like the guy?
MAGS: It's good, just strange
DANIEL: ?
MAGS: She's been single her whole life, been avail 24/7- could I be jealous?
DANIEL: Possibly, I think sibs can become too close, gone thru that with my bro
MAGS: Really? Was that sad for you?
DANIEL: Not like Sami

MAGS: Well, of course not
DANIEL: Plus, sisters are usually closer
MAGS: Ya, we sure r
DANIEL: I miss u
MAGS: Me 2
DANIEL: How's your guy?
MAGS: No more
DANIEL: I'm sorry
MAGS: How's your gal?
DANIEL: No more
MAGS: I'm sorry
DANIEL: Wanna play?
MAGS: Can't now, sis is coming over, but later...
DANIEL: It's a date
MAGS: Mmm
DANIEL: Ta-ta

Katie arrived within minutes of my exchange with Daniel. I think my face was still red from the heat I felt thinking about cavorting with him later.

"You okay, Mags?" Katie said as she plopped a huge bagel on a plate for me.

"Yeah, yeah. Just out of breath lugging a box downstairs. Wow, that looks yummy..."

Pouring a cup of coffee for herself, Katie said, "I can give you a hand with the others if you want, but for now, let's chow."

Apparently, my aptitude for lying—and pulling it off—had increased significantly.

"Okay, start from the beginning," I said while stuffing a wad of bagel in my mouth.

"Just so you know, there was no 'popping the question,' Mags. Believe it or not, Kevin and I have pretty interesting conversations. He's a deep thinker, something I really love about him. So, we've been talking a lot about how our friends are all married with litters of kids and how we really don't fit in. Do you know what he does, Mags? He's a rocket scientist, literally! He designs electronics for space shuttles but those are being retired, so he's working on new stuff, like SLS...shit, I forget what that stands for, but it's the new stuff NASA is doing."

Katie could hardly contain herself. Kevin had captured her heart, mind and soul, and I couldn't have been more thrilled for my baby sister.

With a mixture of joy and just a pinch of sadness, I sunk back into the sofa, polishing off my bagel. I listened to how two very different yet compatible people just committed to spending their lives together.

"You know what he told me after we agreed marriage was a good idea? He said, 'Katie, you make me want to get up an hour earlier in the morning and stay up an extra hour at night.' I know that sounds corny, but I knew after those sweet words, he was the guy for me."

Katie was crying, just barely, and I grabbed her hand.

"You know what Jack said to me? Oh, and by the way, Jack never officially 'popped the question'...I did."

A tear ran down my cheek as I reflected.

"Was it in true Jack form, Mags?" Katie said, a smile replacing her tears.

We giggled, recalling how Jack would simplify things in a way that rivaled a periodic table.

"In fact, it was. After I suggested we get married, Jack did that thing with his mouth—you know? Twisting it, the way he always did when he had to mull something over, then sat back on his chair causing the damn thing to rock on its two back legs, and said, 'It makes sense, Maggie, it's like I've found the exact part for my truck in a giant junk yard... what are the odds?'"

"Holy shit! That is hilarious!"

Katie cracked up and I joined her. Reminiscing had become very effective medicine these past few months, and I savored another few doses.

After a round of guffaws, I continued, "I know, right? So, I said, 'Honey, did you just compare me to a spark plug?' to which he replied, 'Of course not. You can buy those at any auto parts store. I was thinking more like an intake manifold.'"

Concerned our bagels and coffee would find their way back

up, we laughed our way to the kitchen, leaning on the counter to chase side cramps.

Catching my breath, I said, "God, Jack was so damn funny. He never set out to be, but he just was."

Still giggling, Katie said, "Mags, that is the funniest damn story I've ever heard. Why am I just now hearing it?"

"Oh, I don't know, really, maybe things get funnier as time passes."

Or when people pass...

We talked for another two hours. Wedding dresses, locations and guest lists made up the majority of the conversation. Still, stories of Jack and our wedding occasionally surfaced and plenty of happy tears were shed.

My stomach ached from all the snorting, giggling and guffawing. Laughter may be the best medicine but the after effect is excruciating. Still musing over our sidesplitting afternoon, I cleaned up the kitchen and resumed my post-holiday organizing.

Sting's "Brand New Day" blared from my iPod while I finished packing the last of my Christmas curios. I'd lost track of time, oblivious to the waning sunlight and growing shadows in the house. Still bloated from the bagel I gobbled up hours earlier, I decided to forego solid foods for dinner; a nice Malbec left over from the Christmas Eve bash was more appealing. I opened the bottled and let it breathe while I showered. Daniel came to mind as I rinsed my hair, and I remembered our date.

"What the hell time is it?" I said out loud, fully aware I was the only living thing occupying the steamy space.

In less than five minutes I'd managed to dry off, throw my robe on and pour a glass of wine. Phone in hand, I texted Daniel,

Today, 9:42 PM
MAGS: I'm squeaky clean, cozy and feeling oh so coquettish!
DANIEL: I'm hard, hungry and oh so horny
MAGS: Can we start with hungry
DANIEL: Absolutely, been craving your pussy for a long time
MAGS: She's been dying for you, too

DANIEL: I'm gunna call you, want to hear your
voice, send me a pic?
MAGS: Only if you send me one
DANIEL: On its way ...

We fell into our familiar rhythm; Daniel coaxed, teased and expertly led me to an insanely passionate orgasm. Just minutes later, he came with even more intensity, a shock ripping through my body as I heard him cry out, almost in agony. Neither of us spoke in the moments following one of our best fantasy fucks. We listened to each other's heavy breathing, gradually slowing; there was no rush to talk, to confirm or compliment. It was the first time I truly desired Daniel's body next to mine. I wanted to feel his hands roaming every inch of my flesh, his mouth on mine.

Pillow talk was rarely on our agenda, but tonight was an exception. Both of us had something to say.

"I had a first time tonight," I said flatly.

Jokingly, Daniel said, "Oh yeah? You've been faking it all this time?"

"No, seriously, Danny. Normally, I'm so damn satisfied. In most cases, I can't remember ending our call—I fall asleep that fast. But tonight I missed you, physically I mean. I wanted to feel you next to me. Is that strange or what?"

"Not strange at all. I've had those moments, Mags, several in fact. Didn't want to say anything because, honestly, you seemed so indifferent. I often wondered how a guy like me could get so wrapped up in something so distant, so impossible, really. I've mastered the art of staying on the surface, Maggie. I'm not proud of it, but it's how I've coped, especially now Sami is gone. I have no one in my life who I care deeply about...except you."

Complete silence encased the virtual space we shared. Irrational thoughts filled my mind, leaving little room for objectivity. What was Daniel really saying? Did he expect a response?

Barely audible, I said, "I am not sure what to say right now. Funny, I've felt the same way at times. So, this picture comes to mind whenever I think about 'us.' It's not erotic, so don't get your hopes up. It's an image of a graph, with sine waves. Silly, I know, especially since I hated math in school. Bear with me…there are these two waves, never *ever* in sync. This infinite graph shows the waves missing each other at every bend and turn. They never line up."

More silence, deafening and emotionally debilitating.

I was ready to end the call when Daniel spoke up, "But how do you know they never line up, Mags?"

"I don't, I suppose. But the pattern is so damn consistent, never *ever* in sync, you know? God, I hate sounding so scientific. I have no idea where all this shit is coming from. What I'm saying is you and I have this thing, it comes and it goes. In between, our lives go on, we meet people—we fuck 'em if we're lucky, maybe we even get close. But all of that is *real life* Danny, ours isn't. And I think we have to accept your 'up' is my 'down' and vice versa. We are so damn lucky to have each other in times of need…we provide a kind of port for each other's storms."

Exhausted, I shut up and welcomed my newfound friend, *Silence*. She didn't hang around long, though.

A little angry this time, Daniel said, "A port? Like a shelter, where beaten up dogs are kept awaiting some fucking do-gooder's good deed, and if that doesn't happen then he's fucking euthanized? Geez, Mags, that's just awesome. So glad I could be of service."

I was stunned by his interpretation and couldn't think of anything to say.

"I'm a fool to have opened up, Maggie. Disregard everything I said. Jesus Christ."

"Danny…"

"Don't fucking call me that, Maggie. Just don't. You're a real piece of work, you know?"

Pissed didn't even come close to how he sounded. Daniel was lashing out, his intention to inflict pain quite clear.

"Okay, okay. I just wanted to clarify something. I didn't mean it the way you color it. You are much more to me than a *shelter*. But come on, we have to be realistic, you know? We live a zillion miles away from each other…"

"Sixteen-hundred, Maggie, not a zillion. Who's being unrealistic now?"

Flustered, I said, "Fuck, okay. I'm all twisted here. God, why can't you understand what I'm trying to say, Daniel?"

Much more calmly this time, Daniel said, "Because I think you're afraid to say what you really think and feel, Maggie."

My friend returned. She was generous this time, affording me several minutes to think carefully about what to say next.

I began, "Daniel, I care for you, a great deal in fact. I think I've said that before. But you and I come in and out of each other's lives, and that's not what a relationship is built on—a friendship, sure, but nothing beyond. God knows I'm no expert, but I am a realist. I believe what you and I have is a very fulfilling *virtual* connection, but it's not something that will eventually grow into a long-term thing. How *can* it?"

I really didn't want Daniel to answer, but he did.

"Gee, let's think about this for a sec. I think if two people want it bad enough, they'll find a way. Hell, there are books, songs and movies that tell *that* story—a very old, indisputable and applicable story. But hey, I guess I'm no expert either, and it appears I'm irrational and unrealistic. We better defer to your rational analysis of our situation, right?"

Daniel made sure to lace his surrender with acid.

Hoping to close the conversation, I said, "Thank you for understanding, Daniel. Though your tone suggests you may be ending things. Are you?"

"No, Maggie, I'm not. The end of us came by way of your fear of love after loss, and your resignation your life is as good as it will ever be. I won't take the fall for this stalemate, you have to own it, darling."

Daniel didn't wait for a reply; he ended the call just like. I held my phone out to confirm the disconnect, staring at the screen that read, "Call ended, 11:19 PM."

❧

I couldn't sleep after the call with Daniel. Torn up and splattered with emotional blood, I felt like I'd been in a boxing ring with no access to the rulebook. My awkward punches missed every mark because, in truth, I knew I was to blame. Daniel's remark about my fear and resignation was the knockout punch needed to win the match. With no possibility of a re-match, I'd have to deal with the loss permanently.

The clock glowed 2:01 A.M. and I hadn't dozed, even for a second. Coffee sounded good, so I slogged to the kitchen with my groggy-eyed dog at my heels.

Noticing the confusion in his eyes, I said, "Cody buddy, it's not time to get up yet, go back to bed, okay?"

Cody knew the word "bed," but his confusion remained. I walked over to the sofa and coaxed him up.

"Here you go, hang out here for a while, it's okay."

My sweet old dog didn't protest and instantly fell back asleep.

"Maggie, what the hell are you going to do with your life?" I'd asked out loud, a recurring question for which there never seemed to be a meaningful answer.

Feeling exceptionally vulnerable, I gave in to the longing for the way things used to be and for the people who filled those moments.

"You can't have it back, Mags. Jack's dead. Michael is *dead*! And you keep killing off men like bowling pins."

I woke Cody with my angry rant and lured him back to the sofa, promising to keep it down.

As the coffee brewed, I grabbed my tattered notebook and a pen. My problem, I concluded, required a thorough and objective examination of recent encounters. I scratched out a list of questions first,

Who?

Relationship status
When do I think about him?
Why do I think about him?
Am I crazy (Y/N)?

Then I began to elaborate,

Tom
> *Never was a "status"*
> *Occasionally*
> *Wonder about sex with him*
> *N! Just horny*

Bill
> *It's over, but I really miss him*
> *More than occasionally*
> *I think I loved him and vice versa*
> *N, he needs time*

Brett
> *SO done!*
> *Picking up dog shit*
> *Smell reminds me of him*
> *Nope, NO WAY!*

Greg
> *REALLY done!*
> *Never*
> *I don't*
> *Hell no!*

Adding one more, I finished the list,

Daniel
> *It's really over*
> *24/7/365*
> *He moves me*
> *Y, cuz he's a <u>zillion</u> miles away and I still want him!*

A fresh cup of joe in my hand, I stared at the results of my pragmatic analysis. Thinking back on a correction he made just hours ago, I made quick change to my adolescent embellishment,

Daniel
It's really over
24/7/365
He takes me places I've never been
Y, cuz he's 1600 miles away and I still want
him!

Furrowing my brow, I examined my scribbles then inhaled sharply, "Holy shit. I love Daniel."

CHAPTER 12

Something's in the Err

"**A**re you sitting down?"

"I'm still in bed, Katie. Christ, what the hell time is it, anyway?"

Katie was obnoxiously intrusive since the day she officially began planning her wedding. Quaint enthusiasm had turned into excessive micromanagement, and I was quickly tiring of it.

"Here we go again, ol' lady. It's almost six and I know for a fact you get up at five during the week, so don't give me a hard time, *sis*."

How Katie could be so oblivious to my mood was beyond me.

"Can I get a fucking cup of coffee first, or is that task not included in your wedding plan?" I said, each word hurled with precision.

"Okay, fine, make your coffee and I'll be over in a few. And enough of the 'F' bomb," she said, hanging up before I could object.

It was Saturday and cold as hell outside. I wanted to stay in bed, maybe turn on the tube and watch a movie, or dust off the paperback on my nightstand and finally finish the damn thing. The one thing I *didn't* want to do was deal with Katie at six in the morning. Shit, the sun hadn't even come up yet.

Cody sensed my agitation and offered a sweet wake-up kiss—a gesture I rarely took for granted.

"Thanks, buddy, I love you, too."

Wiping the slobber off my leg with my robe, I found my slippers and lumbered to the kitchen.

January turned into February as uneventfully as I turned

56. My folks couldn't make it to Denver, and Katie was overly consumed with where, exactly, her destination wedding was going to take place. She'd emailed an apology, haphazardly embedded in a message about the location of her nuptials,

> *Mags, help me! I love the idea of Napa, but not in July. It's getting too late anyway. The venues book up so fast. What do you think about somewhere sunny, with lots of beaches, like the Caribbean? Would people travel there? Would you? Oh shit! Today's your birthday! I'm sorry, Mags...do you have anything planned?!*

In fact, I did. I'd made a reservation for one at my favorite little Italian place. After a fabulous four-course experience, I'd ducked into an indie movie theater and saw a charming foreign film, *Gloria*. Apparently, life can begin at any age, in Chile anyway. Home was my destination after the movie, though I was tempted to stop off for a glass of wine. Not comfortable throwing a pity party in public, however, I drove past The Grille, secretly wishing I had someone to share it with. Birthdays had become a nuisance, and I made a pact with myself that night: Only two more birthday celebrations for me—my 75th and 90th (if I'm lucky), amazing milestones worthy of celebration.

The buzz of my phone roused me from my daydreaming. It was Katie.

Coating my words with persuasive sap, I said, "Hi Katie. I'm almost put together, just come on over."

"Mags, it's Daddy. He's in the hospital."

Wet sobs followed Katie's dry announcement.

"What? Katie, what happened? Please tell me."

My heart raced, and I sprinted to the bathroom with the phone held to my ear. I ran my fingers through my hair, stripped out of my pajamas and jumped into yesterday's attire. I'd be at her house in less than five minutes.

She told me he was at University Hospital, the new one; its fancy name had escaped me, too. Denver's roads weren't bad, but it was so damn cold. All I could think about was the long and dangerous ambulance ride from Georgetown, where they'd been visiting friends. And then there was the record snowfall we'd had in the mountains. Consumed by fear, stark images of a lifeless man being pulled from the still screeching van taunted my raw emotions. I raced to Katie's house, hoping to elude the grim mirage.

I didn't know how long I'd been holding my breath when my mother called, "Maggie, where are you? We need you here, dear."

Mom's few words triggered ages-old feelings of insecurity. My mother was extremely critical, a trait fortified over the years. She was the last person I wanted to talk to.

"Mom, I know, I'm on my way to pick up Katie, almost there in fact. Then we'll be on our way. Do you need anything? Have you eaten?"

Changing the subject sometimes worked. Not this morning, however.

"Oh Maggie, what makes you think I could eat anything right now?"

Unexpectedly, I was teleported to the time I suggested we plan a surprise party for Dad while Mom dismissed the idea and continued washing the dishes, reminding me he hated being surprised.

"Ok, Mom, I'm just concerned about you, too. We'll be there in 30 minutes. While I have you, though, are there any updates? Have you spoken with the doctors yet?"

All I could get from Katie and Mom was Dad had awakened in the middle of the night, a common occurrence lately. They'd been staying with friends, an unfamiliar place, which didn't help. He'd run a shower as if it were morning and fell. Mom had heard the *thump* and found him unconscious. She'd called 911 and they transported him to Denver. Older and weaker than Mom and Dad, their friends opted to stay home, begging Katie to keep them posted.

"Dear, if I knew anything more, I would have told you. Please just come quickly."

And with that, our call ended.

Beware of growing into a cold-hearted, bitch, Maggie. It runs in your genes.

Katie and I rode in silence. Her face was red, blotchy and

tear-stained. Strangely, I hadn't cried at all. I was in work mode, gathering data and beginning to draft a project plan, albeit a mental one—it would make its way to paper at some point in the day.

"Katie, honey, we'll find out what's going on with Dad. Until then, please don't make it worse for yourself. Here, hold my hand."

I reached over and took her hand, which was cold and lifeless. My heart hurt for her as much as it did for Dad just then. Katie was the baby, and our father adored her. I knew he loved me, but it was different, a logical sort of love. She could do anything and Dad would be delighted. I learned to sit back at watch the fireworks,

Surprise!! Happy Birthday, Daddy!

Katie, my sweet Katie! My goodness, look what you've done!

Yes, Daddy! I planned it, and Mommy and Maggie helped. We knew you'd love it—isn't it funny? I love you Daddy.

You did a fine job, sweet pea. I love your decorations, sort of...who says I'm 'over the hill?' And would ya and look at that cake, I bet you and Mommy made it from scratch.

We did! We did! How did you know, Daddy?

Mom was right; Dad didn't like surprises. But the year he turned 40, I wanted to do something special. He'd been joking about becoming an "old fart," and it seemed like the perfect time to plan something different. Still, dad never knew the surprise for his fortieth birthday was my idea. After Mom shot it down, I told Katie to carry it out; I did all the planning, while she took center stage. Some things never change.

We found Mom sitting on a bench in the ER waiting room, staring unaware.

"Mommy! Oh my God, why are you out here?"

Katie ran over to our mother and hugged her, not letting go for an awkward amount of time.

"Dear, please. It's okay. I came out here to meet you two." She gently pushed Katie away and looked over at me.

"Hello Maggie, thank you for coming," my mother said, as if it were a unpleasant chore.

"Mom, come on, of course. He's our dad as much as he's your husband. Christ."

Stuffing my irritation several layers down, I reached over and, giving her a one-arm hug, said, "So, what's going on? Any news?"

"They say he might have had a stroke. Some big shot doctor said so."

Irked, I said, "You should be glad he's being cared for by a *big shot doc*, Mom."

How had my mother grown into such a bitter woman? Looking at this stranger, I couldn't recall when the shift took place.

Hours of waiting took its toll on all three of us. By the time the neurologist walked over to provide an update, we'd sunk into a state of vigilant silence. The last time I was in a hospital was last year, when Tony's partner was hit by a car; before that, Jack's cancer treatments. The palpable recoil to the sights, sounds and smells of my surroundings kept me sharp, and I took the lead after dad's doctor introduced himself.

Objectively, I said, "Thank you for caring for our father, Dr. Simons. What can you tell us?"

"Yes, how is my *husband*, doctor?"

Mom just couldn't help herself.

"Well, ladies, Mr. O'Leary is doing much better. I am a neurologist and was called to examine him because he showed signs of a stroke. We ran lots of tests, most importantly an MRI, which showed negative for stroke. We ran labs, too, which showed Mr. O'Leary is hypoglycemic," he said slowly, eyeing each of us to see if we were following.

I wasn't. Confused, I asked for clarification, "I'm sorry, did you say hypoglycemic?"

My father had never been diagnosed with that or any other major disease before.

"Why didn't the EMTs find that on the way?"

Attempting to clarify, Dr. Simons went on, "Yes, I said hypoglycemia. And, good question. It's a common mimic to a stroke, and not all EMTs and their units are trained to test beyond the obvious symptoms, in this case, a stroke. Often, patients with hypoglycemia present with confusion, one-sided paralysis, even coma, all of which look like a stroke. Add to Mr. O'Leary's symptoms his age and most first responders will diagnose stroke."

Still unclear, I said, "Why hasn't his doctor detected hypoglycemia before?"

Mom and Katie listened attentively, noticeably relieved I was managing the conversation.

"He probably didn't have it until now. Mr. O'Leary isn't diabetic, is he?"

"No, not at all," I said, not entirely sure, given how Mom and Dad had increasingly kept their health issues to themselves.

"Hypoglycemia can occur at any age, though more common in diabetics. Has he changed his diet recently? Increased drinking, alcohol I mean? When were his last labs, or his last physical?"

Dr. Simon and I were in sync, and I rattled off the information I knew of, looking to Mom for supplemental facts. In the end, it was good to know Dad would be fine, as long as he followed up with his doctor and did as instructed.

"Thank you, Doctor, may we go see him now?" Mom said in an increasingly anxious voice, hoping the sight of her husband would be the reassurance she needed.

"Of course, Mrs. O'Leary, I'll show you the way."

It was more important for Dad to see Mom and Katie right now, so I held back and took a seat outside of his room. I also wasn't ready to see my father as a hospital patient. He'd been a steady figure my whole life, one of strength and power, and I couldn't bear to see him in such a weak state. Roles change as people age, but I wanted to postpone our about-face as long as possible. For now, he was still my larger-than-life father, who stood vigil those first few days after my crippling loss,

Maggie, honey, I'm right here. Your Mom and I are here with you. Come here, honey, I'm so, so sorry, my sweet Magpie. I won't let you go...

I leaned on him a lot after they died. He and mom stayed with me for over a month. They handled every aspect of the services, kept the fridge full, tried to get me to eat and sleep, and took care of me as best as they could. Mom busied herself with house chores, while Dad just sat with me, reading me uninteresting stories from Reader's Digest. It was Katie who finally insisted they head back home. She swore she'd look after me and keep them posted. Dad cried the day they left; I was completely unable to say goodbye.

Convinced Dad was going to be fine, we left the hospital. It was just after 1:00, and Colorado's winter sky was a brilliant shade of blue—not sky, more like royal—lifting my mood considerably. Cold as it was, the high altitude sun made it feel warmer. As was the custom, Mom stayed at Katie's house. Thankful for my privacy, I took a long hot bath and contemplated death; not from a gloomy place, but from a semi-objective, who's-going-to-die-next perspective. After counting all the people close to me who had passed, I decided to make a U-turn and head down another rabbit hole. This time, I counted all the people close to me still living—a lengthier list, indeed.

One name stood out and I instantly felt pangs of guilt for not staying in touch. The last time I saw Tina was Christmas Eve, but the festivities prevented us from having a serious heart-to-heart. Before that, we'd had lunch on Memorial Day, during which I'd told a pretty big lie. Tina had sensed it, but I never followed up. Having lost track, I wasn't even sure if she and Trish were married; I'd received no invitation.

"There's no time like the present," I said with a dose of courage, hoping the silly cliché would sink in and convince me to adhere to it. I'd survived the past eight years cemented in the past, and it was time to quit armchair living and break out of my rigid cast.

Quickly drying off, I threw on some sweats and picked up my phone.

"Hello?" Tina answered in a curbed tone.

"Chica! Hi, it's me, Mags."

I hoped my friend would warm to my enthusiastic greeting, but she didn't.

In the same flat tone, she said, "Oh, hi Mags. Sorry you caught me at a bad time. We're having a heck of a time with Rose."

Barely audible, I said, "Who is Rose?"

A few seconds ticked by before Tina spoke, her reply a complete shock, "Mags, Trish and I adopted a baby girl; her name is Rose."

Waves of emotions flooded my body. Love for my friend

and her partner, joy for their new baby, and sadness for now just finding out about it. I'd lived so selfishly lately, it never occurred to me to reach out to my dear friend.

A sob barely escaped and, quickly swallowing it, I said, "Oh Tina, I am incredibly thrilled to hear this news. Congratulations! My gosh, it's so much to take in."

In a shaky voice, Tina said, "Maggie, I'm sorry you had to find out this way, I feel really bad."

"Please, please, don't feel bad, Chica. It's me who should and does feel bad. I've neglected our friendship for stupid, selfish reasons. I'm to blame. But enough, there's a baby in the house, and you don't want her sensing all this crap. Oops! No more cussing, either."

I was giddy with joy and couldn't contain it.

"Can I swing by sometime, please? I'd love to meet little Rose," I whispered as if I were there, trying to keep the commotion to a minimum.

"Of course! In fact, what are you doing now? Trish and I are exhausted and could use some help from an expert."

It was as though no time had lapsed. Threads of love and respect connected the two of us and forgiveness sealed the bond.

"On my way!"

෴

I had no idea what or if they needed anything for Rose; besides, I'd dust off my sewing machine and make a beautiful quilt soon enough. Nevertheless, I had a very clear idea what these new parents needed, and pointed Beater toward the neighborhood wine store.

"I'm an auntie, Jerry!" I proclaimed to the owner, a short and squat bachelor who gave bears hugs to all his regulars.

"Congrats, Maggie. Time to celebrate then?" He said after squeezing all available air out of my lungs.

"Yes, it is…and time to stock my friends' wine rack. What can you set me up with that won't force me into foreclosure?"

We walked to the back where he kept a few cases of really nice stuff. I smiled, and Jerry winked back. In 10 minutes, I was back on the road, two cases of *Zenato Amarone della Valpolicella* in the back seat of Beater. I also grabbed one bottle of *Banfi Brunello di Montalcino Poggio all'Oro* so we could toast to—in the words of Tevye—life.

A new baby. I was ecstatic and went a few miles over the limit, anxious to hold their new bundle. Tina and Trish would be amazing parents, and Rose was one lucky baby. Admitting life was moving right along for everyone—hell, the world—but me, I punched the accelerator in an attempt to vaporize the subject of my rumination.

Nevertheless, questions still arose: Had I been idling at a subconscious rest stop, waiting for...what, a toll-free highway to happiness? Christ, the energy I'd spent over the past seven— wait, eight—years pleading for salvation, a place free from agony and despair. I'd duped myself into thinking the manufactured life I'd been living was fulfilling and safe; half true, it also kept me from the people I loved. Yes, Jack and Michael died, but I still had my beautiful grandchildren, spirited sister, faithful parents, devoted friends and my loyal, four-legged best buddy.

As my gratitude survey came into focus, I silently affirmed more truths: I had my health; a peaceful home; a career that kept me sharp and engaged; and several more decades to live, I hoped.

Tina and Trish were standing at their huge picture window as I pulled into their driveway. It must have been Trish's house because Tina lived in a small flat in downtown Denver, last I knew. Heck, so much time had gone by, maybe they bought this place together. Either way, it was perfect. Two blue spruce trees framed the older, ranch-style home just outside of the Bonnie Brie neighborhood in southeast Denver. Many shrubs and garden beds lined the perimeter of their front yard; even in its dormant state, I could imagine the backyard was even lovelier.

Jumping out of Beater, I headed for the front door when I completely forgot the wine. I turned around, opened the back and stacked one case on top of the other. As I made my way back up the walk, I saw Tina laughing and Trish just shaking her head, clearly amused. Once inside, Tina slid one case off the other and made a beeline for the kitchen, and I followed. Everyone was whispering when I noticed sweet little Rose sleeping soundly in the Baby Bjorn Trish wore so expertly.

Excitedly, I whispered, "You said Rosie was a difficult baby—she's sound asleep!"

I stroked her tiny head tucked inside the contraption and cooed instinctively.

"She fell asleep right as you pulled up. She must have sensed 'Nana' coming."

With a look of apology spreading across her face, Tina looked over at me and said, "Oh, Mags, I know you're only Nana to your grandkids. I'm sorry."

Playfully nudging her arm, I said, "Auntie, please. 'Auntie Maggie.' Is it possible to preserve whatever youthfulness I have left before committing me to an assisted living facility?"

Having successfully diverted the issue, I bent to kiss their baby's head. In truth, it wouldn't feel right being Nana to anyone but Timmy and Lisbeth.

We moved into the living room, where Trish carefully sat in a rocker, a furniture tag still hanging from one of the delicate spindles. Tina and I plopped on the overstuffed sofa facing a slowly dying fire that had warmed the room comfortably.

Trish rocked slowly, singing, "All the Pretty Little Ponies," a lullaby I used to sing to Michael,

Hush a bye
Don't you cry
Go to sleep my little baby
When you wake
You shall have
All the pretty ponies...

Gazing through their picture window, I secretly hoped Michael was able to dream of pretty things before he died.

Coming from the kitchen with two glasses of the *Brunello* I'd chosen for us, Tina said, "Is Trish putting you to sleep, too?"

"Naw, just daydreaming. What, only two? Surely lactation isn't an issue!"

Tina snorted, and was quickly hushed by the much more serious mommy, who gracefully stood up and stated she'd be in the nursery. Trish's smile said she wasn't angry, recognizing the need for two friends to reconnect.

"Chica, you look amazing. I know you're tired, but seriously, you look like a different person. So does Trish. Motherhood has done you both good!"

Feeling weepy, I quickly took a sip of wine and savored the velvety liquid.

"Mags, I'm sorry I didn't call you. I know this is a big surprise and you just have to know things were just so crazy..."

"Stop it, Tina. We're past that. Please, let's celebrate new love and new life."

"Okay, deal. Want to hear about how we found Rose?" Not missing a beat, she continued the story, "You know I was assigned to Denver's Juvenile Court last year? I resisted the move and didn't make a lot of friends along the way. One day, a caseworker who'd investigated several of my cases approached me with a question. She asked if I'd ever consider adopting a baby. I laughed so hard, everyone in the building stopped and looked over at us."

Tina cracked up as she recalled the event, which made me giggle.

"So, once I stopped laughing, she insisted she was serious and asked if I wanted to know more. I was curious, so she took me back to her office where she had all this information on kids in foster care needing to be adopted. Jokingly, I said, 'But I want a baby, not a grown-ass kid.' She goes on to say, 'I figured, look at this,' and she shows me a picture on her phone of a newborn. I mean a still-bloody baby."

Riveted, I leaned in and said, "Holy shit, Tina, this sounds almost 'black market.'"

"I know, right? That's exactly what I said, 'Is this a black-market baby?' You know what she said? 'No, this is my sister's baby.' I was dumb struck. So, her sister's 16 and can't keep her. The family is Latino and no one really trusts the *system*. This caseworker, who I'll never name, says she thinks Trish and I would be great moms."

Tina took a huge gulp and I simply stared at her. I had so many questions—legal and otherwise.

I collected a few and said, "Was it a legal adoption, honey?"

I didn't want to offend, but I had to know.

"Of course it was. Come on, I have connections and ways of navigating the system, Mags. But I did lie about whose baby. I said someone dropped her off with a note—one Trish artfully wrote in an anguished, unwed teen mother's style. Thank God she's a writer."

"Is it bulletproof, Tina? I don't want this to backfire. What if the mother wants her back?"

The amount of worry I'd begun to take on was adequate for the both of us.

Tina took another gulp and went on, "I have a friend in private practice who drew up 'bullet proof' paperwork, as you say. It's an open adoption; our only condition. The entire family gets to see her once a month. Trish and I are fine with that, Mags. They are wonderful people and I'm thrilled Rose will have a large, extended family."

Her smile spoke volumes. It really was going to be okay.

"Oh, chica, I am so happy for you, Trish, and little Rosie. A real win-win it seems. Cheers!"

We clinked glasses then Tina began to cry.

"What? What did I say?"

Not sure what I said to induce tears, I reached out and touched her knee.

"I'm not sad, asshole, I'm happy!"

I let go of my emotions, too, and tears welled in my eyes. We hugged for a good while, enjoying the warmth of our persistent love and friendship.

"Now, when do I get to hold baby Rose?"

ง๑◅๛

Cody's nose investigated every square inch of me when I got home. He loves babies, though he wasn't prepared for the time Carrie came to Colorado right before the twins' first birthday; the poor guy was completely baffled. Once able to make sense of seeing double, however, his delight quadrupled. Recently, a neighbor had a baby and took daily walks by my house; Cody couldn't wait to greet the pair whenever I was in the front yard gardening. I shared the love of babies and their smell with my dear old canine, and was glad Rosie's sweet scent clung to me like dryer lint.

My phone went off and I picked it up, realizing I'd forgotten all about Dad.

Anxious, I answered on the second ring, "Hey, Katie, how's Dad?"

"Where have you been? I tried calling a million times."

The panic in Katie's voice made my heart race and, pacing the floor, I said, "I'm sorry, sis, I had it on silent while I was at Tina's. Is everything okay?"

"Daddy? He's fine, Maggie. Even ate some dinner with Mom. No, it's my wedding, I don't think I want to do a big wedding after all, especially with Daddy's condition now."

"Katie, don't scare me, Fuck!" I was more than furious.

"I didn't mean to, Mags. I've just been talking with Mom and Dad and we think it's best to stay in the country. And I really I don't want to do the mountains; it's too late to plan something up there anyway."

Katie was in wedding planning mode and it occurred to me we were supposed to go over her plans earlier. Dad's emergency had trumped all that, however.

Silently forgiving her *it's-still-all-about-me* state of mind, I said, "Well, isn't it going to be late for any venue at this point? Are you still thinking a summer wedding?"

I knew folks who planned destination weddings years in advance, several months just didn't seem like enough time.

"Well, that's just it, Mom's college friend, Alice, has a place in Florida, the Keys to be exact. And here's the cool part, we can do it as early as next month! Of course it will be much smaller, but that's okay. Kevin and I really like the idea and, given what's happened, it makes me think we just have to 'seize the day,' you know Mags?"

A smaller wedding sounded terrific. And in the Keys—who could argue with that?

"Katie, I think it's a wonderful idea. It will be quaint, just right."

"I know, I know! So, can you help with the details? You are so good at putting a plan together quickly. I really need you, sis."

I'd always been there for my sister—good times and bad. Likewise, she, in her own way, had been there for me. There was no other answer to her question but "yes."

"Tomorrow's Sunday, let's start early with Mimosas and waffles."

My suggestion was an easy sell; Katie's energy level was nearing depletion and I was happy to help, particularly since it involved early morning libations.

❧

I woke very early the next morning, not a groggy bone in my body.

Jumping out of bed, I called out for Cody, "Hey, buddy, how 'bout a walk?"

He whirled in several circles before settling down for the bowl of kibble I just poured.

"Eat first, then we'll head out."

There was a protein bar sticking out of the fruit bowl, and I quickly washed it down with a glass of water. I'd make coffee when I got home.

I took my time, enjoying the crisp February air as dawn broke. Sunday's were quiet in my neighborhood, and I cherished the silence. I left my iPod at home so I could drink in every sensation along the way. Cody sensed my calmness and we quickly fell into a respectable pace. The Chickadees and Nuthatches scraped for the few remaining seeds hidden beneath the frost; the lucky ones had staked their claims on my feeder back home.

Yesterday had been exhausting and I was glad it was over. I'd ridden an emotional rollercoaster from heightened worry about Dad to sheer joy holding little Rose, and everything in between.

There was no need to analyze; a behavior I'd typically fall into. Brimming with a deep sense of gratitude for all the people in my life, I wanted to immerse myself in the love all around me. Flawed, crazy, unrealistic and erratic, my friends and family were also kind, generous, loving and loyal. Daniel wasn't excluded from my pondering. I still missed him, terribly. Not just the sex, either. Oddly, I hadn't thought about it since our last tryst, well after Bill's departure. After a summer like I'd had, my nightstand drawer should have been jammed full of colorful and ridiculously shaped...tools. The only thing brimming was my head, Daniel's last words bobbing at the surface,

The end of us came by way of your fear of love after loss, and

your resignation your life is as good as it will ever be. I won't take the fall for this stalemate, you have to own it, darling...

After he'd hung up, I curled into a tight ball, hoping my contorted body would permanently expunge those words. With a good dose of humility, I'd asked God to blanket me with peace, offering my apologies for all the blame I'd cast, having taken Jack and Michael too soon. Surprisingly, he answered and I'd slept better than I had in years.

A car horn blared, shocking me back to reality. Apparently, I'd been crossing the street out of turn—an impatient motorist messaged loud and clear Cody and I were hampering his schedule. I wanted to flip him off but decided against it. I wasn't about to jeopardize the gift of peace I'd been given just hours before.

"Buddy, it's probably time to head back. Katie's coming over and I am almost positive she'll have a treat for you," I said, gently steering him home.

Four hours later, Katie and I had settled on the first Friday in March for her wedding day, allowing guests the entire weekend for fun outings or lazy days on the beach. The number of guests worked out to be manageable, topping out at 25—family and non-family together. Mom's friend had room for the bride, groom and immediate family, while the rest of the party would stay at a local B&B. The remaining guests had several choices, and we passed lodging information along in an email; invitations would simply be symbolic at such a late stage. After we made our flight arrangements, Katie left, meeting Kevin for dinner to go over the details of their newly revised nuptials.

I had less than a month to find a dress and coordinating accouterments suitable for the tropics. Scanning high fashion websites, I decided to go for a new look, perhaps a chic haircut, even highlights. Not sure if Katie's was rubbing off on me, but I felt a new chapter coming on and I was excited as hell about it.

March weather in Colorado is unpredictable—ridiculously so. Spring storms can dump several feet of snow as yellow and purple crocuses strain to break through the thawing ground. Suffering from heightened cabin fever, young and old ignore

Mother Nature's threats and hit the parks, bike paths and hiking trails. Meanwhile, "traveler angst" reaches its summit; closed highways and canceled flights the result of spring's meteorological sense of humor.

I wasn't laughing the day I was slated to leave for Katie's wedding. My flight to Miami was scheduled for 8:12 A.M., but it'd been snowing for the past several hours. Wet, heavy slop had blanketed the streets and, unfortunately, the airport runways. Too anxious to think about checking the status of my flight while in the comfort of my warm cozy house, I resorted to accessing the airline's traveler's information site from my phone while sitting at a red light.

"Great time to check, Mags," I muttered sarcastically after noticing my flight had been postponed.

I decided to make my way to DIA anyway; didn't mind hanging out at airports and watching endless streams of people following each other like cattle. Besides, it was the day before Katie's wedding and I had to get to Miami—come hell or high water.

Thankfully, the economy lot had a few remaining slots. I quickly parked Beater and jumped on a shuttle to the main terminal. The snow continued steadily, and I cursed it, apparently quite audibly. The shuttle made its final stop at DIA's Terminal East, so I had to move quickly to get to the other side, just in case United Airlines' flight number 547 resumed its 8:12 A.M. departure time.

It didn't. In fact, it was cancelled altogether. The main terminal was buzzing with frustrated travelers and I had to think fast. Smiling, I approached the ticket counter and asked what the alternatives were to Flight 547.

Avoiding my eyes, the serious clerk said, "Where is your final destination, Ma'am?"

Pouring it on, I explained, "Miami, and I must get there today. I'm hoping you can help me make it to my sister's wedding."

"Let me see. Are you determined to get on a direct flight?"

"Gosh No!" Taking it down a few decibels, I continued, "Uh, I mean I can understand if I need to connect. Colorado's spring snow storms, what can you say?"

My charm resuming, I handed the clerk my ID.

"Your flight was cancelled because of mechanical matters, Ma'am."

The clerk clicked away on the keyboard, determined not to make eye contact.

Convinced my attitude would yield positive results, I said, "Well, that's probably a good thing! Honestly, Sir, I'm happy to connect, twice if necessary."

"Well, if that is your position, we do have a flight leaving Denver at 10:57 A.M., arriving in Atlanta at 4:14 P.M. Then, it looks like I can get you on a flight to Miami at 6:24 P.M., arriving there at 8:37 P.M."

As much as I wanted to ask if there was anything earlier, I didn't want to piss this guy off, so I said, "Book it, please."

Successfully navigating security was the least of my problems. Throngs of angry travelers lined the terminals, some elbowing their way through in hopes of finding one of the few remaining seats at a nearby bar. Bypassing the bar for the time being, I knew I'd want—or *need*—a drink later on.

The flight was surprisingly uneventful and we made it to Atlanta 12 minutes early, making my layover almost two and a half hours long. Indeed a drink was in store. Ignoring my bladder, I claimed a barstool at *TGIFridays,* an otherwise obnoxious restaurant chain but a welcome sight given the few choices in ATL's Main Terminal.

"A house red, please," I called out to the bartender, a beautiful blonde who was oblivious to the attention paid by her customers—men and women alike. I pulled out my iPad and jumped onto the airport's free Wi-Fi. It had already been quite a day, and I wasn't even through half of it.

Just go with it, Mags. Play a few levels of Candy Crush *and you'll be fine.*

I made a quick trip to the restroom and, upon my return, the bar was packed with antsy travelers; apparently a flight or two had been postponed. Nabbing my seat, I took a giant swig, thinking it would drown out the unintelligible chatter. Earphones would have been ideal, but mine were in a case I used when traveling for business.

I ordered another glass of wine, hoping it would come soon

because my flight would be boarding in about 20 minutes. I began packing up my things when I overheard a conversation a few seats away.

"Sami? Sami, you there? Damn this phone and damn AT&T! Oh, honey, there you are. How are things? What's it like over there? Okay, okay! I'll let you finish..."

A familiar voice caught my attention, as did the topic of his conversation. I scoured the bar looking for the source but couldn't see past the fat guy whose legs splayed so wide they touched the patron to his left *and* to his right, who happened to be me.

Then I heard the call for my flight. I had five minutes.

"Wow! The Cologne Cathedral..."

Where the hell is he sitting?

Another announcement, "United Flight Number 547 is now boarding at Gate 21."

Fuck! Where is he?

Panicked, I scanned the bar one last time, Calling out, "Daniel? Daniel?"

His voice was no longer audible and, just like that, he was gone. My heart sank as I made my way to Gate 21, unable to hear my name being called out from the bar where I'd left a full glass of red wine.

Epilogue

"**A**ren't you coming with us?"

Katie was still giddy from her picture-perfect wedding ceremony; excited her guests were on board for the ten-minute ferry ride to the classic Sunset Celebration in Mallory Square.

Watching the setting sun from the southernmost point of the United States had captivated tourists and locals for ages. Hemmingway made Key West his home, as did Tennessee Williams. Both great writers; both tortured souls.

The day left me feeling melancholy, longing for my home and missing my dearest companion, Cody. I wasn't interested in swimming through heaps of sweaty tourists, craning my neck trying to catch a glimpse of an over-enthusiastic juggler or starving artist who made their living off the ones and fives dropped into tattered straw hats.

Hollering from across the great room of Alice's private and luxurious beach house, Katie asked again, "Mags, are you coming or not?"

Standing in line, waiting to board the Key West Express from the tiny Island of Sunset Key didn't tickle my fancy; watching the sunset from where I stood suited me just fine.

With feigned cheer, I hollered back, "No, honey, I'm going to hang here with Dad."

Surprisingly, Katie didn't insist. Her small but effective entourage escorted the overjoyed bride and groom out the door, eager to share their celebration with other nameless tourists.

"Well, haven't you become a fuddy-duddy," Dad chided from an overstuffed chair facing an enormous floor-to-ceiling window that framed lapping waves of aquamarine, azure and bright cerulean.

"Takes one to know one," I said, failing to subdue the smart-ass in me.

Standing at the center counter of an enormous gourmet kitchen, I blended a couple of fruity margaritas, heavy on the tequila. Alice, we came to know, had not only married well, but she'd also become one of Key West's top elite real estate brokers. Alice's Bentley was worth what I could get for my little bungalow in Denver. Nonetheless, I'd never been inclined to chase so many zeros. They'd just turn around and bite me in the ass. I preferred intangibles, or at least I used to.

My mind wondered to the rhythm of the sea...Had I resigned myself to a lifelong relationship with Agape, a divine messenger of unconditional love who admonishes romance? Could I somehow capture my elusive adversary, Eros, taming him to feed my desires?

Get outta your head, Maggie!

"Here you go, Dad," I said, handing him a strong margarita garnished with a fresh slice of lime.

Spotting a chair next to his, I moved to sit but underestimated how deep it was, and let out an, "ooof," nearly spilling my drink.

A restrained chortle escaped before my dear father said, "Thank you, Magpie."

Taking a hefty gulp and savoring it for just a second, he said, "When are you going to start living, Maggie?" He took another quick nip then added, "After I got out of the hospital, I thought about my own mortality and what's left for a man my age. A somber lesson, for sure. But it brought me back 'round to you, sweetheart. You've stalled, and I'm sad about it."

His sucker punch caused me to choke on my first sip.

"Dad, what are you talking about?"

You know exactly what he's talking about, Magpie.

"You might be able to fool everyone else in your life, Maggie, but not your good ol' Dad. I know we don't see each other often, and while I'm at it, we don't see eye-to-eye on most things. You keep your distance, always have. But that's not what I'm talking about."

After a good-sized swig, I scoffed, "Then please enlighten me, I'm stumped."

Not stumped at all, I was curious about his perspective. Normally I'd have built an impenetrable emotional firewall, dismantling the threatening conversation in mere seconds. For the moment, I was entranced by the pink and orange hues of a magnificent sunset; with gentle sounds and balmy smells of the sea in the background, I gave into my dad. I wasn't threatened by his words, more like consoled.

"*Magpie*. Do you know where that comes from?"

Not giving me any time to respond, he went on, "When you were about four, we were driving to the market, just you and me. There was a Magpie in the middle of the road, picking at a hunk of road kill. You shouted at me to slow down so I wouldn't run 'em over. I did as you asked and slowed to a crawl. Then I explained Magpies are scavengers, they eat dead things and follow bigger birds of prey in hopes of finding their leftovers."

Sipping in unison, Dad continued the story. *My* story.

"You asked me how they found dead animals, and I told you they had a unique sense of smell, unusual in birds of their type, or any type really. They were clever birds, I said, and somewhat solitary, making them one of the most proficient of their kind."

Chewing on a piece of ice, Dad went on, "You know what you said next? 'So, they are smarter than the other birds and know how to do things other birds don't?' Maggie, you saw through what most folks think about the noisy critters and focused on their true and often misunderstood nature. Most people shrug them off as loud pests, but you recognized their ingenuity. That's who you are, a resourceful, clever women with a keen sense of things. Putting aside the fact Magpies eat road kill, you are a survivor, Maggie."

A familiar chuckle ended Dad's account, while memories rustled in my head, mixing with the alcohol.

"Did you know my very first research paper was on magpies? I was in fifth grade, I think. You'd been calling me Magpie a lot and I wanted to know more about them. Didn't have the Internet back then so I pulled out the 'B' volume of our Britannica set. Remember how thrilled you were when you bought the entire set for us? Now that I think about it, they weren't alphabetized, were they? There was a range, like 'Buggy' through 'Crest,' right?"

Recalling my youth, I sighed before taking another sip.

"Anyway, besides being scavengers, I found out Magpies

collect things, shiny things it was thought. Often regarded as thieves, but that's just lore."

Glued to the story, Dad smiled at me, warm and tender.

Smiling back, I continued, "Last summer, I was stretched out on the hammock, Timmy was playing with Cody and Lisbeth was snuggled next to me. She noticed a magpie hopping around the yard and I told her what I knew of the bird. Then I explained Magpie was my nickname."

I stole an extra moment recalling my summer with the twins. Memory lane, once a side road, had become a clogged freeway of late.

"Lisbeth has the cutest voice, Dad. She was so excited to tell me they studied magpies in school. Sitting up in the hammock, Lizzy said, 'Did you know they are one of the smartest animals, Nana? They know who they are when they look in the mirror!'"

Seconds ticked by before I picked up where I'd left off, "She'd watched a video on the self-awareness of magpies. Never knew birds could be so contemplative. Strange, really."

Reliving that slice of summer triggered a sense of longing and I slumped in the chair.

Noticing the change in my mood, Dad piped up, "Huh, I had no idea, but I don't doubt it a bit. About the bird and about you, Maggie."

Settling into the deep chair, he went on, "You are smart, clever, and yes, you collect things like your sister. I think it's a woman thing, though your mother doesn't. But that's another story for another time. You, my dear Magpie, have always been keen to who you are. Not in a conceited or self-absorbed way, but sort of like taking stock of yourself, like you do with your gardens."

Pleased with his analogy, Dad sat back and sipped the remainder of his margarita. Allowing his words to seep in, I took another sip of mine, swirling the liquid in my mouth.

A little disgruntled, I said, "Hmm. I'm not sure about that, otherwise why the hell would I be so damn confused? It all comes down to not wanting to be stuck with the label of *widow*, and the need to *move on*—God how I hate those words. Dad, I'm tired of trying to figure all this out. I know you come from a place of love, and I know you and Mom are so anxious for the day I miraculously overcome things and move on. But the harder I try to get over losing Jack and Michael, the more they settle back in, fighting for their place in my heart."

Choking back tears, I guzzled the rest of my margarita, hoping for the buzz to set it. During the past year, I've had the same conversation at least a half a dozen times; Tina, Katie, Tony, hell, even my neighbor Silvia all hoped and prayed I'd *get over it*. I'd counted on dating as my cure. But it hadn't. Not completely.

With a dose of humility, I said, "Dad, you know I love you. You have been such a rock since they died. I'm the luckiest girl in the world having you for my father. But I've tried. I really have. Katie talked me into dating again, which I did, to a point. I had some good, and not so good times. The highlight was Bill. I really fell for him. Did you know I never heard from him after Christmas, when he explained the events surrounding his son's death? How does someone walk away from what we had?"

Tears welled, and Dad reached out and placed his hand on mine, "Magpie, I don't know. But I'm not sure it matters. We all have our stories, honey—stories that challenge every ounce of our being. Quit looking for excuses and focus on life's opportunities. Isn't that what magpies do?"

Discouraged, I grumbled, "I just don't know what else to do to prove to you and Mom I'm okay, and I don't need a man in my life to be happy."

Pointing his finger at me, he squinted his eyes and said, "You don't fool me, Maggie. First of all, I never said a man is what you need to be happy, that's your fiction."

Dad was on a roll and I knew better than to interrupt.

"In fact, I never told you what you needed in life. Ever. You've managed your life pretty damn well without the help of me or anyone else for that matter. All I can tell you is what I see and have witnessed for the past eight years..."

"Dad, please, this isn't the time or..."

"You bet your ass this is the time and place, Maggie. No one has the guts to confront you, they know better. But I'm your father, and as long as I'm alive, I will work to scrape away the tough veneer so you can see what everyone else sees and hopefully learn to live *and* love again."

Wiping an unexpected tear from my cheek, I said, "Okay, Dad, what do you see?"

Tightening his lips a bit, he said, "I see my lovely daughter, encased in sadness and fear. I see my Magpie, who loved to explore open spaces and equally enjoyed playing house with her baby sister, living a cocoon she's designed to isolate her from the world..."

Dryly, I interrupted, "Dad, I'm right here, you don't have to speak in third person."

It took everything I had not to drop an F-bomb or two.

"Dammit Maggie, stop that crap. Quit pushing me, and those who love you, away. Christ you are as stubborn as your mother. Where was I?"

With a little venom this time, I spat, "You were saying how cute I was when I was younger but somehow I've grown into a curmudgeon."

Pulling himself from the overstuffed chair, he leaned in, and said, "Indeed I was. Honey, I love you. We all do. Don't you see? You don't need to go looking for happiness; it's all around you. In your sister, your mom and I, even Cody. I know you don't see the twins as much as you like, but dammit, Maggie, they are your blood and Michael's. If that doesn't bring you happiness, I can't imagine what will."

We locked eyes and, feeling his love blanket me, I smiled at my devoted father.

Smiling back, he said, "You share so much in every-day ways, like inviting family and friends to enjoy a little piece of heaven you call your home. That's happiness, my dear Magpie. People, family, food, music, laugher—it's what we all seek and there it is, right in front of your goddamned nose. You're just too stubborn to realize a good thing, even when it flashes in blazing neon colors."

Dad downed his drink and sunk back into the bottomless chair, oblivious to the fact he'd struck a chord, a major one, indeed.

It's in front of my goddamned nose, blazing in neon colors...

Clearing my throat, I said with a good dose of moxie, "Dad, I hear you, thank you for talking with me. I know I'm stubborn, heck I'm 50 percent Mom, right?"

Dad signaled his disapproval of my attempt to lighten the mood with a classic harrumph, leaving me feeling frustrated and spent.

"Seriously, everything you've said makes sense; I just need to quit trying so hard. I love you, Dad. I'm heading off to bed now, I'm pretty pooped."

I got up, kissed him on the forehead and turned toward my room, looking back to see if he'd taken the bait. He hadn't; slumped and looking more shrunken than ever, he was staring blankly at the floor.

Unwilling to leave my father looking so defeated, I ran back, bent down and said, "Dad, I promise, I heard you. I'm going to do what I should have done a long time ago. Forget swimming upstream, I'm going with the current from now on. I'll find the neon sign and give it a good charge, I promise. I love you, Daddy."

The little girl who'd grown up years ago nuzzled him, feeling safe and very loved.

Unaccustomed to hearing that moniker, he squeezed my hand and, smiling ear to ear, said, "Go get 'em, Magpie, I love you to the moon and back."

∽∾

Sleep didn't come for me; butterflies, it seemed, had morphed into wild bats that wreaked havoc deep inside my gut. Squinting through the blaring light of my laptop, I reviewed the reservation I'd made just hours before. A new, metallic blue X-Terra would be waiting for me at the Hertz counter just a ferry ride away; emotionally, I needed to retire Beater. Soon, I'd be on the road, but this time with a sense of purpose. I left a note on the kitchen counter before I snuck out at dawn,

Dear Dad, Mom and Katie,

Thanks for such a wonderful time. Please pass on my appreciation to Alice. Mom, why have we only now heard of her? LOL! Best of luck, sis, you and Kevin are perfect for each other. And Dad, please take it easy—I need you around for at least the next 25 years.

I'm ducking out...I couldn't resist the opportunity to take a road trip through this part of the country. I'll call you when I get to Atlanta.

XXXOOO Magpie

Acknowledgements

To P, your consistent, loving and guiding support gently ushered me to the finish line. You are along for the ride whether you like it or not.

To J, your keen eye, genuine spirit and continued encouragement guided me through some fretful times. Cheers, my friend.

To D, my chief creative advisor, I hope you realize the value of your contributions.

To Mom, Judy (since passed) **and Dad**, Eddy (still living) who instilled the love of reading and established a home with creative outlets of which I never tired, "thank you" doesn't begin to describe the measure of appreciation I have for you and your loving efforts.

To my dear friends and family who, with great diligence, kept me from laying down my pen—you rock.

To all my contributors: CS (artist), FR (Photoshop wizard), MWM (writer's group leader and advisor) and all collaborative geniuses, thank you from the bottom of my heart.

Finally, and most sincerely, **thanks to all the readers and fans who purchased my book and took the time to read it!** If you enjoyed it, please take a moment and write a review on Amazon, or your favorite online retailer.

I welcome contact from readers, so please feel free to drop me a line:
MAReyes.AUTHOR@gmail.com
or
www.facebook.com/M.A.REYES.Author
Follow me on Twitter:
@MAReyesAUTHOR

www.ingramcontent.com/pod-product-compliance
Lightning Source LLC
Chambersburg PA
CBHW020326200626
46814CB00006BB/2432